A Delightful Debut

Mary Pat Johns makes a delightful debut with *Countin' On Jesse*! The book's cast of characters are so well-crafted that they quickly start to feel like friends, complete with realistic, emotional backstories that will tug at your heart and keep you turning the pages... She kept me guessing, and the ending had me on the edge of my seat! This story sparkles—you won't want to miss it!

LAUREL BLOUNT, AUTHOR OF *JOHNS MILL AMISH ROMANCE* SERIES AND LOVE INSPIRED *CEDAR RIDGE* SERIES

A Sparkling Christian Rom-Com

Countin' on Jesse by Mary Pat Johns is a sweet and sparkling Christian Rom-Com with a poignant edge. Written in a breezy and realistic style, the book pulls the reader in from the first chapter and doesn't let go.

MARBETH SKWARCZYNSKI, AUTHOR OF *THE ROSE COLLECTION* SERIES

A Top-Notch Romance

I loved Countin' on Jesse! Mary Pat Johns did an excellent job of grabbing my interest from the first page and never letting go. I loved the opening scene... and had to keep turning the pages to see what would happen next. Mary Pat took my emotions and heart for a fast-paced roller coaster ride of romance. I was cheering for Jesse and Brenna all the way. Good humor, good suspense, excellent romance!

I highly recommend the book, and I can't wait to read Book Two in the series.

SHERRY SHINDELAR, AUTHOR OF TEXAS FORSAKEN

Their Relationship Is Worth the Steep Price

If you're a romance reader, you'll love *Countin' on Jesse*. Brenna and Jesse must both face and overcome past major losses if anything can grow from the obvious spark between them... Brenna's mom tells her that dealing with life requires more than black and white thinking. "Life isn't so clear-cut. Emotions are messy." I loved seeing them pursue deeper faith to lay their pasts to rest for a chance to build a promising future.

DELORES TOPLIFF, AUTHOR OF THE COLUMBIA RIVER UNDERCURRENTS SERIES, A TRAVELING GRANDMA'S GUIDE TO ISRAEL, ADVENTURE, WIT, AND WISDOM, AND WILDERNESS WIFE

ROMANCE IN VALIANT BOOK TWO

LOVIN' ON RED

MARY PAT JOHNS

Scrivenings
PRESS
Quench your thirst for story.
www.ScriveningsPress.com

To all veterans of war who returned home with life-changing injuries. I salute your honor and your bravery as you adapt to a new life. Your willingness to keep fighting infuses the rest of us with courage.

When Vi Summers' phone chirped for the second time in fifteen minutes, she counted to ten under her breath. Mom's name appeared on the screen, and the ten-count stretched to twenty. Patience was a virtue, right? Stepping back to the stove, Vi continued to sauté the green beans. She had already explained her role as hostess for Paige's Thanksgiving dinner, but when Mom didn't like an answer ...

C'mon, girl, no meltdown today.

A voicemail notification flashed. If the phone calls continued, it'd be a win if Vi made it through the next hour.

Vi's foster dog sidled up, gazing at her with droopy eyes. He caught the green bean Vi tossed mid-air and gulped it down. She lifted a brow. "Food tastes better when it's chewed, Thunder." At his hopeful look, she flipped him another. "No more though. Here's the deal, buddy. I'm gonna find you an owner who can't resist your soulful eyes."

With a half-smile, Vi turned her attention back to the skillet. Conflicting emotions rushed to the surface, threatening to undo her fragile poise. But Daddy wouldn't want her to be upset on Thanksgiving or mad at her mom, no matter how badly Vi grieved his absence. She turned the phone off and slipped it into her skirt pocket.

Rich coffee aroma overpowered the odor of burned toast, a casualty of housemate Brenna's ongoing feud with the toaster oven. Vi would fortify herself with liquid courage, then add more butter to the green beans. Crossing to the corner counter, she poured herself a cup of coffee. One sip later, she grimaced and set the cup back on the counter.

"Did I mess up the coffee too?" Brenna stopped rubbing the turkey with spices to look at her. Brilliant, beautiful Brenna, who found good in everyone. She'd moved in with Paige shortly after Vi. "Jesse prefers it super strong."

Of course he did. Vi bit her lip, guilt-ridden over her uncharitable attitude. After way too much drama—though most of it hadn't been their doing—Brenna and Jesse, the handsome co-owner of People's Gym, aka Peeps, had worked through their issues. Now they contended for Couple of the Year.

"Nah, I'm good," Vi said. The beginnings of a headache tightened like a band around her forehead. She rubbed her temples and studied her prep list. Ah. More butter. Her boots echoed on the pier and beam floor as she carefully skirted around Paige, her other housemate. Heart big as Texas, Paige had insisted Vi move in with her when Daddy died. Declared living alone had passed its expiration date. She didn't mention the other part. Without Paige, Vi would have broken into irretrievable pieces. A rush of cold air cooled Vi's face as she peered into the cramped space.

"Rory should be here any minute. He's making his famous mashed potatoes. Heaps of salt, heavy cream, and butter." As if nothing was wrong, Paige wrestled a bright Fiesta bowl from the cabinet.

The unwelcome news jerked Vi's brain off balance. *Everything was wrong.* She knew Rory's type all too well.

Vi stared into the fridge, attempting to resume her task. Rory, the *other* co-owner of Peeps, belonged to their same close-knit group of friends, but Vi kept her distance. Aside from outrageous good looks, Rory's extroverted personality grated on her last nerve.

"Good luck with that. I can't find the butter." Vi lingered at the fridge, still stunned. Rory would join them. And cook.

His electric presence would overwhelm Paige's tiny kitchen. And Vi.

"I saw it last night when Paige and Rory brought in the groceries. Green beans burning!" Brenna stepped over and shut off the fire. Gray smoke spiraled up from the pan.

Vi dashed to the stove and grabbed a spatula, prying the charred beans loose. An acrid stench rose to her nostrils, making her cough. The smoke alarm noisily alerted—as if the billowing haze might go undetected.

Beside her, Brenna fiddled with the oven timer. Totally unrelated to the shrill bleating, the large pale turkey awaited its fate in a roasting pan.

The doorbell rang. Paige slipped out and returned with Rory. Decked out in navy slacks, a gray Peeps' hoodie, and black cowboy boots, his red hair spiked upward. Vi suppressed the urge to seek cover.

In one second, Rory assessed the chaos, then strode through the cloudy kitchen to the back door and flung it open. Next, he stepped to the window, unlatched the lock, then shoved it upward—all with military precision. Paige and Brenna scurried out of his path as he nabbed a cookie sheet from the counter and waved it in a wide arc. The smoke alarm stopped its incessant shrieking as if bowing down to the male in the room.

Ears still ringing, Vi pivoted, dumping the scorched green beans into the trash. Rory appeared next to her. "You got this?"

Well, bless his heart. "I got this," she spoke through a tight throat, warm with embarrassment.

Spreading his arms wide, he announced, "Crisis under control, ladies. It's Thanksgiving, so hugs and kisses for all."

Vi's spatula clattered to the floor. From Rescuer to Romeo in less than a minute. The man didn't possess an ounce of humility.

The meltdown she'd been staving off mushroomed.

Rory wrapped his arms around Paige and placed a modest kiss on her forehead. Then he draped an arm around Brenna's shoulder, smooching her on the cheek.

When he headed for her, Vi caught the scent of his woodsy cologne and gazed into his face. Big mistake. His gray eyes churned, similar to waves in the ocean. As if he knew and understood every bit of her pain. A questioning look creased his features. Ever so slowly, he held out his arms. The comfort of a hug tempted her. For a nanosecond. If his strong masculine arms embraced her, she'd unravel like a loose thread. She backed away with the grace of a wet hen.

"I'm going for butter," she squawked, brushing past him, certain he'd guessed her fragile state of mind. What if she spilled her guts? Told him that her first holiday without Daddy was breaking her heart. And the calls from Mom weren't helping. Would he understand or downplay her pain? The questions had her bolting out of the kitchen.

Even as she brushed past, he winked at her and said, "We have butter." As if he recognized her flimsy excuse—but she didn't stop.

The man redefined enigma. He seemed to have a tender caring side, though in the same breath, he'd get cocky. Vi knew one thing for certain—Rory could hug and kiss all the women he wanted—just not her. Grabbing keys and purse, she dashed out of the house.

So much for not having a meltdown.

She slipped into her yellow Volkswagen and stomped on the accelerator. As if voicing her inner turmoil, the car squealed down the empty street.

"THAT COULD HAVE GONE BETTER." Rory pivoted toward Paige. A frown turned her lips down. "What? Who doesn't need a hug?"

The frown dissipated into a patient look. "Boss, your hugs are the best. It's too bad Vi shies away from affection—even from women."

"Why?" His brain rebelled at the idea. Physical contact soothed him more than anything. Truth be told, he'd kind of hoped Vi would be up for a hug. He'd been itching for a reason to touch her hair. Crazy long with the perfect amount of curl. A color no dye or paint could replicate. With effort, he attended to Paige.

"I don't know. Vi's a tough nut to crack." Paige picked up a colander of orange yams, then dumped them into a glass container.

Paige's pursed lips indicated a closed subject though Rory had every intention of pursuing it later. Vi fascinated him. She'd always been a part of their group. Lately, however, he'd found himself drawn to her in ways he couldn't fathom. The women he seemed to attract weren't cutting it. Any conversation with his former flame had revolved around the latest hair salon or getting her nails done. Did Vi even pay attention to girly things? Her gruff exterior suggested a tomboyish streak, but her little hourglass figure begged to differ. *Knock it off, Spence.*

He bent one leg into a kneeling position and peered into the fridge, mindful of his artificial foot. Opening the bottom drawer, he lifted a bag of apples and pulled out the box of butter. Rising carefully, he shot a *thank you* to the Lord for the mobility the prosthetic provided. The worst thing in his life had also gifted him with a lifelong dream—he'd build a regional rehabilitation center to provide therapy for other amputees.

"Where was it?" Paige asked, nodding toward his hand.

"Right where I put it last night," Rory replied through tight lips. Vi's leaving bothered him more than he wanted to admit.

"I'll let Vi know."

Rory grabbed the bag of potatoes and then searched through drawers to find a scrub brush and peeler. Once he found them, he concentrated on the process, often interrupted by mental images of sky-blue eyes, rife with pain.

Vi's prep list lay on the counter next to a tasty-looking pan of green bean casserole. Since she hadn't returned, a fact he'd already pushed to the back of his mind several times, he recruited Paige's help to interpret the list. While the potatoes boiled, he tackled the first item. Vi's hasty exit had been his doing, so he'd pitch in where he could. Hugs helped too, though Vi obviously didn't share his opinion.

Long after Rory finished the prep list and taste-tested the mashed potatoes, he caught Paige's eye again. He'd already pestered her into texting Vi a couple of times—okay, maybe four or five—but she still hadn't made an appearance. Despite Paige's assurances Vi simply needed space, a disquiet he couldn't ignore chilled him from the inside out.

The doorbell rang again as guests arrived. Rory opened the door to a distinguished silver-haired man standing on the veranda next to a younger man with red hair brighter than Rory's. "Dad." Rory hugged his father, then addressed his younger brother. "Mark. Glad you could make it."

"Never pass up the opportunity for a home-cooked Thanksgiving dinner," Mr. Spence boomed. He entered with Mark on his heels and cast an appreciative eye around the festive living space. Brightly hued cornucopias decorated two eight-foot tables. A decked-out Christmas tree stood in one corner, multicolored lights twinkling a welcome. The distinct smell of yeasty bread vied with other fragrant aromas. Two women greeted one another as if they were old friends. Brenna's brother and his friend had already become pals with Thunder, Vi's foster dog.

The homey scene made Rory's heart ache. It had been years since Mom had passed, but he still missed her during the holidays. Dad told him once that Mom's hospitality skills had been extraordinary. Rory suspected her giftedness had been the vehicle she used to share Christ's love with everyone she met. People adored her because she radiated grace and mercy. Like his personal assistant, Paige. No way he could juggle Peeps' expansion plans and run his contracting business without his PA.

Did any warmth exist beneath Vi's prickles?

Rory's lips curved upward as Dad charmed a roomful of strangers. Mark, however, possessed an introverted nature from the cradle. Thorny as a Huisache tree. No worries. Today, he'd stick close to Dad and let the older man's gregarious nature pave the way.

Zero chance Vi would call *him*, but Rory checked his phone anyway. Almost time to eat, and she still hadn't shown up. Unease morphed into a hard ball of worry.

CHAPTER TWO

Daddy's last gift. *Thank you, Lord.* Vi gazed at the Victorian house in dire need of a facelift, then took in the land and lake surrounding the house. Twenty acres of prime land in Valiant, Texas. The only place she'd ever been happy. And the first place she ran to when life became difficult. If she were totally honest, helping host a massive dinner distracted her from the real issue. Clear direction on how to move forward was what she needed most. Deep down, she sensed the answers would be here.

Best of all, Rory wouldn't find her here. Talk about a distraction.

A gusty wind whipped the hair from her bun into an unruly frizz as she walked to the front door of her childhood home. Twisting the key in the lock, she let herself in. Stillness reigned as if the memories had left at the same time as she did—too sad to stay. A slight musty odor of smoke lingered in the air. Vi's lip twitched. Daddy had smoked his pipe outside, but the telltale scent always found its way into the house.

Her cell phone buzzed. She fished it out of her skirt pocket and groaned. Mom again. Maybe if Vi answered, the calls would stop. A snort pushed through her nose and throat. Sure they would. "Hey, Mom."

"Where are you?" a strident voice asked.

She shifted from one foot to another, holding back a sigh. "Same place as this morning." Not on her way to Houston.

An impatient noise. Then, "Vi, you're wasting your life in that awful little town. Bored out of your mind, no doubt. Rodney and I are sitting here all alone on a family holiday. He misses you, darling. Say you'll come tomorrow. It will be Black Friday. Great opportunity to update your wardrobe on me."

Mentally, Vi shuddered. Mom would buy styles Vi would never wear. And it wasn't Rodney who missed her. "Mom, I enjoy living in Valiant. You're the one who finds it boring. I can't come at all this weekend."

"Christmas then. You'll be here, won't you?"

Vi heard past the loud persistence to the desperation in Mom's voice. Her lifestyle among society's elite didn't lend itself to deep friendships. Vi relented. "I'll be there on Christmas Day."

As if she hadn't heard Vi's response, Mom said, "Oh, we'll make a week of it. Shop and dine to our heart's content. We'll scour the town for every little niche store—"

"I can only promise the day, Mom. After Christmas, my massage schedule fills up quickly."

"We'll see once you're here."

Mom didn't consider massage a real job. After a firm goodbye, Vi hung up. Not quite a win—no such thing—but she'd redirected Mom's focus on today to three weeks from now—all kinds of time for Mom to dream up outings that weren't going to happen. Vi swallowed hard, tamping down the scream rising in her throat.

Vi's phone chirped again. She clicked a button and held it to her ear. "Hi, Paige."

"Are you headed back?" Concern etched her friend's voice.

Keeping her tone mild, Vi said, "Y'all go ahead. Eat without me. I'm fine. I need a little alone time before I come back."

"It's Thanksgiving, Vi. Everyone is asking where you are. You're going to miss something special if you don't get home." She nattered on about Rory's famous mashed potatoes, while Vi's attention snagged on the "something special." She listened, only to hear, "... Rory's also been asking where you are. He feels bad about the way you ran out this morning ..."

Right now, Vi didn't care how Rory fared in her absence. At every turn lately, the guy invaded her space. Her only thoughts about him revolved around *not* being the man's latest conquest.

"The sooner I get finished here, the sooner I'll be home. Gotta go. Love you." Vi ended in a breathy whisper. She clicked off the phone, tears blurring her vision. Oh, bother. These all-over-the-place sentiments were her primary reason for coming here. Since Daddy's death, the past she'd thought buried away forever had sprung to life with a vengeance.

RORY'S THUMBS ached from rubbing them together. The rich scent of pumpkin pie still hung in the air. Vi had been gone for hours. Her absence gnawed at him. Paige mentioned this was Vi's first holiday without her dad. Firsts in the grief cycle were tough. It explained why her stormy blue eyes had held such pain. Without knowing, he'd yearned to comfort her.

But she ran.

He could tell her from experience the flight response

wouldn't work—not ever. She'd figure it out if she could settle long enough to catch a breath.

They'd finished prepping the dinner and waited until everyone had arrived. Still no Vi. Paige had asked him to say grace. Then everyone chowed down on the delicious holiday food. He vaguely remembered eating, but the food had no taste.

Worse yet, Paige said her last calls and texts to Vi had gone unanswered.

The afternoon's only bright spot occurred when Jesse proposed to Brenna. She glowed, and Jesse looked as if he'd bench-pressed a planet. Thrilled for his best friend, Rory couldn't keep ignoring the urgency in his spirit about Vi. He fidgeted in his chair, not hearing the conversations floating around him. Her well-being had leaped to the top of his chain.

He leaned over to where Paige chatted with two of her siblings. "Give me the address to Vi's house."

"She won't want to be disturbed." Pools of worry in Paige's brown eyes communicated she hoped he'd do it anyway.

"I'm going out there." His gut wouldn't leave him alone until he checked on her.

VI GLANCED around the living area. She'd packed her belongings the evening of the funeral, Daddy's death still too fresh to process, and moved in with Paige. *Thank you again, God, for my housemates.*

She pulled a tissue from the pocket of her skirt, wiped her cheeks, and stepped into the galley-style kitchen. Daddy had always talked about enlarging it. The seed of an idea pushed through her grief. What if someone ushered the dated space into the twenty-first century? Added flair and panache, but kept the quaint Victorian features?

Her steps slowed as she walked to the bedroom where Daddy had spent his last days. She turned the old-fashioned crystal knob and peeked in. The door hinge squealed in protest. Stale air greeted her.

Meds and reading glasses on the nightstand, rumpled sheets on the bed, a basket of once-clean pajamas and towels, now dusty. Everything was untouched from the last time she'd seen it. Before Daddy's final trip to the hospital. Why hadn't she returned sooner? Six months of neglect made it harder to bear.

Tears streamed down her face. The tissue she'd used earlier had turned into a soggy mess. Her boots echoed across the planked floor. As she perched on a corner of the bed, a specific knowing flashed through her being. The silver lining of death in all its redemptive glory awakened within her, and she knew without a shred of physical evidence. The most crucial part of Daddy—his spirit—had achieved freedom. Unshackled from his sick, earthly body. Because of Christ's sacrifice, Daddy had gone to a place she couldn't go yet. But someday ...

The subtle seed crystallized into a concrete plan. She would restore this place. Make it a home again—her home. Daddy had left her a tidy sum. Restoring this place would be a dream come true and provide the strength to stay. Consulting with a professional seemed the next logical step.

Solid purpose filling her, Vi shut the squeaky door with a firm hand. She strode to the wraparound porch, peering out to the lake. A gray sky had darkened the water to charcoal. Stormy white tips frothed the waves. The smell of rotting marsh reeds filled her nostrils.

Two boardwalks spanning the lake could use a coat of paint and more bracing. She navigated around unstable porch steps. *Thank you, Lord.* Her sadness had turned a corner onto a fresh track. Renovation had crossed her mind before, but now the timing seemed perfect.

By coming to her childhood home, she'd discovered what she needed most. She would restore this old wreck and cocoon herself in, all safe and snug. Daddy's love echoed through the walls. He and this house would provide the strength and insulation she needed to live her own life. She'd always struggled for balance anywhere else. Why hadn't she seen it before?

And maybe ... it would alleviate the cost of her own poor decisions.

In the distance, a slight movement caught her eye.

CHAPTER THREE

Vi squinted for a better look. A black dachshund with a saggy middle, her enlarged nipples dragging on the ground. Intent on her mission, the little dog paid no attention to Vi. Ever a softie for new moms, Vi surmised the dog's puppies must be nearby.

The stray went to the back of the house. Vi followed, careful to avoid clumps of weeds and crumbles of sidewalk concrete, only to find the dog had disappeared.

"Mama Dog," Vi crooned, trying to coax the dog into reappearing. The wind whipped harder. Out of excuses, she sighed aloud. No use putting off the inevitable. Her friends needed her. At least Paige did. Her stomach yowled as if in agreement.

The wind brought a distinct chill, raising prickles on her bare arms. Vi rubbed her temple. The sip of bitter coffee she drank earlier had only been a teaser. She'd return triumphant, and make her own pot of brew. Vi would stay immune to Rory's friendly overtures, concern, or any other feelings on his part. From what little she'd noticed, the man didn't lack for female attention. She sniffed. The men in her life had proved dismal failures, Daddy being the lone exception. With him, she'd felt protected.

And after she'd eaten a piece of pumpkin pie, she would tell the others about her restoration idea. Test the waters, so to speak. She was so hungry even Rory's mashed potatoes sounded appetizing.

High-pitched yips sounded close by, making Vi's mouth stretch in a smile. Mama Dog's puppies. Tall yellow grass brushed her legs as she hurried toward the noise.

She spied two squirmy black creatures, and then a buzz of activity swarmed around her ankles. Minuscule missiles spiraled around her skirt, flying into her hair. Fear petrified her movements.

Gasping for air, she splayed a hand across her face. With the other, she clawed at her hair, lurching away from the collective menace—one step, then another. Tiny barbs stung her arms and legs, then protracted like super-long needles.

She stomped instinctively, desperate to dislodge the bees.

Crack!

Boards gave way beneath her. Windsock-style, her arms flailed. One foot slipped, then the other.

She fell. Everything went dark.

RORY SPIED Vi's yellow car parked in a driveway of sorts where she'd lived with her dad. The old Victorian beckoned him to come and explore. However much it piqued his curiosity, he first had to find Vi. The holiday meal he hadn't tasted turned to concrete in his stomach.

Where would she go? He stepped onto a driveway badly in need of fresh pavement. "Vi! Can you hear me?"

Dry brown leaves blew with no rhythm as the wind sharpened. A chill dampened his skin beneath the hoodie. A dog barked close by. Rory strained to hear. His prosthetic chugged to keep up as he ran to the source of the noise.

Not far behind the house, a small black dog stood sentinel-style, barking incessantly. Rory's gut clenched. Could it have to do with Vi? He'd heard of dogs playing the role of guardian angel. "Easy, there. What's upsetting you?" The animal shied away as Rory approached. Then it turned, scampering into the weeds.

Rory took in several things at once. Flat boards. A jagged hole. He drew even with the hole and peered inside, his eyes meeting darkness. Pulling out his phone, he knelt on his good leg, shining the phone light into the hole. His heart lurched when he recognized Vi's purple shawl. Her eyes turned violet when she wore it.

"Vi! Can you hear me? Vi!" Not a muscle moved. She lay unconscious; her red hair flowed over her shoulders. The anxiety Rory had felt all morning roared to new heights. *Lord, help!* His fingers punched 911. When a person came on the line, he explained the circumstances and gave the correct address. As he clicked off, the person on the other end insisted he stay connected. *Sorry. Not happening.*

Frantic to find a ladder, he rose. "What the—" Something jabbed his hand, and a buzzing noise flew around his head. Ducking, he stumbled away to study his palm. A sting. As gold and brown insects swarmed, he ran, his mind computing the circumstances. Vi had fallen into the hole. She was unconscious either from the fall or—he clicked a number on his phone. Holding it to his ear, he spied a decrepit outbuilding. He hurried toward it as the phone rang.

"Have you found her?" Paige's whispery voice dripped with fear.

"Yes. Is Vi allergic to bees?"

Her soft gasp highlighted his worst suspicion. "That's a yes?" Then, "I'm at her place and nine-one-one is on their way." He stood before the shed door. No lock. *Thank You, Lord.*

"What can I do?" Paige asked.

"Confirm the address with nine-one-one." In his haste, he might have spouted off the wrong one. "And Paige—" The words choked their way past his tight throat. "Pray it's not too late."

Rory crammed the phone into his pocket. He grabbed a dust-covered ladder, then sprinted to his car as if his boots were on fire. Clicking his key fob to open the trunk, he grabbed the red first aid kit and rummaged for an EpiPen. Having seen anaphylactic shock firsthand with his brother Mark, Rory found it hard to breathe past the fear crawling up his throat. The wind whistled in his ears as he dashed back to the hole.

The instrument clamped between his teeth, Rory stuck the ladder down the hole, then stepped down, rung by rung, alert to every creak. A damp, moldy smell assaulted his nostrils. Spider webs swept across his face and clung to his beard. He blinked and continued to descend, leading with his natural foot. For the thousandth time, he thanked God he still had two good knees. Flesh and blood joints made climbing more manageable. He'd had a rock wall installed at the gym, scaling it regularly to understand and stay in touch with the limits of his prosthetic. For times such as this, apparently.

His boot hit a damp, slick surface. The wall felt slimy under his hands.

Body weight balanced, he pivoted in the cramped space. He pulled out his phone, flashing it around for a visual of the area. The narrow opening at the top fanned into a bowl shape no more than eight feet across at the bottom—an old, abandoned cistern.

Vi lay inches from his feet.

When he kneeled, moisture seeped into his pants. Goosebumps rose on his arms. How long had she been down here?

"Vi, can you hear me?" He shone the phone light next to her face. When she didn't respond, he nudged her collarbone with his fingers. Angling his body closer, he lifted a limp hand —clammy to the touch. A chill curled around his spine.

"Wake up, Vi. Talk to me, babe." He'd wanted to say those words for a long time, as if they were good friends who chatted often. The truth existed as something quite different. Even within the intimacy of their tight-knit group, she'd always evaded him. He took a deep breath, savagely cutting off the musings. Just as well. They could never be more than friends.

Rory forced his emotions into a detached state. He noted facial swelling and rash-like symptoms. The shadows hindered any closer inspection. He pressed two fingers against her carotid artery, bending lower as if to hear her pulse. When weak bumps vibrated beneath his fingers, his breath swooshed out.

She stirred the tiniest bit and wheezed. Not getting enough air. *She needs help now.* He scooted into a better position, uncapped the blue lid of the EpiPen, and wrapped his fist around the cylinder. Beset with a desire to preserve her modesty, he smoothed her skirt and injected the EpiPen through the fabric into her outer thigh. She could fuss at him later. He gripped it until it clicked and gave thanks when it released properly. "You're on the mend, Vi." His lips moved silently as he commanded her body to cooperate with the injection.

The state of her hair tugged at his heart. When he pulled it away from her face, a bleeding lump on her forehead appeared. He inhaled sharply at the deep cut. Small wonder she'd fallen unconscious.

Rory's shoulders slumped in relief when sirens sounded in the distance. Then Jesse's head appeared at the top of the cistern, diminishing the light. He turned and yelled for a flashlight, then peered back into the hole. "How is she?"

"Non-responsive. Full-blown anaphylaxis. Probably a concussion. Plenty of scrapes and bruises. She'll hurt all over and have a doozy of a headache. Accumulated layers of leaves and debris here at the bottom may have cushioned her fall."

"You remembered how to use it?" Jesse perched on the ladder, directing the light at the discarded EpiPen.

"Some things get buried so deep you can't forget." Rory pressed two fingers against her neck again. Her pulse imitated a faulty light bulb. Not the response he wanted. He took hold of her icy hand.

Topside, Vi's dog bayed a long mournful note. Rory looked up at Jesse's lined face. "She's in bad shape—what's taking nine-one-one so long?"

"Paige and Brenna went to flag them down. It's a maze if you don't know the way."

Rory continued to monitor Vi until more faces appeared, blocking the gray sheet of sky behind them. A brighter flashlight shone around him. An official-sounding voice called down, "Sir, we need you to climb out so we can assess the situation."

Rory rubbed his beard. His emotions were swinging trapeze-style. They had the equipment and the know-how to get Vi out of this blasted hole, yet he didn't want to leave her.

For her sake, he would.

He rose carefully and glanced down. His breath caught at her still form. Her hair, normally bright enough to kindle a fire, had darkened in the flickering light. The vibrant color had disappeared from her lips. He placed his good foot on the bottom rung and murmured, "Hang in there, Vi. I'll catch up with you later."

CHAPTER FOUR

Hospital rooms had no character. Rory had resided in enough of them to know. He glanced around the private room. Insipid beige walls, squeaky clean linoleum, a mottled mix of gray and grayer. The antiseptic stench made him want to hike to the hill country and breathe fresh air. He wouldn't be here at all, if not for the woman lying in a bed twice her size.

The blanket covering Vi moved. Rory approached the bed with light steps. He and Paige had traded shifts. So far, every doctor and nurse who came through the door had reminded him she needed to rest. As if his presence threatened their goal.

Brenna and Jesse came for a while. After twenty minutes of awkwardness, Rory gently nudged them back out the door. Their whispers and dreamy gazes at Brenna's brand-new engagement ring were more than he could handle at the moment. Through the window, the last embers of sunset ebbed, leaving a dusky twilight in its wake.

"C'mon, Vi. Show me those baby blues." Rory stroked her

arm gently around the bandages and IV tape. Her supple skin enticed him closer.

With reluctance, he took a step back, sliding his hands into his pockets. Touching Vi only made him want to touch her more.

He inspected her injuries. Her elbows and forearms bore scrapes and bruises, but her hands seemed fine. One side of his mouth rose. As a massage therapist, she would consider it a gift.

Yeah, well. Those healing hands could bring relief to anybody but him. Several years ago, a brief infatuation with his physical therapist during rehab had cured him. He'd thought he'd fallen in love and assumed she loved him too, only to overhear her say she wanted a whole man. In retrospect, God had protected him, even if his butchered self-esteem begged to argue. Never again would he start a relationship with a woman in a health-related profession.

In awe of Vi's heart-shaped face and delicate brows, he watched her sleep. One hand escaped from his pocket, despite his intentions. His thumb trailed down one creamy cheek, then the other. The rash had receded quickly with the proper meds.

The swelling had diminished where her forehead hit the cistern ledge, though the cut had required a few stitches. Would she fret over a scar? His ex-girlfriend would sue and demand cosmetic surgery, but Stella lived for drama. No comparison with what he knew of Vi.

However, much as he enjoyed the opposite sex, he'd keep it light. No more serious relationships for him—he'd been burned enough. The wistful notes banging around in his heart begged to differ.

With a sigh, he stepped away to the window and peered at the parking lot. Headlights gleamed as cars left for the evening.

A foam cup sat on the sink counter. He picked it up,

swirling the murky contents. Cold, bitter coffee. Pouring the remaining liquid down the drain, he crumpled the container and tossed it in the wastebasket. He whiffed a musty scent and followed the source. The hem of his pants remained damp. He'd only found a fresh shirt in his car. No clean slacks. It didn't matter. He had to see this through—Vi's well-being remained the priority.

Settling in the uncomfortable chair, he automatically checked his phone. The business calls he'd transferred to Paige. She knew where to find him if anything new popped up. Once Vi recovered her feisty self again, his world could continue on its axis.

As if she mattered to him. Which she didn't. Except she was hurting.

He found it difficult to separate her as a person from his emotional desire to help her through this ordeal. He'd come to terms with never having his foot back. But her? For reasons he couldn't fathom, he needed her to recover and be herself again. Blunt. Sarcastic. Hopelessly cute when she was mad.

Machines whirred and clicked, reminding him of days he'd worked hard to forget. A nurse entered, giving him a bright smile. Entering numbers from the devices into her computer, she exited the room with a jaunty hip swing. The old Rory would have at least struck up a conversation. However, his accountability pact with Jesse and the horrible breakup with Stella had changed his outlook. He'd lost interest in flirting. The feeling struck him as surreal. Hunting for his next date had once been his favorite pastime.

Vi stirred. He hastened to her side and scrutinized her pale features. Too pale.

The desire to touch her again overwhelmed him. "You'd make my day if you'd wake for a bit."

Earlier, he'd lifted her so Paige could pull her waist-length hair over one shoulder. He ran his thumb and forefinger down the loose braid Paige had plaited, then peered closer. Clusters of tiny purple crape-myrtle petals snagged in her hair, casting a fairy princess sort of spell in the room.

Her eyes remained closed. The hive on her face and neck had pretty much faded. Rory's gaze traveled downward. Those lips. Adorable. Would she wake up if he kissed her? A machine beeped, and a red light flashed as if to warn him. He pulled back and stroked his beard.

Bad idea, bud.

Her long lashes lay serene in sleep.

Worst idea in eons.

At the last second, he amended the action he longed to take, settling for a sweet kiss on the forehead. One tiny smooch. Nothing creepy.

COMING out of an endless black corridor, Vi dreamed about mashed potatoes. The melt-in-your-mouth, buttery variety. Creamy. Perfect consistency. Starving didn't begin to describe her hunger pangs.

Something touched her forehead, all woodsy and cinnamon. A feathery sensation brushed her cheeks.

Vi cracked one eye open and slowly looked around. What was Rory doing here? As a matter of fact, where was here? She gazed back at him. Elbows propped on the bedrail, his chin rested on his intertwined fingers. She raised a hand and touched her forehead. Had he kissed her?

"Wake up, Sleeping Beauty," his rumbly voice teased, confirming her suspicions.

How had this happened? She'd never allowed Rory this close. She glanced at a bandage on her arm, then sniffed hospital antiseptic. Her eyes arrowed back to Rory. Oddly enough, his nearness didn't bother her. Quite the opposite. She found his presence almost comforting. A thought pushed through her groggy mind—did this Casanova kiss as good as he looked? He hadn't retreated but seemed to judge her reaction. Her gaze trailed to his lips.

As if he read the yearning she'd newly discovered, twin flares of delight warmed his gray eyes. His mouth stretched in a wordless grin.

Rory leaned toward her, his enticing mustache twitching a tad. Her eyes closed as his lips gently covered hers. Mm. The kiss deepened into pure pleasure. Vi forgot all about mashed potatoes.

ENGAGED IN TOTAL BLISS, Rory didn't hear the door open.

"My stars, Violet! What are you doing?" a female voice demanded.

Rory froze in place. Vi jerked those soft, come-hither lips away. *Bummer.* He straightened, searching for the noisy source of outrage. Blast it. That lovely kiss had him all fuzzy-headed.

A small woman bearing an uncanny resemblance to Vi stood a couple of feet away from the bed. Clad in a teal-colored skirt and matching jacket, her hands balled into fists. Her behavior suggested Rory wasn't even in the room.

She paused for breath and plowed on. "I let you out of my sight, Violet, and immediately, you go off and ... and ... I find you kissing—*kissing.*" Ending on a shrill note, she threw her hands in the air.

Rory wanted to call a timeout.

"I'm fine, Mother. Thanks for asking." Vi sank deeper into the pillow, her eyes looking everywhere but at him.

Rory frowned. This indignant creature passed as Vi's mother? Not exactly how he planned to meet her, if ever. She and Vi could have been twins. However, at the moment, they acted nothing alike. Vi usually stayed on an even keel—unless she was hightailing it away from him. He much preferred the way she'd been kissing him back.

Meanwhile, the woman continued to fire off volleys of words. "You are most certainly *not* fine, or else you wouldn't be here." She favored Vi with an icy blue stare. "Why, you're covered with scrapes and bruises. What happened to you? No one would tell me anything!" She crossed her arms, apparently waiting for a full explanation.

Vi spared him a glance before she gazed with a bored expression at the ceiling. The plea in her eyes had been so fleeting he could have missed it.

Rory jumped into action, clearing his throat with gusto. "You know, ma'am, none of us knows the complete story. And" —he paused while his mind leapfrogged to a solution—"until Vi recovers enough to help us piece it together, any explanation will have to wait. The doctor gave strict instructions for her to rest."

"That's what she was doing when I walked through the door? Resting?" Her mom's perfectly tinted brows mocked him. "Who are you?"

"Rory Spence. And you are …?"

"Tru Marshall. What line of work are you in, Rory?" His name jerked from her mouth.

"Mo-ther!" Vi's face pinked, objection rolling off each syllable.

Bring it, Mom. He'd had plenty of practice with aggressive females.

"I'll be glad to tell you over a cup of coffee, ma'am. Guaranteed to taste terrible, unless the in-house coffee shop is open, but Vi needs to rest." Rory had spent a couple of years perfecting friendly-no-wiggle-room negotiator-speak. It'd be worth every dreary meeting if it worked now.

Though Tru still wore an irritated expression, Rory walked around the bed to stand by her. When she turned slightly in his direction, he gave a silent cheer. Her I'm-in-charge perfume argued with the antiseptic smell of the room.

Nothing else to do but go for it. Rory edged toward the door, inclining his head. A delicate balance of courtesy and suggestion remained crucial.

Suspicion in her narrowed gaze, Mother huffed and marched toward the door, high heels stabbing the floor. "Coffee will do."

Dare he touch her? What if Vi got the hands-off attitude from her? The words of his father replayed in his mind. *There are times, Rory, you have to take a risk. Zero risk, zero-gain.*

Rory gently took Mom's elbow and glanced back at Vi. Her head turned sideways, she gazed at him, her rose-petal lips opening in a small O. He winked and ushered the woman out the door.

FIVE MINUTES HADN'T PASSED when the door swooshed open again. "*Mija*, you're awake!" Paige entered, her black boots click-clacking across the floor. She swathed Vi in a careful hug. "How are you?"

Vi's eyes filled with tears. If only she could bat away these blasted emotions. "I'm fine. A little banged up." She hurt all over. "What happened, Paige? Mother came, and I couldn't even tell her why I was here."

"Yes, I saw them in the hall—"

"Why was Rory here?" Vi couldn't keep the tartness out of

her voice. No one else needed to know about their kiss. It was embarrassing enough Mother caught them as if they were a couple of teenagers. Shadowy memories of high school days poked into the present. She shifted uncomfortably, her lips still tingling.

Paige's dark eyes widened. "Rory and I took shifts so you wouldn't be alone. Only when my turn rolled around, he wouldn't leave. He paced the hall and drank coffee. What do you remember?"

Vi's eyes squeezed shut. This morning happened ages ago. "Uh, I needed space, so I drove out to the house and walked outside. I heard puppies ... there were bees. I ran ... and fell into the old cistern Daddy boarded up years ago." A shiver raked through her body. She reached for another blanket.

Paige helped her unfold it, then tucked her in. "We got worried when you didn't return. Rory left to search for you, then he climbed down and injected you with an EpiPen."

The ache spread to a dull roar in Vi's head. "What? How did he know?"

"Rory found you first, then saw the bees. He called to ask if you were allergic, but he'd already put it together."

"Rory?" Vi couldn't imagine the man being useful in a practical sense. Well, he scooted Mother out of the room. That kiss ... She looked through the blinds. City lights dotted the darkness.

Paige's voice rose. "The paramedics said his quick actions saved your life."

"Surely, it wasn't that bad." Even as the words left her mouth, Vi knew the truth. Her parents had lectured her about the seriousness of anaphylactic shock ever since she could remember.

"*Mija*, they had to give you oxygen down in that awful hole." Paige's voice shook, tears sliding down her cheeks.

Vi grasped her hands. "I'm okay now, Paige." The sterile room grew smaller by the second. None of this would have happened if she hadn't run off this morning.

They were both silent, contemplating the unthinkable alternative. Vi shook her head weakly. She had to move forward. Think about anything but Rory Spence. Then she remembered her idea. "Who knows about remodeling? I finally figured out what I want to do. Updating my house is the first step."

Amusement crept into the other woman's expression.

"What? Do you know a consultant?" What made this funny?

A snicker escaped before Paige covered her mouth. "Yes, *mija*. I know the perfect person. You know him too."

"I do? Someone from church?" Her current brain fog rendered her thinking capacity to soggy leaves and dirt.

Laughter lurked in Paige's melodic accent. "Aside from co-owning Peeps with Jesse and his dad, Rory is a contractor. If anyone in Valiant knows what to do and has the right contacts, it's him. Want me to set up a meeting?"

The aroma from the diffuser streamed a light lavender scent into the small, dim room. Vi used deep, kneading petrissage strokes to roll and release the knots on the upper back of a woman lying on the massage table. Sweet lady with neck and shoulder muscles that resembled the stretchy part of a straw. Vi could empathize. Her foot, encased in a walking boot all day, felt cramped. She longed to rub her aching instep.

Vi's conscience smarted right along with the pain in her foot. She'd deliberately scheduled a last-minute massage over her appointment with Rory. A face-to-face meeting would be embarrassing, considering their kiss in the hospital. What a dreadful mistake. The client flinched, and Vi realized her fingers had tightened into weapons. "Sorry," she murmured.

Stepping back, Vi slathered her hands with oil for one last round of circular stroking movements, forcing her mind away from a certain handsome redhead. When she finished, Vi bid the woman goodbye in a low unhurried voice, then slipped out the adjoining door to the women's dressing room. Clients deserved an unrushed feeling to complete the massage experience. Vi couldn't control what happened once they left—most of them trotted back to their stressful lives—but a restful hour of tension relief helped.

Vi glanced at the white bandages on her arms and grimaced. When Paige had filled in the gaps of what had happened on Thanksgiving Day, she'd not minced words. *Rory saved your life.* How did a person deal with that?

She moved to the sink and washed her hands carefully, drying every bit of excess moisture with paper towels. Germs remained an occupational hazard. She licked dry lips and headed back to change the massage table linens, beyond ready for this day to end. Her body ached as if someone knocked her stuffing loose.

The perky, upbeat music floating through the speakers signaled Peeps' evening environment, making Vi more than ready to leave the energetic pace. A yoga class might soothe her weariness, but the mental picture of striking a warrior pose with the cumbersome boot eliminated the idea. Thankful her injuries never encompassed more than a sprained ankle and a few scrapes, she finished with the linens and trudged from the women's dressing room.

Oh, no.

The absolute, no-holds-barred, last person on earth she wanted to see sat in the nearby waiting area. Rory thumbed through a magazine, one ankle crossed over a knee as if he had all the time in the world. Her face burned.

His gaze caught hers. He flicked the magazine aside and stood, then closed the short distance between them. His lips formed a no-nonsense line. "We had an appointment."

"I had a massage." Her insides cringed. Then, as if tattling on her half-truth, the infernal boot snagged on the carpet, and she stumbled.

Fast as a whip, Rory grasped her upper arms and steadied her. "No more tumbles, Vi."

The compassionate words robbed Vi of her last defenses. "I'm sorry." She choked out. To her dismay, her eyes filled. She sniffed, blinking back the tears.

Rory's eyes softened, as if he recognized her exhaustion. He took her elbow gently. "The deli's closed, but we can still talk in there." Vi let him guide her across the lobby, since her steps compared to putty.

Was it wise to meet with him now? Probably most unwise. With Vi's emotions running so high, no telling what she'd do or say. Her head turned toward the double doors leading to the parking lot. His grip firmed around her elbow as if he'd guessed her thoughts. As they walked lockstep across the carpeted area, Vi felt the slight hitch in his gait. The close way they covered ground, an onlooker would have assumed ... She forced her mind away from the obvious conclusion. Her brain rattled with annoyance over the boot and questions about their non-relationship. But what about Rory? His lifestyle included a boot of sorts—forever.

He opened a deli side door most members didn't know existed and led her to a table. The roll-down metal curtain kept them out of sight from the brightly lit lobby—Peeps' public eye. He pulled out a chair for her, then took one across the table. Vi sank into the chair, relieved to be off her feet. Rory's drawn features suggested he'd had a long, busy day. However, a steely determination still seeped through. She hadn't noticed that attribute before. Pulling a tiny orange from a pocket of her scrubs, she stuck her thumb in the top and separated the peeling from the soft fruit.

The silence stretched. The dim room helped to shield Vi's observation of him. Broad shoulders and muscled biceps pulled his white dress shirt taut. Brick-red hair spiked in wavy tufts. Firm jaw. Nice lips between mustache and beard. *Don't look at his lips, girl.*

Rory shifted. "Vi." His tone held no judgment.

Music sounded in the distance. Weights thudded and exercise machines clattered from upstairs. She had no idea what to say. *Sorry I blew off our appointment? Sorry I got focused on my foot and forgot you lost one? Hey, loved the kiss. Can we do it again without Mother?* Cheeks warm, she stared at the peeled orange in her hands, picking at the white membrane.

He cleared his throat. Even in the weak lighting, she could have sworn his eyes twinkled. "Um. Paige mentioned you're looking to remodel a house and need consulting advice. Is that the gist of it?"

She nodded, unable to trust her voice. Rory made it sound so reasonable. The truth smacked her in the face. Her preconceived opinions of him were causing her to doubt his skill. Paige had made it abundantly clear Rory's sharp business acumen rated a consult at the very least, though Vi had tried to forget the expansive list of adjectives that had flowed forth— Integrity. Professional to the bone. Excellent communicator. Yada, yada, yada ... Would it be so terrible to ask him a few questions?

Transparency had never been easy for her, but if he could be determined, so could she. She looked him square in the eye. Oh, dear. Big mistake. "Sorry. Emotions have been getting the best of me lately. And I haven't thanked you. Paige says you saved my life."

When he didn't answer, she rushed on, "Daddy left me a house and property. I haven't known what to do with it." His interested expression encouraged her to continue. "When I went to the house on Thanksgiving, um, before the bees ..." She laughed shakily and set the orange atop the peelings in a neat pile. "I got the idea to remodel. I lived there as a child." Good. She'd said it, even though she swiped at a tear.

Rory didn't seem perturbed with her emotions leaking like a drippy faucet. "I heard about your dad's passing a few months back. I'm sorry for your sake he's gone." His eyes shone with compassion. "We lost Mom when I was a teen. Don't deny your emotions. Grief can be unpredictable. One minute you're fine. Then, almost in the same breath, you're crying and mad at the world."

Vi's brows raised. He'd described the rollercoaster she'd ridden the last few months with scary accuracy. "You're on the other side," she whispered around the lump in her throat.

He nodded. "The heartache will heal eventually. Doesn't mean you won't miss him. It's been fourteen years, and I still miss Mom." He paused a moment. "Vi, are you sure you're ready to move forward with a project as extensive as a remodel? Fixing up your childhood home may prove more difficult than you think."

The slender fingers of his hands clasped together easily, and he still didn't appear in a hurry. Neither did he seem reluctant to help. He wanted to make certain the remodel path fit her needs. As if he cared not only in a professional sense but for her overall well-being. Wow. This perspective of Rory boggled her mind. A far cry from the flirty guy she'd kept at arm's length. Even though he'd always been an integral part of their friend group, they'd never had a serious conversation. She'd been too busy avoiding him.

Rory continued as if he hadn't shattered her preconceptions of him. "The remodel itself isn't an issue. I know and use the best subcontractors in my line of work. I can help you through the bidding process for supplies and labor, guide you through the financials, and let you know what it will cost versus how much you want to spend. That's the easy part."

"What's the hard part?" Vi's hands twisted in her lap.

For the first time since they sat down, his eyes flickered. "We, um, will have to work together. Up in each other's grill, so to speak. Phone calls, texts, meetings, errands—it will be a much smoother ride if you trust me."

Things with no name crawled through Vi's stomach. He would say the dreadful T-word. Because of her own bad choices, the only man she trusted without reserve had been Daddy. "Let me think about it." Her voice trailed into a squeak.

"Take your time. I won't rush you." The deep soft murmur calmed the wriggling horde inside Vi.

Wait. They were talking about business, right? Vi's head spun. Overthinking his motives wouldn't help. Her gut fluttered with unease.

Rory rose in a fluid motion and extended his hand. "Here. I'll walk you to your car. It's getting dark outside."

Despite her conflicting feelings, Vi wouldn't refuse an escort. Since word got out about Brenna's abduction, everyone at Peeps had become more vigilant. Vi tossed the orange and peelings into the waste container and fell into step beside Rory. A sliver of the moon beamed through a sky striated with clouds. Shrub roses near the entrance perfumed the air with a delicate sweet fragrance.

A vehicle rumbled, red taillights glowing as it exited the parking lot. Almost to her car, Vi's traitorous boot slid on the gravel. Twice in one evening. Could she evaporate into the asphalt? Rory kept her upright, his arm encircling her waist. At the very least, the man deserved kudos for *not* commenting on her clumsiness.

He released her and stood back, hands in his pockets. She

fumbled with her keys, though managed to open the door without mishap.

Safely inside the car, she risked a peek at him. Darkness hid his features. He stroked his beard with his thumb and fingers.

Amusement lacing his voice, he said, "And Vi? I won't initiate any more kisses."

Vi's teeth ground together. Of course, Rory would bring up what she wanted so badly to forget. She slammed the gearshift in reverse and backed out, unwilling to acknowledge the remark. She sped out of the parking lot lightning-bolt-style but peeked in her rearview mirror. Rory hadn't moved an inch.

She braked at a red light and tapped the steering wheel with impatience. *He* wouldn't initiate any more kisses. As if she might? Her conscience pinged. They both knew she'd invited the second kiss.

Waiting for the light to turn, she debated. Her place or Paige's?

CHAPTER SIX

Rory squinted at Vi's yellow car. He knew perfectly well his reference to their marvelous kiss would make her mad. He still needed to say it on the off chance she might want to repeat it. He snorted at the thought. Most unrealistic, given her reaction. However, her drag-racing out of the parking lot worried him. Similar to the way she'd run off Thanksgiving morning and fallen in a hole. His pulse ratcheted all over again when he remembered her feeble response to the Epi injection.

The rational side of his brain waged war against his gut. If Vi went to Paige's, the traffic would slow her driving to normal. If she went to her place, she'd be alone in an empty house. Criminals loved out-of-the-way places.

Ignoring Vi's probable reaction, he turned and ran for his car. Her reckless driving combined with her destination—he needed to ensure she didn't get in trouble again. Why Vi was his business remained unclear.

Once he reached the access lane, Vi's car turned the corner onto the road to her place. Christmas lights from local businesses blurred into a red and green haze as he whizzed down the road after her. Following her taillights, he turned onto a bumpy dirt path. He gritted his teeth, hoping his vehicle's undercarriage would cooperate. When he saw her car parked next to the house, he exhaled with relief. Indirect light shone from a window, but nothing about the place seemed familiar in the darkness. When he'd been here previously, he'd had other concerns. Now here he'd come again, to make sure nothing worse had befallen her. He pushed aside the questions rising in his mind.

A smoky haze in the distance spun him into combat mode. Rory opened the console and slid his pistol from its holster. A strong sense of danger prickled at the back of his neck. He climbed out and stuck the gun in the waistband of his pants. What had Vi gotten herself into this time?

Locusts sang their eerie one-note song. A chill wrapped around Rory's spine as he approached the porch. A burning scent hit his nostrils, harkening him back to Afghanistan. With stealth, he eased up the steps and opened the door without making a sound. The front room stood empty.

Then Vi yelled, "Hey!" Male voices grunted curses. Rory dashed across the living area, noisily slamming his boots against the floor. He hoped whoever had surprised Vi would suppose an entire army had arrived. Almost to the doorway, he slipped the pistol out, pointing it down.

He entered the room and quickly took stock of the situation. Hands on her hips, Vi glared at two young men. Their filthy clothes and matted hair suggested the vagrant living conditions of homeless illegals. The fear in their eyes mirrored Vi's, but it would disappear the instant they realized she was alone—good thing he'd listened to his gut instead of his head.

Rory pointed the pistol at the men. "*Necesitas irte ahora, dozd.*" He held his breath, backing his order with a wave of his gun toward the door.

They scrambled out the open door, dropping boxes of food. Canned goods thudded on the floor and rolled. Rory strode through the kitchen, gazing through the window as they raced into the scrub brush.

When he turned, Vi's blue eyes had darkened with emotion. "What ..." She leaned over, steadied her hands on her knees, and inhaled deeply for a few seconds. When normal breaths returned, she lifted her gaze. "What are you—you followed me!"

A shrug lifted Rory's shoulders, his breathing erratic. He hadn't used a gun since deployment.

Bewilderment etching her features, Vi asked, "What did you say to them? They blasted out of here like the house had caught fire."

"A botched-up mixture of Spanish and Farsi that made no sense." Rory shook his head. "The gun convinced them to leave." Frowning, he put the pistol back into his waistband. Thoughts of what could have happened haunted him.

Vi stepped over to the small dining table and plopped into a chair. Her fingers absently combed through her long, curly hair. "I guess I'm glad you showed up, but it still doesn't explain why you followed me." Her brows arched in a "this better be good" look.

Okay. Not ready to process two strangers in her house, so he'd deal with the fallout from his remark about the kiss. He sought a chair and settled into it, not as controlled or nimble as he preferred. The immediate relief in his right leg made it worth the nick to his pride.

When Vi's eyes turned purplish, his attention mimicked the cans rolling everywhere. With effort, he finally said, "Hey, I know you're mad about what I said, but I hated the way you tore out of the parking lot. I didn't want you to get in trouble again." Exactly what would have transpired, had he not shown up? His gut tightened at the thought.

When her brows arched even higher, he steepled his hands and rubbed his thumbs together. Yeah, his explanation made it worse. Time for a Hail Mary. He said carefully, "Vi, could we hit the reset button? You know, do the grace-thing with each other?"

The wariness abruptly left Vi's expression, replaced with an emotion Rory couldn't read. She said, "Yeah. That'd be good," and rose to leave the kitchen.

Hmm. Did she mean it, or did her quick capitulation involve an ulterior motive, one he hadn't seen yet? Stella always had an agenda. If their friendship had any chance of survival, however remote, extending grace to each other only made sense. With the additional stress of a remodel, it would be crucial.

An awful thought sobered him. What if Vi turned into one of those women contractors hated? When the unexpected happened, they turned into fire-breathing dragons, incinerating anyone who got in the way. Detail-obsessed, continually dissatisfied … the list went on and on. He stared at the fiery red hair trailing down her back. Cute little package, but if she considered him a pushover …

"Do you think they'll return?" She tossed the words over her shoulder.

Starting this minute, Rory would clarify his position—a man who wouldn't sugarcoat a dangerous situation to coddle her feelings. "Probably. You shouldn't be out here alone, especially at night."

Her shoulders slumped as his meaning hit home. "That's a hard one. I depend on those walks. When Daddy died, I stopped, then found … well, I need the habit again. Besides, they're trespassing, right? This is private property." She turned, drilling him with a part-stubborn, part-pleading look.

Rory could relate to Vi's need to walk. The bench-press machine had become his go-to stress reliever. He softened his stance. "My guess is they're illegal immigrants who set up camp in an out-of-the-way place—which is your land, so yes, they're trespassing. I'll notify Tavo. They'll scatter for a while with regular patrols, but it's still risky out here by yourself."

Her lips twisted. "This land belongs to me. Walking around the lake keeps me sane. If I can't ..." She turned and stumbled into the living area. Empathy kicked into gear when he noticed the wide boot hampering her progress and her look of frustration. Crankiness stemming from a physical issue proved an ongoing battle—one with which he stayed intimately familiar.

Her words convinced Rory. The property belonged to her by rights. Nothing wrong with her desire to walk in the comfort of her inheritance. He envied her for having a place she loved. Especially since he hadn't felt a deep connection to any place since Mom had died.

"I get it. If you'll be patient ..." Her dejected look had his brain firing piston-style. "I'll figure out a way for you to take those nighttime strolls. Deal?" A shift took place on the inside. Even if he had to hire a bodyguard, Vi would get her walks.

They stepped onto the porch. She stopped and faced him again, her heart-shaped face wreathed in a smile. "Deal. When can we get the remodel started?"

The little vertical crease between Vi's eyes deepened at his slacked jaw. "I think fast."

Excitement made his pulse race. Maybe Vi was wired to make quick decisions, but for him, it answered a prayer he hadn't known how to articulate. Remodel options cut rivers through his mind. He shifted the weight from his sore leg.

Development for the subdivision continued to flourish. Updating this old Victorian would challenge and expand his skill set while he waited for the right piece of land to build the rehab center. He gazed around the large wraparound porch through a contractor's eyes. Missing boards, windows with cracked glass, peeling paint. What little he'd seen of the interior needed a significant update. He had the know-how to redeem this place and restore it into a real home.

Vi gazed at him with a pinched expression. "It needs a ton of work, doesn't it?"

Rory chuckled in sheer relief. Construction, he understood. The workings of a woman's mind? Not so much. "This is your house, Vi. Nothing will happen until we're both sure what you want and how much you're willing to spend."

When the worry in her eyes eased a bit, it pleased him. Too much.

The dim stars struggled to shine in the muddled sky. The burning scent persisted, though now it had a meaty aroma. Rory shuddered to think about what animal roasted over a makeshift spit. Possum or squirrel came to mind first. From there, it went downhill. He'd call Tavo about the squatters on his way home.

She pivoted and faced him, legs planted, and arms crossed. "You're limping." It wasn't a question.

"It happens. Not a big deal." Rory tried to lighten his tone despite the surging irritation. For once, they'd been on the same page. Then she had to spoil it.

"It *is* a big deal." Her gaze swept his face. "It's wearing you out. A massage would help."

He refused to go there. If she put her hands on him, he'd turn into a mushy ball of whatever-you-do-don't-stop. "I'll be fine." It came out as a growl.

"Not if you don't treat your leg better." Her stubborn look had returned.

Rory grunted and turned to his car, hating that his leg seemed to agree with her. He fumed, all but crawling in behind the steering wheel. He'd find a way for Vi to take her walks. Then he'd remodel her house exactly the way she wanted it.

Once those two things happened, he would say adios. No massage, ever.

Her car door slammed.

Yeah, he'd made her mad. Rory punched the ignition button of the Lexus. It was better this way. No matter how much he wanted to kiss her again.

CHAPTER SEVEN

A corner of Rory's mouth lifted in a knowing smile. He checked the time on his phone while Dad wrapped up a conference call. The older man's steps increased, and his words clipped as he paced a well-trod path behind his executive office desk.

Rory's spacious suite adjoined Dad's, but Rory preferred his Peeps' office. Despite the small space, he treasured the breathing room. Far less chance of being pulled into discussions that didn't concern him. The role of Dad's glorified errand boy remained a bothersome image. One he'd worked hard to overcome. His last name might be Spence, but he craved an identity apart from his legendary father.

The office reflected Dad's taste—well-crafted wood furnishings and comfortable seating. Nothing ultra-expensive. Dad never wanted to forget his humble beginnings. One issue they agreed on.

"Confounded phone meetings. Those calls suck the life right out of flexible thinking and creativity. Everybody's focused on saying their two cents. About what it's worth too." Dad's bright blue eyes sparked.

Rory steepled his fingers on his lips as his father plopped down across from him in a rawhide-colored suede chair. He thunked his phone on the coffee table. "Let the thing rest so I can think." He stood with the energy of a much younger man, strode to his desk, and pushed the intercom button. "Becca? Coffee, please."

Moments later, a fortyish rail-thin blonde wearing a don't-mess-with-me suit and fashionable high heels entered the room with a coffee tray. She set it on the coffee table between the two men and turned to leave.

"How're you today, Becca? Is Dad treating you right?" Rory grinned, anticipating her response.

"Rory, you been askin' the same thing for years, and the answer ain't never gonna change. The man's an absolute tyrant. Don't know why I put up with him." She stalked from the room, nose in the air. Rory's smile broadened.

Dad chuckled, totally unperturbed. "Becca needs a raise. She's been here so long she knows what I'm going to say half the time."

"Yeah, she's loyal to the core—and you *can* be a tyrant." Rory considered any long-term relationship a blessing. Well, the positive ones, anyway. What if a woman embraced him as he was? His dream of having a family, a loving wife, and a passel of kids, had fallen silent in the loud, ever-present noise of his disability. He'd come to accept his limitations. On good days, he gave thanks for the painful journey that had molded him into a better man. Most women never made it that far.

Dad sipped his coffee. "Tell me about High Meadows." The new subdivision they'd been developing the last couple of months had taken off. Scads of calls were flowing in from young families who wanted to settle in Valiant's newest upscale neighborhood. When the idea first formed, Rory had contemplated building a spec home and moving in, yet a fancy designer home had no appeal in his solitary state. Homes needed families to fill them.

They continued to discuss the subdivision development for the next fifteen minutes, then the older man said, "I'm working to procure the tract of land you and Jesse want for Peeps, but my surveyor says the adjoining acreage is an even better deal."

Rory straightened. "Bigger?" The size of the lot they'd purchased meant scaling down their expansion plans. More land would resolve the issue.

"Yep. About twice the size. I'll send directions so you and Jess can see for yourselves." He swirled a finger in the air, a signal to move on. Rory nodded. Busy schedule aside, he wanted to broach the subject of remodeling Vi's house.

"If it's okay with you, I want to push the nuts and bolts of Peeps' expansion to next week." Rory held his breath. Dad preferred set talking points.

The older man eyed him while sipping his coffee. "What's on your mind, son?"

Here it came. Rory loved and respected his father and wanted to keep him in the proverbial loop. Unfortunately, he had a pretty good idea of where Dad stood on the subject. "I've been asked to remodel an old Victorian. It looks and sounds like a project I want."

His father huffed and set his cup down too hard, splashing large drops on the oak coffee table. Rory snatched tissues out of the holder and wiped up the mess. Dad's opinion had made itself clear before he'd ever spoken a word.

"I've always steered clear of remodels—not enough money in old construction. Nasty problems lurk behind existing structures. Hard to estimate costs. Messy work. Owners get sentimental over junk when it's better torn down."

Yep. At least he'd gotten the short version. Rory couldn't explain how the old house beckoned him. Whenever he thought about it, something deep inside wiggled akin to a baby tooth. Part ache. Part joy and wonder. He'd already said yes on his end. Still waiting on Vi's yea or nay. He placed his mug on the coffee table.

"Is there a woman involved?" Dad's stern countenance reminded him of the countless times he'd gotten into trouble as a boy. He'd hoped the subject wouldn't come up. Dad knew him too well.

He hedged, "The homeowner is a woman." The woman he couldn't quit daydreaming about. Even if her feelings didn't match his.

Dad pushed out his lips and nodded, but he only said, "Be careful, son. A young contractor is only one bad deal away from losing his shirt and his reputation."

Advice Rory had heard before. "I know, Dad. I got this." Even as the words hopped out of his mouth, he hoped he could follow through. What if Vi didn't have the funds for a major remodel? He'd gotten carried away with the prospect of restoring the home and forgotten the contractor's golden rule —if the job wasn't cost-effective, it wasn't worth the risk.

The project hadn't left the starting gate, and he'd already goofed. *Get your head in the game, Spence.*

Dad's shrewd look shut down his musings. "Talked to your brother lately?"

Another worn-out topic. Rory grabbed for his ebbing patience. Dad always asked about Mark, as if Rory and his brother were still in high school. "Nope. Not since the last time you asked." His brother embraced his anti-social nature to the max. Apparently, he included family in his wide sweep of everything he couldn't bother with. "Want me to swing by the zoo? You know he doesn't return calls."

"Well, one of us should check on him. Make sure he's alive and well." Dad ran a hand over his face. The crow's feet deepened around his eyes.

"It's Mark's choice not to communicate, Dad." Rory kept his voice even.

The older man went on as if he hadn't heard the last remark. "We need to reach out. Your mom's death took a toll on him."

"Dad, it happened fourteen years ago. It affected all of us, not just him." Rory stood. He'd had this conversation with Dad many times over the years with varying degrees of heat.

"I know." He leveled a look at Rory. "Mark has always marched to his own drummer. But this deliberate separation concerns me. As you get older, you think more about these things."

"I'll catch up to him." Rory wiggled his good leg, then the prosthetic.

"You do that. Remind him he still has an old man. You got a meeting?" His dad stood, hands in his pockets.

"Always. Don't know what I'd do without Paige to keep me straight." Shooting a quick prayer heavenwards, Rory hoped Vi would give a thumbs up on the remodel. Once he knew, he'd get Paige in the loop.

"Sweet little gal. Good head on her shoulders."

With effort, Rory kept his eyes at face level. What Dad didn't say flapped through the air on bulky wings. "Bye, Dad."

His dad barked out a single-syllable laugh. "Don't want to go there, huh?" He stood and clapped a hand on Rory's shoulder. "I'm proud of you, son. You're a fine young man. When you find the right one, you'll know it."

"Thanks for saying so, Dad."

Despite the not-so-subtle references to settling down, Rory hugged the older man with affection. They'd adapted the practice shortly after Mom died. Once they realized somebody you loved could be gone in an instant.

A smug look passed over the older man's face, and his eyes glinted with mischief. "I won't even play the grandkid card —today."

With a wry look, Rory adjusted his gait and strode to the door. His thoughts were elsewhere. Why did a little woman with fiery red hair flit through his mind faster than his dad could say the g-word?

CHAPTER EIGHT

Alone in the deli, Vi pushed her salad away after listening to Mother's latest voicemail. Thoughts of Mother only entrenched Vi's desire to remodel her childhood home. Vi wanted to meet with Rory, but calling him felt awkward. Why couldn't she have held her tongue about the limp? Touchy subject. A little discretion on her part might have helped. Or not.

With a sigh, she gazed out the artificially frosted window. Upbeat Christmas music floated from the upstairs speakers. *Dashing through the snow …* Yeah, snow in South Texas happened once a decade, if then. A ten-foot-tall Christmas tree shimmered with red and silver decorations. Essential oil wafted throughout the lobby, a pungent mixture of pine and cinnamon.

She bit her lip and cringed. The tender flesh had already suffered through previous nibbling. Her heavy massage schedule and the unknown remodel costs were taking a toll. Resuming her walks around the lake would help with the anxiety. However, the vagrant incident spooked her more than she wanted to admit. Absorbed in her thoughts, she shrieked when Rory slid into the seat across from her.

"Gotcha! How's my favorite redhead today?" His gray eyes widened.

The unintended remark made Vi laugh, even as a pleasant sense of belonging splashed against her walls of solitude. Unfortunately, her mind chose the moment to replay their kiss, making her cheeks flush with warmth.

Rory returned her grin as if he knew where her thoughts flew.

Vi tore her eyes from his and struggled for coherent thought. This ... this *twitterpating* would never do. She stammered, "We need to talk."

He nodded as if in agreement, glancing at her uneaten salad. "Not hungry?"

Then Vi remembered why her appetite vanished. "I'd be hungrier if I could figure out what to do with Mom."

"Ah. Mother."

Another chuckle rose in Vi's throat at Rory's wry inference. "You got a firsthand view of how she acts when things aren't going according to plan." She'd never asked about his "coffee date" with Mom. It brought up memories she preferred to avoid.

"I got the impression she loves you, but doesn't know how to show it." Rory patted her hand. "She'll figure it out."

"We've always butted heads." Vi's relationship with Mom normally stayed private. However, Rory had already met the woman. "This latest round, she's insisting I move back to Houston."

"What's in Houston for you?" Rory's thumbs rubbed together.

"Bad memories. I lived there off and on for several years. Big city life is not my tamale."

"Seems to me you've got a good life here. If you haven't changed your mind, we need to talk next steps about your house."

His sensible tone cheered her in a way she couldn't explain. She bit her lip again when reality knocked. "How much will this cost, Rory?" Staying cool and professional about a subject so close to her heart had become increasingly difficult.

The depths of his eyes swirled. Deep. Intense. "Depends. I'll need to walk through your house and get an idea of what you have in mind before I can even quote a ballpark estimate. The price range can vary by thousands."

Gratitude eased her tight throat. Straightforward. Upfront. This kind of communication she understood. She glanced at the clock. Not quite 12:30. "I don't have another massage until 3:00, then I'm booked through the evening. How's your afternoon?"

Rory pulled out his phone and clicked through several screens. "I'm good until 4:00. Let me grab a sandwich first. You tell me what's important to you house-wise, then we drive out there." His gaze trailed to her uneaten salad. "You want anything when I order?"

His calm take-charge manner set her at ease, even if it bugged her. This was a job to him. She swatted the thought away as if it were a noisome fly. "Excellent plan. And I'd love a pineapple smoothie."

"You got it. Don't get me started on the smoothie bar though. I can wax eloquent on the topic longer than anybody wants to listen."

Vi giggled and reached for her purse, but he ignored her. As she gazed out on the sunny day, Mother's depressing voicemail dissipated. Talking to Rory had drained off most of the tension. And the bit about waxing eloquent? She found the humility refreshing ... and endearing. But he was male. To the core. She didn't dare forget.

Rory set the smoothie next to her, settled in his chair, and held out his hand. "Want to bless the food with me?"

Oh, dear. Their group held hands during prayer. Since she'd removed herself from his vicinity whenever they gathered, this twist threw her off balance. The spark in his eyes revealed he knew she'd avoided him. The challenge lurking in the depths spurred her to action. She touched his hand with her fingers.

The floor-to-ceiling window emitted a perpetual chill, but there was nothing cold about Rory's gentle grip.

RORY'S INSIDES *whoop-whooped* as they drove to the house. Vi had taken his hand when they prayed over the meal. Not that he would have let her off the hook. If this project had any hope of success, her days of running from him were over. He cast a side look at her compact frame in the leather seat. The slate blue Peeps' hoodie over navy scrubs and the long braid flowing down the front of one shoulder made his pulse whoop too. Steady there, bud. She's complying because it's business. Let go of the fantasy and get real.

He opted for small talk. Jesse had no patience with chit-chat, but Rory had discovered it opened a lot of doors. "How many massages this morning?"

"Two down. Three this evening.

"Do you enjoy the work?"

She yawned. "I do. It's, um, fulfilling to ease people's physical pain." She stifled another yawn. "Sorry. Don't know why I'm so sleepy."

Rory's hands tightened on the steering wheel. Sleepy meant relaxed. Another box checked. A decent outing would help her trust him—though the why remained a mystery. He sensed a deep, protracted root. No expert on relationships, he defaulted to what he knew. A house was built in layers. He'd build this relationship with a sound foundation. Strong as cement. Mixed with care and poured in increments.

A question or two at a time. "And your ankle? How much longer in the boot?"

"It's healing. Not fast enough to suit me, but now it only hurts if I overdo. About four more weeks? It'll be after Christmas."

Vi's timeframe sounded optimistic. Far be it from him to dash her hopes.

The Lexus bumped along the ruddy dirt path, arriving at her place slightly indignant. Rory climbed out of the car and gazed at the once-majestic house. The fresh territory whispered his name. Dry brown leaves danced around his face, mirroring the excitement rising in his spirit. He looked at Vi to see if she noticed anything different.

Consternation had settled in her lips and jaw. "I need help to visualize a finished product. All I see is peeling paint, rotten boards, and way too much landscaping for one person to accomplish." She pointed. "I love the curlicue wood cutouts in the corners."

Rory forced his rising emotion into a professional box. "Gingerbread. You'll get to pick out all you want so long as your budget agrees. Fresh paint and new siding will fix the exterior. Once it's restored, you'll have a classic up-to-date Victorian home."

A stiff wind gusted under a bright white sky. More leaves blew across their path. A hint of smoke drifted in the breezy currents of air. Rory extended a hand, relieved when she took it and helped her up the uneven steps. Their footsteps echoed on the wooden porch.

Vi unlocked the front door, and they entered the living area. Alit with curiosity, Rory gestured around the room. "May I?"

At her nod, he slipped into contractor mode and began a tour of the premises. The joy slow-waltzed into a tango as he inspected bedrooms, bathrooms, and closets. Vi had silently followed at a distance, hanging back when he climbed the stairs.

On the second floor, Rory surveyed a master bedroom with small closets and an even smaller bathroom. Trademark of an era when people didn't require as much. Easy makeover. More closet space and a bathroom extension would be a snap in this large room. An alcove nestled into a wall near the bathroom. Perfect setup for an infant.

After a quick peek at a balcony overlooking the property, he clomped back down the stairs. Vi waited for him in the living area, apprehension masking her pretty face. Man, he wanted to make her worries go away.

"You've got a magnificent house, Vi." His enthusiasm spilled over—no smoke to blow here. His exhilaration climbed to a fever pitch. Seeing this place come to life would satisfy an itch he hadn't even known existed.

"Daddy said the house had good bones," Vi murmured.

"He was right. There's always the possibility of things cropping up we don't foresee. I've learned how to work around most of those issues."

Her jaw had loosened, even if her eyes remained wary. "Did you see the kitchen?"

Enthusiasm stretched his lips wide. "I save the best for last. It's cliché, but I've always thought the kitchen is the real heart of the home."

Vi's lips tweaked. Adorably so. "If that's the case, this kitchen is on life-support."

She led the way while Rory angled his head to look at the ceiling joists and corners. No weaknesses to the visible eye. Still, he'd have a roofing crew check it over. When Vi stopped, he stood behind her. The view from over her shoulder proved enjoyable for reasons having nothing to do with the house. He adjusted his attention and gazed into a small galley way. Enough space for the essentials. No extra footage for anything else.

Vi shied away from his nearness and motioned to the area. "I first got the idea to update here. Bringing the kitchen into the twenty-first century is a priority, though it probably needs an add-on." She shot Rory a wry look. "If I can afford it." Quickly turning, she picked up a stray can from under the counter, no doubt from where it rolled the other night when the vagrants had fled.

"I'll run projections, so you have an idea how much the renovations will cost. Updates on the bathrooms and kitchen, bigger closets, and creating two more bedrooms within the existing space would summarize the interior, I think. Then we'll prioritize."

Her delicate brows knit as she viewed the room. "I don't need extra bedrooms."

Hmm. He swallowed, chalking it up to simply not knowing. "It's a matter of looking down the road, Vi. What if you get married and decide to live elsewhere? The house will be easier to sell if it's updated."

"I don't want to live anywhere else." Vi's jaw resembled a brick.

"Okay. What if you have kids? They'll need their own rooms. The master bedroom already has space for an adjoining nursery." Uh-oh. Her face shuttered. He'd lost her, only he didn't understand why.

She brushed past him, her boot dragging. Fumbling in a

pocket, she pulled out an orange, put it back, then pulled out her phone. "I have to get back."

"But you said—"

"I remembered an errand. Can you take me back now?"

Rory stroked his beard, trying to keep up. "Not a problem."

She lit out the door as fast as the boot would allow. Rory caught up to her and helped her down the steps. They got in the car without a word. He punched the ignition button. As the vehicle purred to life, he turned to her. "What did I say?"

Vi stayed silent for a moment, then spoke quietly. "It's not you. It reminded me of … unhappy times."

Rory stilled. Whatever the unhappiness, she hadn't gotten over it. "Wanna tell me about it?"

Vi's braid flew sideways in a vehement no.

He waited a few moments. When she didn't volunteer any more, he put the car in gear. "I've enjoyed working with you. Now that I've seen the house and have an idea of what you want, I'll work on the numbers."

Small talk reigned as Rory drove back to Peeps. He cheered on the inside when Vi appeared to shake off her funk and answered a few non-threatening questions.

Parking in the Peeps' lot, he turned to her. "I won't belabor the point, but I'm a safe place, Vi."

Her blue eyes glinted, and a smile ghosted her lips. She leaned over and tapped him on the nose. "Rory Spence, … you're not safe at all."

CHAPTER NINE

In the cozy little room, Vi flicked her braid over one shoulder, inhaling the subtle lavender scent emanating from the diffuser as she draped sheets on the massage table. Dimming the lights, she left to get Tavo from the waiting area.

"Hey, bud." She eyed the man cramped into a chair too small for his girth.

"Hey, yourself." He rose, towering over her. The tic above his eyebrow signaled pain.

Vi nodded to the swim trunks clutched in his hand. "You know the drill. Slip into those and crawl under the sheets." Helping Tavo and other public servants unwind from the stress of their jobs had become part of the reason Vi loved massage. She turned toward the women's dressing room. With a glance over her shoulder, she said, "When I come in, be ready to tell me where it hurts." When clients could verbalize their pain, they felt validated.

Vi studied Tavo's stride as he hobbled into the room. Pinched nerve? Sciatica? The man loved powerlifting, despite the strain on his body.

Minutes later, he lay on his back, covered up with the sheet. Vi pushed down on his shoulders. Rearranging the sheet to leave his arm free, she kneaded the exposed limb. A regular client, Tavo knew what to expect, and his breathing evened into a relaxed rhythm.

As her hands continued with the gliding strokes, Vi's thoughts drifted to Rory. He'd texted earlier, saying they would start the demo phase today if the crew stayed on schedule. Her emotions impersonated a mallet plinking up and down a xylophone scale. Happy the project had gotten underway, even if doubt assailed her regularly. The ultimate cost of the remodel had caused sticker shock, but Rory had gone over a mammoth cost breakdown with her. He seemed as jazzed about the project as she.

Dare she hope this remodel would be everything she dreamed of? Daddy would have loved this. Vi's lips stretched into a grin. Probably what he envisioned from the get-go. *Her* fixing up the house. Daddy had possessed many positive qualities, even if follow-through didn't make the list.

When she had finished Tavo's arms, legs, and feet, she said in a low voice, "It's time for you to turn onto your stomach."

A giant bear waking from slumber, Tavo hefted onto his stomach in stages. Vi settled the sheet across his torso and legs and began the process again. The exertion it took to get the muscles in his tight back pliable dampened her neck with perspiration.

Her musings shifted to Rory again. What on earth had she been thinking, tapping his nose, and teasing him about not being safe? She didn't flirt—not normally anyway—but seeing his eyes pop had been worth it. For once, she'd ousted a reaction out of the suave, debonair Mr. Spence. He excelled at getting a rise out of her, so let the roles be reversed for a change.

The hour complete, Vi's body drooped with fatigue. Tavo, however, was much improved. She glanced once more at his sheer mass and giggled. Without fail, he fell asleep during a massage. She left him on the table snoring lightly, knowing he'd wake up in minutes.

Soft strains of music floated from upstairs as she moved to the small waiting area. She sat in the same chair Rory had occupied the evening he'd confronted her about dodging their appointment. Surreal. The man occupied far too much of her mind space. She reached for her phone as it chimed with a text.

> Demolition phase uncovered an issue.
> We need to talk. Meet you out there?

Bricks settled on her already-tired shoulders. An unforeseen contingency Rory had warned her about? She texted back quickly, saying she'd be there in thirty minutes.

Tavo exited the room. "Hey, Magic Hands." The tic had vanished, replaced with a broad smile. "I can breathe and walk again, thanks to those hands of yours." He stood straighter in a pair of faded jeans and a long-sleeved shirt.

Her mind still on the text, Vi remembered the reason she'd waited for him. "Thanks for saying so. Paige wanted me to mention she's having a Christmas party in a couple of weeks. Are you up for grilling the meat?"

"If I'm off. What day?"

"Hmm. Sunday evening next? She'll text everyone the info."

Shuffling a gunboat-sized shoe, Tavo asked, "How's she doin'?"

Vi caught the wistful note even in her distracted state. "Paige? She's fine. Stays busy." She peered at Tavo's carefully masked expression. "Need me to give her a message?"

The two creases deepened on either side of his face. "Nah." He fiddled with a tattered baseball cap. "Ro filled me in about the vagrants out at your place. We've been patrolling. They've moved on for now."

She blew out a relieved breath. "Rory worried about the possible danger they posed, but if they're gone—"

"No. Vagrants multiply. It's still not safe for you out there." His raised brows gave more authority to the decisive words.

Vi slipped the holder from the end of her hair, unplaiting the braid. "This is my property we're talking about."

"Yeah, I know. Rory mentioned it. He's working on a solution. You need to be patient." He slipped the cap on, adjusting the bill.

Vi's fingers stilled as she looked at Tavo. Those had been Rory's exact words.

As if Tavo read her thoughts, his deep voice rumbled. "Now don't go gettin' worked up. Be smart, doll. I'm not the only one who needs your hands." He touched two fingers to the bill of his cap in salute.

"But—"

Tavo strolled away, giving her a backhanded wave. Vi huffed. Nice to know *someone* had relaxed. Even if her hands still trembled with the effort to get him there.

SOFT PINK TWILIGHT covered the evening sky by the time Vi pulled into the driveway of her old house. Sheetrock, rotten wood, and pieces of old carpet lay nearby in a dump trailer. Rory stood on the porch. The yellow light shining over the door backlit his hair, making the auburn color blaze. He hurried down the creaky wooden steps with long strides.

Vi shivered despite her light jacket. The word *charming* so underrated Rory's appeal. His genuine desire to help with her house had overshadowed any traits she'd found disagreeable in the past. Not a stretch to believe he'd become the most sought-after contractor in Valiant. A shadow overtook her musings. It probably applied to his bachelor status as well. She tucked the errant thought away, not sure why it bothered her.

He reached her car door before she could unbuckle her seat belt., His actions seemed clipped, though he remained the consummate gentleman. She stole a look at his profile. Seeing chagrin etched into his attractive features morphed her fear to a new level. "What's going on?"

When he shook his head, she let him steer her up the steps and into the house. Demolition dust assailed her nose and lungs. White sheetrock powder danced in the air, making her cough. Recognizing the signs of an asthma attack, she rapidly glanced around the room before her lungs staged a complete insurgency. Bare studs stood where walls had once existed. Rory had said the house would look worse before it looked better, yet this nakedness took her by surprise.

When Rory opened his mouth to speak, Vi touched two fingers to his lips. Whatever the news, she needed a few moments to absorb this new beginning. Sidestepping a pile of rotten wood, she walked to the kitchen and superimposed Rory's build-out plan over the stripped space. He'd been so patient with her vague ideas, then drew up a blueprint and let her tweak it. She'd found the process enchanting. Even as her heart stirred, the tickle in her throat increased.

Vi coughed again, backing into Rory's solid chest. He grasped her elbows as she wheezed, losing the battle for air. He swiveled her around, searching her face, then slid an arm around her. "We need to get you out of here."

Her eyes smarted with tears as she allowed him to lead from the house. Rats. She could add old house junk to her list of allergies. She patted her skirt pockets for her keys. Finding them, she held them out. "My inhaler." The words squeaked through her rapidly closing throat.

Before she'd finished the words, Rory grabbed her keys and ran.

Another coughing fit took over, accompanied by lightheadedness. Not good.

In record time, Rory handed her the inhaler. His somber gray eyes studied her as she plopped onto the porch steps. Gasping, she pressed on the spray button, inhaling from the nebulizer. As the medicine took effect, her oxygen-starved lungs relaxed, and breathing became easier.

Rory sat beside her on the steps. His presence brought another level of comfort to her foggy mental state.

"I'm all right." She spoke hoarsely. Her hair hung in a curtain around her shoulders. She'd loosened the braid after Tavo's massage. The coughing fit had undone the rest. Embarrassment tugged at her. Her hands shook too much to pull it back. The brief lack of oxygen had robbed her of strength.

"Let me help." Rory scooted behind her, brushing away her hands and gathering her hair. "Do you have a ... what do you call it ... a hair holder?"

A chuckle wisped from her dry throat as she slipped a band off her wrist and held it up. Her arms felt as if she'd worked out with heavy weights. The part of her that normally insisted on distance stayed silent. The mere act of breathing remained enough to keep her occupied in the present.

"Oh, that's handy." His strong fingers combed through her hair all the way to the split ends she'd meant to get trimmed. One of his knees brushed her side.

Rory's hands stilled. She could almost feel his bafflement. "You don't know how to do a ponytail, do you?" Thank goodness, her lightheadedness was receding.

"Nope. It can't be hard." Something she couldn't place reverberated in his voice.

Darkness had fallen. More alert to her surroundings, Vi's self-defense mechanism kicked in with vigor. She tried to rise, betrayed by her knees buckling.

"Whoa, where's the fire?" Still sitting on the step above her, Rory's arm anchored her waist to keep her upright. His cinnamon-y breath warmed her cheek.

Right here. Vi's prickling skin had nothing to do with the cool breeze nipping the air. She snatched the elastic band from his fingers and tethered her hair. Good grief, she had to find her own space again. "Tell me about the issue while we walk." Unfortunately, her rubbery legs picked that moment to imitate the lake water.

CHAPTER TEN

Rory's arms held her steady, as he pointed to the inhaler she held. "Need to use it again?"

Drat! His presence had an uncanny way of making her forget the basics. She raised the nebulizer to her mouth, pumped, and inhaled. Her breathing improved immediately. "How did you know?"

Rory stood and descended the steps. "My younger brother had asthma. When we were outside, my job as the older brother was to make sure he didn't get in a bind. Same with the Epi."

Dismay washed over her as his words sunk in. Only an ingrained response. Duty. Any fanciful thoughts on her part that he might care beyond the job needed to stop.

Vi ached to trail around the lake, but the flare-up had taken a toll.

With a crooked grin, Rory took her hand and tucked it into the crook of his elbow. "Here. Lean on me. We'll make it work, however slow you need to go."

"Thank you," she murmured. "The lake is soothing."

Hanging on to his upper arm soothed her too. She pointed to a dirt path, leaning into him as they walked carefully down a slope. Dad had kept the scrub brush trimmed back. In his absence, gnarly limbs and new weed patches crowded the spacious walkway.

A quarter of the way around the lake, Vi's breathing had returned to normal, yet Rory made no attempt to pull away. Still, this tiny respite couldn't last. Calling on a strength she didn't feel, she asked, "What's going on with the house?"

"Termites." He patted her arm, then untucked it from his elbow and turned away from her. Hands on his hips, he peered out over the silvery water.

It took a second to register. "Termites?" She'd heard of them, of course, but never in a positive light.

He met her gaze. His chest swelled and deflated when he exhaled. "Damage all along the back of the house. It's a hidden problem. Once the woodwork gets torn into, then you find the damage." His eyes held a wary look. "It's an expensive fix."

"How expensive?"

"Stud replacement, new flooring. It will run several thousand dollars."

Vi gasped. "That much?"

Misery carved into his slow nod. In a low voice, he said, "I know you want to remodel the house. However, in light of this new problem, now might be the time to go a different route."

What he didn't say clamored for attention. "You mean sell."

The slight incline of his head signaled his agreement. She looked away to the lake, her eyes seeing nothing. The advice to sell she'd heard before. Well-meant, maybe, but no. "Not what I want to do, Rory."

"I know." His steady gaze indicated he did understand. "If

you sell, the land will bring you a tidy profit. You'll have a nice cash flow, and no worries about old house problems."

The words sliced into her heart ... and dreams with the sharpness of a knife blade. The tickle rose back up her throat. Anybody who bought her land would tear down the house without a second thought. They would only see an old wreck.

Her old wreck.

"I thought you had the same vision I did," Vi said through the hurt.

White teeth glimmered through his mustache, giving her hope. "Nothing's changed there. I'd love to restore your home. The potential for a unique makeover still exists, but the latest trouble isn't something I calculated in. My job as your contractor is to help you understand the options. I'll abide by whatever decision you make, but it is your decision."

Vi's brows knit. Could she afford it? The nest egg Daddy had left was shrinking by the minute. Rory's words about the margin of risk ricocheted around in her head.

"Okay. I heard what you said. Please take off the contractor hat for a minute. What does your heart think I should do?" For a moment, Rory's steady bearing cracked. He stepped closer. As if he wanted to kiss her. Then, he stepped back.

"My heart doesn't get a vote. Only you can decide." His last words ended in a rumbly whisper before the wind whisked them away.

Sudden raucous honking kept her from drowning in his eyes. "The goose hears us coming." She paused on the dirt path next to one boardwalk.

Rory stepped ahead of her onto the bridge. Vi noted the bulge at the back of his waist. "You brought your gun?"

"Yes." He turned, his eyes appearing silver in the moonlight as he searched her face.

Vi froze in place, absorbing the fact Rory carried a gun.

"I'm serious about the danger of you out here at night."

Hmm. Still no backing off. For an instant, Vi missed her former perception of him. Every ounce of flirty behavior had vanished. *This* Rory was formidable.

Rory closed the distance between them. "You get to choose about the financial risk, but your safety is non-negotiable."

Wow. Did he mean it? She'd never met anyone who said those kinds of things. Her mind catapulted back to Thanksgiving Day when he'd insisted on giving hugs. Her insides tingled. Her blatant non-participation still stung. When he stood this close, she wanted a hug. Rather than throw herself at him, she merely said, "I'm okay with the gun."

He put an arm gently around her shoulder and squeezed. "You need time to think about how you want to proceed with the house. In the meantime, let's enjoy your lake."

Oh, dear. Not helping.

His closeness dispelled the chill. Moonlight streamed through the inky sky, and a burning smell floated on the air. A coyote howled in the distance, and the sound of honking drifted in their direction again. Louder. Desperate to focus on anything besides the man next to her, she said, "Harry wants to say hi. You might want to hang back. He's not real fond of strangers."

Vi eyed the bird's flapping wings. Raising her voice, she said, "Enough. I brought a friend, and we're taking a walk. No reason to get upset."

Harry sniffed at Rory, then screeched like a rusty gate. Losing interest, the goose honked his way to the water's edge. His bright orange feet were neon lights in the marshy weeds, and wet plopping noises indicated fish. Vi took a deep breath as her daily cares receded to a much more manageable level. The two puffs of albuterol had served their purpose.

Rory's trim form silhouetted against the moonlight. Hands

in his pockets, he gazed over the lake at the silver waves undulating across the water. The full moon glowed a buttery yellow color. Vi wanted to capture the moment. Her breath caught, and she turned back the way they came.

They crossed the boardwalk, climbing the gentle grade, neither of them speaking. Once she stood at her car, Rory faced her. "I enjoyed the walk. It's easy to understand why you're fond of coming here. Let me know when you've decided about the house."

Turning to go, he pivoted back. "I found an item you might want. Be right back."

Curious, Vi followed him. He opened the passenger door of the Lexus and pulled out a black object.

"This fell out of the sofa when the guys were angling it through the doorway. Probably stashed between the cushions." He handed it to her.

Dad's electronic tablet. He'd tinkered on it the last few months of his life. She'd forgotten all about it. Until now.

Elated, she threw her arms around Rory, kissing him square on the cheek. The impulsiveness she'd worry about later. "Thank you. This means the world to me." She hurried to her car. A connection with Daddy. Maybe he had sage advice about her house dilemma. Should she stay the course, however pricey, or should she sell?

RORY POURED CREAMER into his mug of coffee, anticipating the knock at the door. Jesse strode in wearing jeans and a blue Peeps' shirt. Once Vi drove away, Rory knew he needed to verbalize his concerns. But not to Vi. He was her contractor, for heaven's sake. The description didn't include hugs or kisses. And he'd barely kept from begging her to go through with the remodel. The tremendous pull of her old house mystified him. Restoration beckoned him at every turn.

Jesse would keep him straight. He and Rory had decided to be accountability partners about the women they dated once they'd returned to the States. Though Rory had second-guessed his commitment several times, he would readily admit they'd both benefited from the arrangement. Saying the hard things the other needed to hear had been difficult, even if Jesse's advice had proven to be wisdom in disguise more than once.

"Coffee?" Rory held the mug aloft, its rich, nutty scent filling the townhouse. He settled on the uber-modern couch and grimaced. Stella's taste had made his living quarters almost unbearable. The uncomfortable furniture boasted loud geometric designs. The color palette of gaudy gold and purple made him want to gag. It played a large role in her ex-girlfriend status. On good days, he thanked God their relationship had ended. The rest of the time, he wanted to smack himself for playing the fool.

Jesse placed his mug on the end table, sitting in a glider that didn't match anything. Once Rory's initial horror of Stella's taste in design sank in, he'd retrieved his favorite chair from Dad's house. Stella had objected, of course. Said it clashed with the rest of the room. Her "my way or the highway" attitude had been the last straw. Rory chose the highway.

"Hey, bud. What's up?" Jesse's dark eyes had lost their perpetual flintiness. Falling in love had done wonders for his best friend. The regular counseling sessions for anger and PTSD hadn't hurt either.

"Dad wants us to scope out another tract of land besides the one he's working on for us."

"Bigger?"

"Same thing I asked. Twice the size of the one we're buying. You know what I'm thinking—"

"More land to expand for Peeps—if we can afford it."

"Yep. You up for a look-see? Tomorrow morning works for me."

"Let me check for appointments." Jess studied his phone. "Day after tomorrow I'm free all day." When Rory nodded, Jesse clicked his phone shut. "Shoot me a text whenever you shake loose. Now tell me the real reason you're here."

Rory's throat dried. He sipped his coffee, gathering the courage to discuss Vi and her house.

A half-smirk curved one side of Jesse's mouth. "How about we cut to the chase here—is this about a girl?"

Jesse knew him too well. "Yeah." He drew the word out to three syllables. "I ... um ... I kissed Vi." Rory studied the design on his coffee mug. Shoot! Not how he wanted to start this conversation.

"You what?" The disapproval slicing Jesse's tone didn't bode well.

Rory's back stiffened. "It's not what you're thinking ... at the hospital, she woke up ... and ... those lips ..."

"You mean after she'd fallen into a hole, nearly died from bee stings, and likely in a lot of pain?" Jesse's eyes bored into him. "How did that work?"

Provoked, Rory fired back, "It worked fine ... until her mother interrupted."

Jesse stared at him, open-mouthed. Then he threw back his head and howled with laughter, jerking the glider back and forth. "Unforgettable for sure."

Vi's mom ranked low in his concerns. "I told Vi later I wouldn't initiate any more kisses."

"Uh-huh. Did she bite your head off?" Jesse guffawed again, making Rory's eyes shoot skyward.

"So, you're the expert on women now?"

"I've learned a thing or two, mostly the hard way." Jesse paused for breath. "Bud, you've always liked to kiss the girls. Might be, this gal's a stretch, even for you."

Piqued, Rory tried to defend himself. "I'm drawn to her. I'm also her contractor. Today, we ran into a termite issue." He grimaced. "It's going to cost thousands in cost overrun. I advised her of her options—she'll either have to spend the money or sell and start over. Now though, I'm torn."

"Why? You did the right thing."

"Then she asked what I would do." He stared at the vinyl floor, remembering. "Jess, I nearly begged her to continue the remodel. It's nuts how much I want this job. It's a new twist in my wheelhouse. I'm getting to breathe life into her dream. Moving forward has to be her decision, but I don't know how long I can stay neutral."

"What do you think she'll decide?"

"I don't know. I get the impression the house means more to Vi than a place to live. It's part of her identity. She'll regret it if she sells."

"You have her best interests at heart. Have you prayed about it?" Jesse's demeanor remained non-judgmental.

Peace wrapped around Rory as his hard-won lessons in prayer came to mind. A soft smile curved his lips. "Thanks for reminding me prayer should be our first option."

Jesse set his cup aside. "I understand you're attracted to her. But what about Paige?"

Rory gazed at his friend in befuddlement. "What about her?"

"I thought you and Paige ..."

"Hmm. Maybe way back. Not anymore. Paige is like a sister."

A line creased between Jesse's brows. "You guys are always together ..."

"Because she's my PA ... and a darn good one. She reads my mind, anticipates what I need. Nothing else to it."

"And Paige knows that?" Jesse didn't sound convinced.

"I assume she does. No weird vibes ... we're friends ..." Rory finally caught Jesse's drift. "I've never kissed Paige—on the lips," he clarified.

Jesse's jaw relaxed. "Okay, then." He rocked for a bit. "Maybe you need to start from the beginning about Vi."

The perfect opening to launch into his favorite subject of late.

Two cups of coffee later, Rory wrapped up the conversation with an impression he'd had earlier in the evening. "Jess, it was the strangest thing. I watched Vi interact with that silly goose at her lake. She stood there with her hands in her pockets. God seemed to whisper in my ear it was how I need to handle *her*. Keep my hands to myself until she trusts me."

"And your lips." Jesse's tone could have dried a wet towel.

"The I-won't-initiate-anymore-kisses meant the same thing. And, yeah, it made her mad, but a guy's gotta have hope."

Jesse choked on a swallow of coffee. "As if *Vi's* the one who's going to have a hard time refraining from kissing?"

Rory shrugged and picked up his empty cup. He'd had enough caffeine to howl at the moon.

"Vi has always had a strong 'no trespassing' vibe, but her profession requires it. Can't be a cupcake around men who want massages." Jesse laced his fingers together. "Hard edge or no, members adore Vi. Someone's always singing her praises in the comment cards."

"Yeah, she mentioned giving me a massage once." He

hastily added, "She saw the limp and said a massage would help."

"Good for her."

Rory shot him the stink eye. "I'm not putting up with a woman who feels sorry for me."

Jesse's forehead wrinkled. "For Pete's sake, Ro, there's a big difference between pity and honest assessment. She's trained to relieve pain. I doubt she's feeling sorry for you."

Rory's gut sloshed with too much coffee.

Checking his phone, Jesse said, "It's close to midnight. I gotta hit the sack. A wise person once told me, 'You better take it slow and easy.' When I first dated Brenna, nuts as I was about her, I managed to do everything wrong and scared her so bad, it's only by God's grace we didn't crash and burn." He rose, stretching his arms toward the ceiling.

Rory stood as well. His leg ached abominably, but he couldn't resist. "You crashed all right. More than once."

Jesse popped him on the arm. "So learn from my mistakes. Take your own advice and be careful."

CHAPTER ELEVEN

Vi dragged herself from her car and focused on climbing the veranda steps. One normal step, then heave the boot. Things she normally took for granted had become hurdles. Her last two massages had lasted to infinity and beyond. While her hands worked, she'd used the time to pray about selling the house or continuing with the remodel. Still no direction. Maybe a talk with Rory would help. At the project's start, they'd fallen into late-night phone calls or texts when she'd had a million and one remodeling questions. A tingle zinged up her spine. It had been a few days since they'd communicated. He probably wondered if she'd come to a decision.

Truth be told, she'd missed him. His zest for living in the here and now appealed to her. He didn't hold regrets in a death grip the way she did. Vi's head shook sideways of its own volition. If Rory knew what she'd done, he'd run in the other direction. She couldn't even forgive herself—no use wishing for a relationship that could never happen.

Vi opened the heavy wooden door. Christmas decorations

winked from every corner of the living room. Thunder scrabbled to his feet, woofing. A half-grown cat slipped between gifts under a tree. Carols played, courtesy of Alexa. An odor she couldn't identify floated from the kitchen. Brenna's night to cook.

Dropping her purse and bag beside the cushy brown chair, she headed to the kitchen. Brenna stared into a red skillet on a stove burner.

"Do I have time for a shower?"

"Probably. Jesse's coming." Brenna attended to the skillet.

"Okay. If y'all want to eat, don't wait on me." Vi hobbled out of the room. She couldn't wait to get the boot off tonight. Did Rory feel this way? Maybe when they talked, she'd ask. The bathroom was empty for once, so she showered and dressed quickly. Her stomach yowled with hunger. She hopped back to the kitchen, the heavy boot under one arm.

"Great timing," Brenna said as she and Jesse ladled rice and stir-fry onto plates at the stove, then gravitated toward the small dining table.

Vi filled her plate and sniffed. The garlicky-soy sauce mix made her mouth water. She stood with her plate, leaning next to the cabinets.

Jesse set up an extra folding chair. "Plenty of room, Vi. Come sit down." His dark eyes probed her face. "Long day?"

"It's over now. A good night's sleep and I'll be ready to do it all over again tomorrow." She joined them. A meal with friends barely outweighed the third-wheel feeling she got around these two.

She tasted a bite of the savory stir-fry. "Wow, Brenna. This is good."

"It's fantastic, darlin'." Jesse flashed Brenna a smile, pinking her cheeks. He looked back at Vi. "You'll tell me if something needs to be addressed in the massage department, won't you?"

Vi hid a smile. Jesse's attention to detail had become another Peeps' legend. "Yes. So far, it's nothing I can't handle. A few folks think because they pay, they can tell me how to do my job."

Jesse and Brenna groaned in commiseration.

They finished their meal, chatting about the day's events. Staccato clicks in the hallway caught Vi's attention. Paige entered the room in a high-necked evening gown and silver heels. An elegant updo crowned her head, and earrings dangled to her shoulders. The floral scent she wore competed with the stir-fry aroma.

"Goodness, woman! Where are you going?" Jesse grinned broadly.

"A charity fundraiser. And I'm late. Rory will be pacing." Perfect red lips revealed Paige's showstopper smile. Cramming a box of breath mints in her sparkly clutch, she asked, "Am I all together?"

Brenna screwed her face up in pretend scrutiny, then fisted her hand in a thumbs up. "You look stunning."

"You'll be the prettiest gal in the room," Jesse echoed.

Paige hurried out the door, her scent lingering in the air.

Disappointment flooded Vi's chest. Rory wouldn't be available to chat tonight. He had a date.

After dinner, Vi shooed Brenna and Jesse out of the small kitchen. "Scoot. You know the rule, Brenna. You cooked, so you're off the hook with clean-up." She cast a side-eye as they exited the room. Jesse's large bronze hands rested on Brenna's shoulders. Must be nice.

Vi busied herself putting away spices, stumbling over Thunder on her way to the dishwasher. "Gracious, bud. You better stay out of the way. Neither of us wants me to fall on you." She'd put the word out about needing forever homes. So far, no one had stepped up to claim him or the cats.

Vi stacked the dinner dishes in the dishwasher racks, threw away paper napkins, and hand-washed the pans. She should have listened to her gut. Rory and Paige were a couple.

Any attention Rory paid to her had to do with the house remodel. She wiped the counters with a dish towel, then gazed around the spotless kitchen. Now what?

Brenna and Jesse had already claimed the living room sofa. They would ask her to join them, but she could only take so much of their togetherness. Her original plan had been to hole up in her room and try to crack the code on Dad's tablet. And wait to see if Rory would text first. But now she couldn't sit still long enough for any codebreaking.

She needed to walk around the lake and sort out her whirling emotions. Cicada song and moonlit water would cure her antsy state. However, if Rory found out ... well, she couldn't stomach another safety discussion.

She paced the small kitchen, her ankle aching from the lack of support. Sighing, she maneuvered her foot into the thick sole of the walking boot, then strapped it over her jeans.

Biting her lip in frustration, Vi stalked into the living room. Multi-colored strands of tiny Christmas lights glowed from an evergreen garland. The scent of cedar emanated from the corner where a brightly decorated tree stood. Jesse and Brenna sat, heads close together on the sofa. Smooching, no doubt. Stifling the urge to roll her eyes, she perched on the chair, phone in hand.

"What's going on, Vi?" Breathlessness laced Brenna's words.

Honesty gained the upper hand. "I want to go out to the house and walk around the lake, but Rory says I shouldn't be there by myself."

As the words left her mouth, she thought of who might be available. "I'm going to text Silas. Maybe he'll meet me out there." Silas, a physical therapist at Peeps, stayed on the fringe of their friend group, mostly by choice. Still, he'd been friendly enough to her. He didn't send any creepy vibes either. Her thumbs moved over the screen. She clicked SEND and looked at Jesse and Brenna. "If he can't, I'm going to beg you two to go with me." She hated to sound so needy even if her desperation forced a backup plan.

"No begging necessary. We'll go." Jesse sat forward, his boots scraping the floor. Brenna nodded vigorously. "Thanks. Let me see if Silas ... here he is now." She scanned the incoming text. "He'll meet me there." Vi smiled, relieved Jesse and Brenna were off the hook.

Jesse's brows knit together. "Might be best if you waited in your car until Silas gets there."

Not Jesse too. The need to walk overwhelmed her. "I'm out of here." She snatched her purse off the floor and slung it over her shoulder.

"Stay safe, Vi." Jesse's baritone voice carried. She slowed her steps in a poor attempt at dignity.

Silas proved an excellent walking partner. When Vi mentioned Rory's edict about not being on the property by herself, Silas nodded as if privy to information she didn't possess. His appearance begged for closer scrutiny. Shoulder-length hair, scarred face, and unreadable expression gave off a rough impression, but Jesse would have objected if he had reason to doubt Silas's character.

Vi strolled ahead of Silas on the trail. He didn't offer much in the way of conversation, yet he answered readily enough when she asked him a question. Mostly, he seemed grateful for the company. A fellow sojourner in a lonely world.

Once, she had glimpsed a flash of pain behind the stoicism, but he'd covered quickly and shown her another cat video on his phone. The man adored the silly antics of cats. Fitting. Silas's stealth and quick reflexes reminded her of a feline. Tiny shivers curled through her arms. The air of mystery surrounding him suggested danger, but Vi refused to pry. She had enough secrets of her own.

Harry waddled toward them with loud, rusty honks. The

screeching and flapping of his wings didn't faze Silas. He held out his hand for the bird to inspect. Harry sniffed Silas's hand with curiosity but made no attempt to peck it or any other part of Silas's body. Vi clamped her mouth shut when she realized it hung open. Silently, she added goose-whisperer to his interesting skill set.

After a couple of laps around the lake, Vi's roiling emotions had calmed down, replaced by curiosity about Daddy's tablet. She and Silas climbed the sidewalk's slight grade to their cars.

Silas looked at her, his expression inscrutable. "You okay?"

"Yeah. I'm better now. Thanks." Vi didn't know what else to say.

Eyes alert, he gazed around the area. "It's nice out here. Let me know if you need a walking buddy."

Silas stood there without a word until Vi got in her car. Only then did he head toward his gray truck.

Back at Paige's, Jesse and Brenna were saying goodnight. Vi shrugged the sour thoughts away. Those two deserved a happy ending.

When Jesse made eye contact, Vi gave him a nod, then slipped into her room. Dropping her purse on the bed, she quickly changed into pajamas. As she climbed onto her bed with Daddy's tablet, Paige's stilettos tapped on the wooden floor. The housemates usually gathered in the kitchen to debrief about the day. Tonight, however, Vi had no desire to participate. No desire to hear about Paige's date with Rory. Instead, she propped her pillows against the headboard and snuggled under the bedcovers. What words or numbers might Daddy use as a password?

Her phone chimed with a text.

Whatcha doin'?

Rory. Lightness lifted her heavy thoughts, then

consternation rushed in to fill the vacuum. Vi bit her lip, thinking. The desire to hear from him won out.

How was your date?

Satisfied, she leaned deeper into the pillows. She could do friendship. Friends counted on the plus side.

Not a date. Business.

Hmm. Not a date? Her phone rang with an incoming call from him. She picked up, pushing past her tight throat. "Hey."

"Hey, yourself." Rory's deep voice had an extra layer of gravel. "It's late, but I wanted to hear about your dad's tablet. Did it require a password?"

His lack of sensitivity robbed Vi's speech. For heaven's sake, the man had been partying with her housemate this evening. "Uh, no. No ... yes, it needs a password. I'm working on it now."

"Have you tried your birthday?"

"*My* birthday? Why would Daddy use my birthday?"

His deep rumbly chuckle warmed her insides despite the confusion swirling around in her mind. "I'm guessing, Red, it ranked as one of the best days of his life."

She stiffened. Any oxygen in her lungs vanished.

"What's wrong?"

"Daddy called me Red."

He chuckled again, this time smothered by a yawn. "Well, it suits you. Wish I'd known him."

For the first time, the reminder of Daddy brought contentment instead of grief. "Yeah, he was the best dad ever. I'll try birthday combinations. See if any of those open it."

"You'll figure it out, Red."

"Rory?" She needed to say it before she lost her nerve. "I'm still thinking about what to do."

"You'll make the right decision. I talked to the bug guy and ran the numbers. It will add on about seven thousand to fix the termite damage."

"Ouch. You aren't trying to sway my opinion, are you?"

"Never. You need all the facts to make an informed decision." Rory's playful tone had disappeared. She could picture the earnest look on his handsome face, even if he did sound half asleep.

"Thanks." Torn, Vi wanted the conversation to continue. Thunder pawed at her door. "Good night, Rory."

As she clicked off, Rory muttered unintelligible words about knowing which house option he'd choose.

She got up and let Thunder in. She climbed back into bed, propping the device on her lap. It couldn't hurt to try his suggestion. Her fingers tapped the keys and pressed ENTER. Numbers only didn't work. She spelled out the month, then added the rest. No. Not right either. What about her name? Mother had always called her Violet. Daddy had shortened it to Vi. When she wasn't Squirt ... or Shorty ... or Red. She keyed in RED0601.

Tears smarted when the window changed. Rory had been right. A tentative smile lifted the corners of her mouth. Dad and Rory would have enjoyed each other.

Concentrating on the tablet again, Vi grinned at the game icons. It thrilled her to hold the device Daddy had used—often in the last days when his energy level drooped. Spotting Google Drive, she clicked on it and then touched the File icon. "Did you know how to store pictures and documents?" she asked aloud, holding her breath.

Several documents popped up. She scrolled down and clicked on the oldest date. Skimming down the page, she gasped. Daddy had written her a letter.

Hey Squirt,

You're snooping around on my tablet! I'm glad you found it, but you might wish you hadn't. It's time for you to know a few things. I reckon some of it will be important to you—other stuff, not so much. While I'm still feeling good enough, I'll jot down what I can remember. It took me a while to figure out how to do a letter. I tire out fast these days. You'll be walking in the door soon, and I'd rather talk to you in person.

Vi swallowed hard and opened another file—instructions on how to get around the "dodgy" stick shift on the white truck. Tears spilled from her eyes. She could hear Daddy mumbling around his pipe as he explained *you had to get a feel for it.*

She wiped her palms across her wet cheeks and placed the tablet on the nightstand. Tempting as it was to continue reading the letters, the decision to read one letter at a time and savor Daddy's last words won. Resolutely, she turned out the light. "Night, Daddy."

RORY GLANCED at his phone to see if Jesse had texted, then riffled through the messy pile of spreadsheets, sketches, and sticky notes on his Peeps' desk. Loud music pulsed through the wall with a high-intensity workout in full swing. Those guys were nuts. Mission forgotten, he sat back, staring longingly at the thick roll of plans he'd stashed on top of the file cabinet. Waiting for Vi to decide was taking a toll. He needed to tell her the prices he'd previously quoted would increase the longer she waited.

He shifted position. Too early for his leg to ache. C'mon, Jess. They needed to spy out the second tract of land before his day filled. He'd hoped for downtime after last night, but the chances of a slow day were erased by the second. He and Paige had scored several possible investors at the fundraiser. However, if she felt as disconnected as he did, they needed to revisit their networking strategies.

A single sharp rap on his door, then Jesse entered with no greeting. Rory did a double take at Jesse's drawn face and red-rimmed eyes. He lowered into a chair in front of the desk.

Without knowing why, Rory braced against the chair cushion.

"Manny died last night," Jesse said in a level voice. He clasped his hands together and stared at the floor.

Rory's thoughts jerked back to that terrible day in Afghanistan. Manny had been in the Humvee when the IED exploded. He'd survived with severe and ongoing injuries. Callous or not, Rory thanked God his scarred legs and crushed foot were the extent of his injuries.

"How ... did he pass?" Rory managed around the rock in his throat. Their eyes met with the dark knowledge of what Rory hadn't said. Had Manny accidentally overdosed? Or did he take his own life? Rory had experienced the level of pain that could drive a man to it.

"Rosa said he went peacefully."

Rory blew out a pent-up breath. "I want to believe it."

"Yeah. I do too." Jesse laid his palms on the desk and rocked them back and forth. "The funeral's on Friday. Want me to get us a flight?"

"Yes. Give me a day to get things lined out here. Our plan to spy out the new tract of land will have to wait." Memories flooded his mind. Manny had been the up-for-anything guy until the accident. What followed were days stretching into months of pain, relieved only by heavy drug use. Jesse had stayed in communication with Manny while Rory fought his own battles with surgery and rehab. Rory's life had been a living nightmare for months. However, a still small voice telling him he would not only survive but thrive saved him during those days and nights of pain.

Rory's chest swelled with grief, though his chin lifted in tribute. Honoring Manny's life would be a privilege. No more sorrow over his own missing limb. Rory knew he'd done nothing to earn the grace and mercy he'd received. Nor did he deserve the opportunities handed to him.

But he'd fight every giant in the valley to secure the blessings of his second chance.

CHAPTER THIRTEEN

Rory sat in the same chair he'd occupied the last time he waited for Vi to finish a massage. His eyes narrowed as she slipped from the room. Her grim face and the way her boot dragged telegraphed exhaustion. She made a beeline for the women's dressing room, never looking his way.

Two minutes later, a guy swaggered out of the massage room. Rory's neck muscles bunched.

"Man, massage ranks right up there with sex. That little redhead was all over me. If you're next, she ain't got nothing left," he exclaimed.

Animal. Rory's hands fisted as he jumped to Vi's defense. He stood and stepped toward him, keenly aware of his superior height. *When in war* … "Locker-room talk is off-limits at Peeps."

A sneer curled the smaller man's lip. "I'll talk however I want. Who are you?"

Rory's jaw flexed. *Make my day, creep.* "The guy who can revoke your membership."

When the words registered, the guy brushed past Rory

without comment. Yep. A Peeps' membership mattered. No doubt the guy's identity revolved around the workout scene. And bragging to anyone who would listen about his massage.

The adrenaline rush subsided, Rory steepled his hands, allowing his breathing to even out. Imagining Vi alone with men of *that* ilk gnawed on Rory's insides.

Vi stood in the women's dressing room door. Rory didn't know how much she'd witnessed, but the fury in his heart dissolved at the fine lines etched around her mouth. Even her braid drooped. She looked at him, her gaze clouded with emotion.

Their eyes locked. Vi took a step toward him, then hesitated. Every cell in Rory's body willed her forward. He opened his arms, steeling himself not to move. The last time he wanted to extend comfort, she ran away. Slowly, she took another step toward him. Then another. He refused to break eye contact. *I'm right here, babe.* When she moved within reach, he gently curled an arm around her and closed the distance. Her resistance crumbling, she wilted against his chest. Her body shuddered, then went still. He rested his chin on her head and stroked her hair. "I'm sorry," he murmured into her ear.

Too soon she pulled away, her thumbs flecking away tears. "He was awful."

"No more massages for him. What's his name?" He'd inform the desk there would be no appointment openings for him. Ever. Rory wanted to hold her again but settled for standing close.

Her voice cracked. "After today, I agree. His name is Curtis."

"Consider it done." Rory grasped her hand. She didn't object when he led her over to the waiting area and settled her in the chair he'd vacated. He sat beside her, rubbing her right palm with his thumb.

"Umm." She rolled her head from side to side. "How did you know?"

"When the guy—" Rory couldn't bring himself to say his name. "—left the massage room, he mouthed off. His comments weren't appropriate, so I made sure he won't do it again."

Vi snorted. "Curtis is an idiot."

Rory melted as if butter on a hot pancake when her sky-blue eyes found his. "I'll be gone for a couple of days. Before I leave, I thought you might need a walk around the lake."

Her white teeth gleamed in a genuine smile. "You read my mind. I didn't remember to line up a partner, so your offer is perfect. Thank you." She stood. The hunched shoulders and dejection from seconds ago had disappeared.

"You're lining up walking partners?" Rory immediately disliked the idea.

"Well, yes. Since you laid down the don't-walk-alone edict. Silas walked with me last night." Vi stretched out her hand to him as if to pull him out of the chair.

Rory extended his hand and let her tug a bit. He stood, rubbing the back of his head as he digested this unwelcome news. "Silas walked with you around the lake?"

Vi raised her brows at him, then pulled on his hand. "Well, what choice did I have? You were out of pocket. Tonight, I was counting on Harry for company. Can we go now?"

Rory's eyes narrowed at the thought of a goose for protection. However, Vi's exuberance over a simple walk proved so engaging he let her lead him as they walked to the parking lot. The woman needed a bodyguard in the worst way. He'd sign up for the job in a heartbeat if most of his evenings weren't already busy with clients. But Silas? The notion thrust Rory into a place far ahead of their current status. What would happen if he pushed their fledgling friendship?

He tapped the hood of her car. "Wait for me *in the car* when you get out there."

Her features screwed into an adorable mug as she raised her hand in a mock salute.

HIS LEXUS HAD BARELY ROLLED to a stop before Vi climbed out of her car. Her small, sassy vehicle fit her perfectly. Her hair blew about her face. She secured it with a band, then zipped up her hoodie.

The wind had died at dusk. Traffic from the freeway rushed in the distance. The limbs protruding from gnarly mesquites around the small wannabe backyard stretched outward like bony hands. A few long runners of Augustine grass snaking through the weeds were the only remnant of a formal lawn. The porch light glowed yellow. The smoky campfire smell had vanished.

"I want to walk through the house first," Vi said, drawing him out of his reverie. "The dust shouldn't be a problem anymore, and I need to see the damage for myself." His lingering grief over Manny loosened its grip on her cheerful attitude, and his steps quickened as he followed her up the porch stairs.

"If you decide to proceed with the restoration, these steps need a rail on each side."

Vi swiveled, her face saucy. "You'll be the first to know, Mr. Contractor."

Rory held back a grin. His boots thudded on the pier and beam foundation. Vi's boot clomped in tempo. He showed her the spongy spots in the flooring and the hollow walls. A smug feeling stole over him. The role of Vi's go-to contractor swelled his chest. Dare he hope for more?

"Ready for the lake?" She motioned for him to follow, then pulled the hoodie over her head, stuffing her hands in the broad middle pockets. Her eyes reflected the porch light.

What a kid. Why did this diminutive woman make him think of family? He pulled his hood up and followed her. When she reached the bottom of the steps, she snagged his hand.

He laced his fingers through hers, urging his sulky leg forward. No way he would pass up this opportunity, even if his logical mind posted a TAKE IT SLOW banner.

Moonlight danced on the water. Rory's frosty breath rose, then evaporated into the inky air. Harry spied them from a distance and created a ruckus of splashing, honking, and general disturbance. Water rats glided through the soft waves in straight lines.

Her earlier distress forgotten, Vi moved across the boardwalk with zest. Rory rubbed his hands together and blew on them.

She zipped back to him as he stared out over the water. "Hey, why are you going out of town?"

His lightheartedness spiraled downward. "Funeral. An Army buddy of mine."

Vi's face fell. "I'm sorry for your loss."

"Thank you. Manny's wounds were life-threatening. In one way, it's no surprise. I hope he found peace with the Lord."

Eyes widening, Vi said, "That's the most important thing, right? Recovery didn't happen on this side, yet Daddy looked forward to heaven and seeing Jesus. His perspective on dying helped me more than anything. How old was Manny?"

"Same age as Jess and me. Thirty-ish. Married. No kids."

The nippy air reddened Vi's nose and cheeks. "How sad."

"Yeah, it is." He tweaked her nose. "You're turning into a popsicle. We need to head back."

"Let's say hi to Harry, then we can go." She pivoted, trekking over the creaky boards.

The bushes nearby rustled. Hopefully, all skunks were elsewhere, safe and warm. Harry wheezed like he'd swallowed a chalky eraser. Vi talked to him, and the silly goose rubbed his neck around her legs. She held out her hand for him to inspect. He appeared to sniff, then nuzzled his head on her palm.

She gazed at Rory, her eyes shining. "I did it. Silas showed me how to approach this guy last night. Harry didn't peck him, so I thought I'd try it."

When Rory turned to head back, she followed. Her latest revelation about Silas distracted him. A teaching moment, huh? The fangs of jealousy bit hard, spurring Rory past caution. Yeah, she'd been delighted when he proposed a walk, and uber-cute the whole time. Could she handle more? Could he? When they reached their vehicles, he opened Vi's car door, and she climbed in. Once her car heated up, he motioned for her to roll down the window.

He stared into her sweet little heart-shaped face, almost losing his nerve. He rubbed his hands. "Vi, when I get back in town, will you go on a date with me?"

The instant the words left Rory's mouth, he knew they'd been a mistake. Those blue eyes, so full of light the second before, shuttered immediately. Her lips flattened. The hard edge had returned. But then her countenance softened the tiniest bit, which gave him a sliver of hope.

"I'm sorry, Rory. I'll admit I had the wrong impression of you, and I'm glad we're getting along better now. But—" Vi shook her head.

Rory stamped his foot to regain feeling in it. "Why not? We're good together, Vi." The desire he'd stuffed down barreled right past any reservations he'd had about asking.

Vi bit her lip. "I'm not good relationship material. Rory, you don't know me—"

"Why don't you let me be the judge of that?"

Vi's eyes flashed. "What about Paige?"

Rory felt as if the same brick had hit him twice. First Jesse, now Vi. "What about Paige? I don't understand why people keep asking me about her." His real foot resembled a block of ice. The other leg screamed for relief. He bumped aside the discomfort and pressed on. "Listen, Vi. I don't know what you've heard, but nothing is going on between Paige and me."

"Could have fooled me. Apparently, I'm not the only one either." Her frosty words competed with the air.

Rory detested giving in to the prosthetic, but the cold was wearing him down. "Let me get in the car with you. We'll hash this out."

Embarrassment swept across her face, and she almost relented. Almost.

"There's nothing to hash out. Please, Rory. Let me go." The plea in her eyes finally penetrated his senses.

He backed up. "We're not done here, Vi."

She pushed a button, and her window went up. The yellow bug picked up speed and crunched through the dry leaves.

Once again, Rory stood with his hands in his pockets, staring as Vi ran away. From him. It seemed to be his lot in life. Only this time, he couldn't go after her. If he did, he sensed it would drive her farther away.

He kicked the ground with his good foot. Mentally, he ticked off the things he had to do tomorrow before he boarded a plane. A meeting with Paige topped the list. Time to find out why their close friends considered them an item.

CHAPTER FOURTEEN

Vi's conscience was killing her. Rude and insensitive hardly tapped the surface of her behavior this evening. She smacked the pillow, tossing restlessly. Receiving the comfort of Rory's arms one minute, over the moon when he proposed a walk around the lake, then a horrid knee-jerk reaction when he asked her out. As if she hadn't suspected or even hoped he might.

Back home, Vi had disappeared into her room, not wanting to talk to anyone. Certainly not Paige. Exhaustion wired her tight enough to trip an alarm. Flipping her pillow to the cool side, she breathed in the fresh cotton fragrance. Strains of music from the movie *White Christmas* floated under her door. She glanced at the clock on the nightstand. 11:07 p.m. She grabbed her phone, and thumbed a text.

Are you awake?

She hit SEND before she could change her mind.

Barely.

Her fingers flew.

Forgive me for acting so rude? Delete. *Sorry I left you standing in the cold.* Delete. *A date would be fun.* Delete. She sighed with frustration, then thumbed again.

I want to proceed with the remodel.

She stared at the screen and pressed SEND.

Are you sure?

Rory's hesitation bounced through the text into her room.

Yes. Are we still friends?

Funny how a month ago, she wouldn't have cared or wanted it. Now she couldn't imagine her life without him. Friends were important.

RORY TEXTED PAIGE AT 6:32 a.m.

Meet me for breakfast?

Paige was an early riser. Declared she could accomplish half a day's work before Rory arrived and changed everything.

At home in his townhouse, he rocked in the glider. Well, home before Stella destroyed it. Now it had become a place to crash. He cast a jaundiced eye around the room. A professional designer would help him start over, but he hadn't found the mojo to make it happen. A real home needed a woman's touch. The right woman.

Bible in his lap, Rory took another sip of coffee. Reading Psalms soothed his restless mind. When he tried to pray, however, the heavens were as closed as Vi's face last night when he'd asked her out. After her text about the remodel, he'd called. They'd both been careful to stick to business. Her decision to move forward brought him a level of joy he didn't understand. But he didn't know what to do with her "Are we still friends" question. Only friends with Vi sounded next to impossible. The insane level of attraction arcing between them shredded the notion. He hadn't answered because anything he said would have been a half-truth. She would run from the whole truth.

His phone chimed with Paige asking when and where. Once they'd decided, he drained his coffee mug, mulling over how to approach the dilemma he found himself in.

Why their close friends thought he and Paige were a couple remained a mystery. He leaned forward in the glider, resting his elbows on his knees, fingers intertwined, thumbs on his forehead. "Lord, you know Paige and I work together, so please give me an extra measure of tact. Help us talk this through with no hard feelings on either side. You alone have the insight I need."

"So, boss, what's on your mind?" Paige sat across from him in a booth at a pancake shop. They'd already talked through her to-do list for the days he'd be gone, including the hefty number of calls and appointments to get the ball rolling on Vi's project. Breakfast finished, they drank more coffee as Rory figured out how to broach the subject of their relationship—a delicate blend of work versus friendship. Until now, he'd believed they'd pulled it off.

The aroma of fruity pancakes and salty bacon peppered the air. Hands wrapped around his mug, Rory idly watched a young boy scarf down pancakes, his mouth ringed with a purple line of blueberry syrup.

"Boss?" Paige nudged.

She wore a cherry-colored coat over slacks and a white frilly blouse. Her shiny ebony hair sported a low bun. Silver hoops adorned her ears. Her classic beauty was as familiar to him as his own beard. They were friends with not one iota of romantic chemistry between them. Rory had wanted to take it to the next level more than once, but his mind and body reacted the same way every time. Any measure of peace became a lone grain of sand on a windy day. Right now, Paige's almond-shaped eyes held a note of amusement. The slight smile confirmed it.

Rory gazed at her. "Sorry. I need you to be straight with me." He inwardly winced at her open and trusting brown eyes. Sucking a deep breath, he plunged in. "I've had two people recently ask me about—" The word stuck in his throat. "—us."

"And ...?" Her knowing look sent him into a frantic backpedal.

His breakfast declared mutiny on the way to his gut. Paige was the sister he'd never had. Had the easiness between them caused him to overlook overtures on her part for more?

"They seem to think ... there's ... something going on." He wagged a finger between them.

"What did you tell them?" Paige's smug look and playful tone were more than he could bear.

"I told both people there's nothing between us ... our relationship is friends-only." He said the words quickly, not missing the wistful look crossing her lovely features. Uh-oh. His thumbs rubbed together of their own accord.

Paige set aside her coffee mug and held her hands out across the table. Rory slowly gripped them. "And you're worried my feelings might be more?" Her words conveyed a note of compassion.

Not able to break eye contact, Rory tilted his chin in a wordless *yes*.

She exhaled softly. "I think it's crossed both our minds—" A corner of her lip turned up. "—and we've had our chance."

The wistful look returned. "I believe romantic love starts with friendship and one day … catches fire." Her eyes twinkled. "I care for you, but we've never combusted—into flames or anything else." She continued. "Oh, I've considered *us*. It always left me feeling flat and disappointed. The excitement was missing. Do you feel the same way?"

Rory's body sagged with relief. He'd never loved Paige more than he did this minute. His thumbs kneaded the tops of her hands. "Same as you, I've wondered. But the desire never happened. I finally reached the conclusion it would wreck what we have—friends with an excellent working relationship."

Understanding flashed in her trademark smile. "Believe me, I get it." She slipped her hands out of his grip, wrapping them around her coffee mug. They sat in silence for a while, digesting the conversation.

Paige stirred first. "Who's asking about us?"

The question landed Rory in a tight spot. If he answered, his interest in Vi would reveal itself. Oh, why not? Paige would figure it out anyway. "You know Jesse and I are accountability partners." When she inclined her head, he continued. "I told him about a girl I'm interested in. He objected because he thought you and I were in a relationship." He made air quotes around the last words, still careful to tread lightly. Paige had informed him more than once his "male insensitivity" had lost him points.

She seemed pensive. "Jesse gets protective. When you first mentioned it, I assumed you were referring to business contacts, since we couple at networking events." Her eyes rolled heavenward. "Maybe the pretense spills over? Not for us personally, but the way others view it?" She frowned, shaking her head. "I'm rethinking the party scene, boss, especially after last night. She waved a hand between them. This latest misunderstanding only confirms it. And the upcoming gala ...”

“Are you good for it?” Rory asked. The New Year’s Eve gala remained the pinnacle of Valiant’s fundraising events. Black-tie, who’s-who, old money. Invitations sold for five hundred dollars.

“Honestly?” She dragged the word out. “I’ve been dreading it. The atmosphere reeks of entitlement. I always feel out of place.”

Rory knew precisely what she referred to, but if Paige didn’t attend as his plus-one, he needed to find a date.

She brought him back to the present. “Who’s the other person who thought we were a couple? And who’s this girl you told Jesse about?” Her look warmed him, and his breathing returned to normal. Defining their relationship hadn’t bothered her. “You’ve got to come clean, boss. I can help diffuse wrong perceptions.”

Rory’s collar tightened. “You know her.”

Paige’s brows pinched into concern. “You haven’t rekindled the flame with your ex-girlfriend, have you?”

“Not Stella.”

Paige squinted at him. “Who, then?”

Here goes. “You live with her.”

Paige’s grin could have stopped traffic. “Vi?”

“Yeah.” Yep. Crushing on Vi. Even if she’d turned him down for a date.

Her lips etched into a line. “*Hmm.* That explains a few things.”

Eager for the tiniest tidbit, Rory leaned forward, but Paige didn’t elaborate. “So, what do you think?”

“Vi’s not super affectionate or one to share deep secrets. If you’re interested, you best grab hold of extra patience and keep it in your back pocket." Paige tinkered with a package of sweetener.

Rory's face scrunched. "Great."

Paige smiled at his wry tone. "You'll be good for her." Then her voice dropped as if talking to herself. Rory leaned even closer, and she muttered something about misconceptions.

Not knowing what she meant, he only said, "I'd appreciate all the help I can get." Shooting her a grateful look, he waved for the ticket. Emilio, a Peeps' employee, stood at the cashier counter. Did the guy ever not wear the grungy black hoodie?

"Who's here?" Paige followed his gaze. Then she peered into a compact to reapply her lipstick.

"Emilio. Looking guilty as usual. Wonder why he's not at work?"

CHAPTER FIFTEEN

Hands on hips, Vi stood nearby as Emilio squirted WD-40 on the squeaky door.

The small man swung the door back and forth. Satisfied, he turned to Vi. "I fixed it. Once the oil soaks in, should be no noise." He wiped his hands on a dirty rag.

"Thanks, Emilio. The massage experience works better when the door doesn't squeal like a dying rat." Vi smiled at him. Peeps' maintenance man notoriously disappeared when needed, however, he'd always been quick to fulfill her small mechanical needs.

When he turned to leave, she asked, "Hey, have you seen Rory this morning?" What was the matter with her? She didn't need to talk to Rory.

Her inner antenna perked at his shifty look. "Ya, I seen him. At the pancake place holding hands with his girlfriend. Some guys have all the luck." He shrugged. "This latest one—I seen her around—a real stunner with dark hair, big smile."

Vi couldn't find her voice. Paige. An echo of Rory's voice

haunted her. *There's nothing between Paige and me.* Suddenly, she found it hard to breathe.

"You need me to find him?" Emil's smooth suggestion burst into her dismaying thoughts.

"No!" Oops. Too intense. "Ah, no. I don't need to see him." She shooed him away with her hands. "Scoot to your next task. And stay out of Rory's hair."

Vi entered the massage room and shut the door. Making her way to the linen cabinet, she yanked out fresh sheets. The urge to cry overwhelmed her.

<hr />

NOW LATE EVENING, Vi couldn't justify her procrastination any longer. She'd been driving around with no destination for the last thirty minutes still with no inkling of what to say to Paige. How could the woman act as if there was nothing between her and Rory? Brenna had already texted to find out when Vi would arrive home. She'd tied the question to dinner, but it didn't fool Vi. They were afraid she would fall into another hole or something equally stupid.

Reluctantly, she navigated the busy holiday traffic on her way to Paige's. Her hands had tingled early on and increased. Now they throbbed with pain.

Temps were dropping fast. Same as last night when Rory asked her out, and she slammed the door in his face. Regret gnawed at her. What if she'd accepted? A date with Rory sounded like fun. And freedom. And fire. A yearning for more unraveled her resolve. She blinked away tears, forcing herself to remember why she hadn't wanted to come home. Rory might have asked her out, but he loved Paige. Despite what Rory said, Emilio's hand-holding info painted a picture Vi couldn't ignore. Focused on thoughts of Rory, she pulled into the driveway too fast. Shrieking, she stomped on the brakes, stopping inches from the storage shed.

Disaster averted, she left her car and gazed at the silhouette of the Christmas tree in the big window. A warm fire beckoned her chilled body when she opened the front door. Thunder lay on the rug near the fireplace. His ears pricked, and he woofed softly at her entrance. Christmas lights strategically placed around the cozy living area heralded a comfy aura. Welcoming, even.

"Hey, Vi." Brenna appeared, wiping her hands on a dishtowel. The scent of warm toast wafted into the room with her. "You hungry? We're making grilled cheese sandwiches and tomato soup."

Vi sniffed. The cheesy smell unhinged all thoughts of escape. Her gut roared with hunger. By early afternoon, she'd depleted her mandarin orange supply, and a trip to the deli had never happened. Brenna's earlier text made it clear they were waiting for her. Vi had maxed out on rude behavior, so she trudged into the kitchen, the booted ankle fussing with every step. If she could get through dinner …

At the stove, Paige flipped another grilled cheese sandwich onto a plate with others. She glanced at Vi, then crossed the room, blanketing her in a tight hug. Eyes moist, Vi submitted with the enthusiasm of a paper doll.

Paige released her, then searched her face with warm, friendly eyes. "Let's chat tonight?"

Grasping for a measure of control, Vi rasped, "After dinner." Only then did Paige back away.

Through tears, Vi stumbled over, took the plate Brenna handed her and sat. Paige placed a cup of soup next to her plate, along with a bottle of water. Vi stared at her plate, willing the tears to dry up. She sniffed, wiping her nose with a napkin.

Once her housemates sat, they joined hands and Brenna said the blessing. Vi dug in, salivating over the gooey melted cheese. Despite her misgivings about coming home, she felt much improved after eating. Limited conversation suggested they'd all had busy days.

"Hungry much?" Brenna eyed Vi's empty plate.

Paige laughed. "Did you eat anything besides oranges today?

Mentally, Vi retraced her day. "Does coffee count?"

Brenna looked skyward. "Girl, you've got to keep your strength up."

"Time to chat. Here or in the living room?" The words rivaled the warmth permeating the air, even if Paige's brows arched with determination.

Did anybody ever tell Paige no? Vi sent a silent plea heavenward.

"I vote living room." Brenna held up a finger, pointing in said direction.

Her housemates looked at her. Vi lifted a shoulder as if it didn't matter.

Picking up her water bottle, Paige left the kitchen. Brenna grabbed her phone and followed. Vi lingered behind, flexing her tender fingers. A memory of Rory massaging her palm washed through her consciousness. *Don't go there, girl.*

Once she'd settled into her spot on the sofa, Paige piped up. "How's the house remodel coming along, Vi?" Her soft accent added a lilt to her words most people found charming. It made Vi want to leave the room as soon as humanly possible.

"I had to think through the extra cost of a termite issue, but I've decided to proceed." She groped for words to satisfy her roommates and keep her dignity intact. "Rory,"—her breath swooshed on his name—"says it will take a few months." She choked out the last words and hung her head.

The other two women stilled. The dryer thumped in a repetitive motion off the hallway.

"What's going on, Vi?" Paige sounded infinitely patient.

The words burst out of Vi's mouth in tight staccato cuts. "Why do you and Rory act as if nothing is going on between you?"

Paige lifted her chin. "Because there isn't."

Vi shook her head. "I've seen the way you two interact. Emilio said he saw Rory with his girlfriend this morning. You were holding hands."

Quiet up to this point, Brenna made a dismissive noise. "Emilio is *not* a reliable source."

"Why would he lie?" Vi asked.

"Don't get me wrong. He came in handy at, um, the pickleball tournament, but the guy loves to gossip. Facts aren't important."

Vi chewed on Brenna's take, despite her obvious reluctance to discuss her abduction. They'd all been glad Emilio saw Leo racing through the parking lot with her. Never mind he'd sneaked outside for a smoke break when he'd been needed inside.

"I can explain." Paige held her ground.

Vi wiggled her boot with impatience. Despite all the evidence to the contrary, she wanted to believe Paige.

"Rory texted me early this morning to meet him for breakfast." Paige tucked her hair behind her ears. "We do it when he's about to leave town. From the beginning, he seemed nervous and distracted. After we planned for his absence, I asked him what was on his mind. He hem-hawed around, then spilled it. It upset him that you and Jesse thought we were in a relationship.

"At first, I didn't know he was serious. We don't mind aggressive business contacts to think we're a couple, but the more we talked, I realized how it must look to others." She turned to Vi. "Rory and I are friends—end of story."

Her elegant shoulders lifted expressively. "He's affectionate, no doubt about it. Physical contact—it's air to him. He's kissed me plenty of times. We've hugged too, but it's never been intimate."

Vi scrambled to grasp this new perspective. There hadn't been anything platonic about their kiss in the hospital.

Despite the sincerity in Paige's eyes, Vi remained unconvinced. "What about holding hands?"

Paige's forehead wrinkled, then cleared. "Oh, *mija*. Rory told Jesse we're more like siblings than anything else. It distressed Rory to think I might want more." A soft chuckle rumbled in her throat. "I only took his hands to assure him our relationship didn't go beyond friends."

Vi didn't know if she believed this new spin, but her roiling emotions receded. The raging wound in her heart stopped bleeding.

"Has Rory asked you out?" About to pop, Brenna directed the question to Vi.

Vi grabbed her messy braid. On auto-pilot, she unplaited it. Gazing at Brenna, she inclined her head a fraction.

"Oh, fun! We can be the fearsome foursome on dates." Brenna bounced on the end of the sofa.

"Will you go out with him?" Paige asked.

Vi felt her face crumple.

"Why not?" Brenna demanded.

"I can't. And I can't talk about it anymore." Vi wouldn't subject Rory—or them—to the agony she lived with every day.

After an awkward silence, Paige cleared her throat. "Okay. We've got prep work to do for the Christmas party on Sunday night. How about we divvy up the chores again? It worked at

Thanksgiving." She looked at Vi. "Did you talk to Tavo about cooking the meat?"

"Yes, I told him you would text him the info."

"I need a headcount so he can tell me how much meat to buy."

"What time on Sunday? I'm hoping Jesse will be back." Brenna thumbed her phone screen. "*Hmm.* Their flight arrives mid-afternoon, then the drive from Austin. If all goes well, he and Rory should be back in Valiant by early evening."

Paige shot her a knowing look. "They won't want to miss the food. We can delay, as long as there are plenty of appetizers."

As they discussed the menu and divvied up prep work, Vi unwound by degrees. Well, as much as possible under the circumstances. Her decision not to date would inevitably lead to other subjects she'd rather not share, even with her housemates. She rose, stretching her arms over her head, first one way, then the other. "All this talk about food has made me hungry again. I'm going to raid the leftovers." She headed toward the kitchen.

Brenna hopped off the sofa. "Me too. Nat's marathon workouts make me crazy-hungry." She paused in the doorway, then spoke again, her voice low and husky. "Vi, the way things look can be deceiving. At one point, I had nailed Jesse as the biggest player around. Even though circumstances seemed to back it up, none of it was true."

Vi digested this news as she opened the fridge. She remembered those tumultuous days all too well. Brenna had cried a lot. She'd even moved out temporarily, determined to get away from Jesse. It hadn't worked.

Brenna leaned past her, pulling out the plate of foil-wrapped grilled cheese sandwiches. "Rory's not a player, Vi."

CHAPTER SIXTEEN

Much later in the evening, propped by pillows, Vi nestled into a comfortable position under the bedcovers. She clicked through screens on Daddy's tablet until she reached the documents. Impending dread pulled at her. What made this so hard tonight? In the back of her mind, she knew it had to do with Dad's words in the first letter. "Things you might wish you hadn't read." Licking her lips, she opened another letter.

Hey, Red,

Your mama hated it when I talked country. She'd say, 'Thomas, if you talk like a hick, people will think you're a hick.'

Vi grinned. She could hear them in her head arguing about it

There ain't no tactful way to say this, but it needs saying.

Once we got all the custody issues worked out, things rode along okay for a while until your mom married again. I'll hate 'til the day I die what you suffered at the hands of that sorry bum. Long story short, I noticed things when you'd come stay with me. Getting you to take a bath was worse than ridin' the meanest bull around. You squalled and carried on, and I saw bruises where no little girl should have 'em. You were afraid of everything, whereas you'd always been a tough little tomboy before. I put two and two together, and it broke my heart something fierce.

I looked into getting full custody of you, and I wasn't trying to get back at your mom. I couldn't stand the thought of you living in the same house with him. But two different lawyers told me it'd be a cold day in hell before any judge would give me custody—in Texas, the mother usually gets preference. Your mom had a good source of income, and I woulda had to put you through the wringer to prove anything. She and I fought about it a lot.

When your ma and him split, it made my heart glad. I'd been scared for both of you for so long, it came as a relief.

Vi paused as tears ran down her face. Daddy's perspective ripped off the flimsy emotional scab covering the abuse. Her memories were vague about Mom and Wallace's divorce. She continued to read.

Your mama is a good woman down deep. She acts all gruff, but it hides a tender heart. When she gets her priorities mixed up, her sweetness gets buried. If you haven't already, you need to forgive her. She's always loved you.

I've run out of words for now.

Vi sat still for a long time, letting the tears flow. The abuse had stripped her childhood away. She'd gone from being the apple of her daddy's eye to feeling degraded and worthless. For years, she wanted revenge. Too late, she discovered that path sowed seeds of rebellion. When her decisions led to such brokenness she wanted to die, she finally got honest with God. Life grew bearable again once her relationship with God improved.

For the first time in years, the emotional undertow, the strong current pulling her out to sea, stopped. Daddy's words answered questions she'd never dared ask anyone. Red numbers glowed from the clock on her nightstand. Her eyes burned from weeping.

She sucked in deep, cleansing breaths as the perpetual tightness in her chest receded. The giant, gnarly knot of pain that roared to life whenever she thought about her childhood —or hid from it—had lost its power. Even now, invisible rents snaked up and down her soul, creating a fresh perspective. She'd never been alone. Daddy had known about the abuse. He'd tried to rescue her.

"Thank you," she whispered.

A shell breaking with new life, the horror of her past faded. A greater truth had taken its place. For the first time in a decade, she longed for an honest conversation with Mom. Transparency had never been their strong suit. Maybe if they communicated, Mom could begin the healing process too.

Vi powered the tablet off and laid it aside, the germ of an idea forming. Her mind drifted as she pulled her hair into a careless ponytail. Reading the letter had exhausted her, but thankfulness reigned in her heart.

As her eyes closed, a familiar scene popped behind her

eyelids. An attractive man leaned into her consciousness, tenacity sparking through his gray eyes. "We're not done here, Vi."

"ARE you sure this is a good idea, Ro?" Jesse asked for the second or third time as they waited on the tarmac for the plane to unload. "What if the crate doesn't fit in the back of the Jeep."

"I've already told you, it's foolproof. Vi will want the dog. On the off chance she doesn't, I'll take him to the K9 refuge in Houston." Rory stretched the kinks out of his legs from the flight. Another addition to the list of things the prosthetic disliked—cramped plane seating. Next time he'd go first class. For now, his leg would howl until he could squeeze in a workout and remind it who was boss. Sighing, he zipped his black leather jacket against the damp breeze. *Be thankful you can still walk, dude.*

Gray skies threatened rain. Tawny fields surrounded the flight lanes. Orange cones sat off to one side. A baggage cart rolled their way.

Jesse glanced at his phone. "If we're not held up here, we should make it to Paige's Christmas party."

Rory hid a smile as he scratched his beard. Inserting a deliberately dubious tone, he asked, "You sure Brenna will be there? She might be running around a track and forget."

"She'll be there," Jesse growled.

"What a lovesick puppy." As the words left Rory's mouth, he stepped back to avoid another punch. His arm still ached from the last time he smarted off.

Jesse arched a brow. "Jealous?"

"You know it." Rory pulled papers from his pocket, ignoring Jesse's smug look.

Workers wearing bright safety vests emptied multi-colored luggage from the cargo hold. The baggage cart driver hopped off and heaved luggage onto the cart. Another entered the hold.

"What if Vi's not at the party?"

"Where else would she be? And why am I repeating all this? If I can't track her down, which would be odd, I'll take Cyrus home with me and catch up with her tomorrow."

"Since when do you know anything about dogs, Ro? I think you need to square this latest idea with Paige. Vi already has a dog—and cats."

Jesse had a point. "On the way home, I'll call Paige." He mustered a stern look. "You need to chill. Quit looking at all the reasons it won't work."

A worker stepped down from the cargo hold with a large crate. Rory strode over to it, peering inside at an oversized black German Shepherd. "How you doin', Cyrus? You need water?"

A soft whimper greeted him.

When Rory asked Manny's wife if she needed a home for the dog, relief had etched Rosa's face. One less worry. For the rest of their brief stay, Rory kept Cyrus close. Poor dog missed his master.

They got the dog through the checkpoints, then located Jesse's four-wheel drive. Rory noted with satisfaction the crate fit perfectly.

Rory climbed in the front seat, shifting his leg until he found a measure of comfort, then pulled out his phone. "Sail us home, Jess. I'm calling Paige now."

"You got it. I'm looking forward to Tavo's brisket." The dark slash between Jesse's brows had disappeared.

Brisket? Right. Rory snorted, holding the phone to his ear.

THE MOUTH-WATERING AROMA of grilled meat wafted into Paige's kitchen when Tavo slammed open the back door. "I need a pan and foil. The brisket's done and needs to set." He stomped Sasquatch-sized boots on the backdoor mat. "Getting breezy out there, ladies."

Vi glanced up as Brenna pulled an immense silver roasting pan from the drainboard, placing it on the counter. "A cup of wassail will warm you up." Brenna ladled a hot fruity drink from a pot on the stove into a foam cup.

"Whatsall?" Tavo sipped the drink with a quizzical expression, then grinned. "Good stuff." He exited with the drink cup and pan. Brenna grabbed the carton of foil and followed him.

The cinnamon wassail scent floated from the stove as Vi continued to garnish a pasta dish with cilantro sprigs. Rory's mashed potatoes would have been a better choice with the drizzly weather. Before the holidays were over, she secretly hoped he would make them again. Mere curiosity on her part to taste what everyone had raved about.

Curiosity killed the cat, Vi.

She rolled her eyes, focusing on a small spot on the ceiling. Since the night she and Rory had walked around the lake, self-preservation and desire waged war within. She'd made it clear she couldn't date him, but he'd acted as if their relationship wasn't over. Even said as much. In the deepest recesses of her heart, she didn't want it to end either. However, fun as the texting and calling were now, getting involved with him would eventually lead to greater pain, and she had no desire to hurt him.

Surveying her handiwork, she covered the bowl with plastic wrap. She hoped their trip hadn't been too taxing. She knew from experience, exhaustion rated high as one of grief's sneaky side effects.

Paige's phone chimed. Vi saw Rory's name splashed across the screen as she made her way to the fridge. Her breath hitched. She opened the door, then made room for the pasta bowl. Paige's heels announced her entrance, and she grabbed her phone. She peeked at Vi, then left with the phone glued to her ear.

Vi snatched a leftover cilantro sprig, inhaling the spicy smell. Then she gathered cooking utensils to load in the dishwasher. *Paige works for Rory. He calls her all the time. No reason to get worked up.*

The flutters in her stomach didn't pay a lick of attention to the careful rationale.

CHAPTER SEVENTEEN

Guests milled around in the living area. They drank wassail and indulged in appetizers, all the while chatting while Alexa streamed a holiday playlist. Brenna had parked by the big window next to the Christmas tree, fiddling with the angle on her Santa hat. Her brother and his friend sat on the floor by the fireplace, stroking Thunder. The hound lapped up the attention. Hmm.

"They're here." Brenna sang out, her eyes shining.

A rush of cold air blew in when Jesse and Rory entered, stamping their boots on the welcome mat. Both men wore jeans, jackets, and enormous grins.

"Hail the conquering heroes. About time you guys got here." Tavo's massive silhouette outlined the kitchen doorway.

Brenna quickly made her way to Jesse. He enveloped her in a hearty hug, knocking her carefully angled Santa hat askew. When Rory scanned the room, Vi dropped her head. She couldn't bear to watch his eyes seek Paige. They both declared they were only friends, but their adamant denials still made her wonder.

"Are they here? Everybody circle up." Amid the commotion, Vi glanced up to see Paige looking all festive in her black leggings and shiny gold tunic. Classy. Sophisticated.

Vi wanted to hide. Brenna and Paige insisted Vi wear her elf costume, but now she felt silly. Bright green and white striped leggings and up-turned shoes with jingle bells? Not her finest hour. Letting her hair fall around her face, she took her time joining the others. The playlist merrily chorused, *God rest ye merry gentlemen, let nothing you dismay …*

A pair of boots blocked her way. Head down, she attempted to go around, stopping when the boots mimicked her steps. Slightly annoyed, she looked into Rory's smiling face.

"How's Santa's helper this evening?" His eyes soft, he appeared glad to see her. And his barely concealed amusement proved contagious.

Vi giggled self-consciously. "The costume seemed a good idea before real people showed up."

Rory stroked his beard, then whispered, "You make an adorable elf."

Oh, dear. Her knees nearly buckled at his crooked grin.

He tucked the loose strands of hair behind her ears. A mischievous look crossed his features, and he stuck his finger in her ear.

She ducked away, a smile tugging at her lips. "Behave." She made to move around him. Affecting an air of innocence, he followed, grabbing her hand.

"Everybody ready to pray?" Paige gave Vi and Rory a pointed look, her brown eyes dancing. Standing beside her, Tavo smirked.

Amen pronounced, somebody yelled, "Yeeee-ha! Let's eat." People laughed as they made their way toward the kitchen. Rory didn't leave her side.

"How did your trip go?" Vi studied him as they waited in

line. The tiny crow's feet around his eyes had deepened into creases.

"Tough. Rosa suffers from mood swings, and now her safety net is gone. Manny was the steady one."

"Hard to watch," Vi murmured.

"Yeah. Thanks." Eyes pooling with emotion, he squeezed her hand.

People emerged from the kitchen with loaded plates. The smoky brisket fragrance permeated the air. A snazzy version of "Jingle Bell Rock" blared from a speaker. Jesse's sister Nat hip-bumped Tavo as he waded through the line with monster-sized helpings on a double thickness of paper plates.

Rory sniffed. "Smells divine, Chief." He pivoted back to Vi, leaning in until his beard brushed her cheek. "Got something to show you and talk about after dinner." She shot him a questioning look.

"Nope. It's a secret." He rubbed a hand over his chin. "First, we eat."

Ants gnawed on the edges of Vi's stomach. What was Rory up to now?

RORY YAWNED with satisfaction after a second helping and pushed back in the cushy chair. He'd had to coax her, but Vi had consented to sit with him and share a food tray. She'd insisted on him taking the comfy seat. Any chair would have worked if it brought her near.

This woman. One foot away, and he wanted her closer. Maybe he could finagle a hug before the evening passed.

Vi had eaten well enough, even if she seemed tense. Her questions about the trip weren't probing or nosy, and she'd listened when he answered. Still, something seemed off. She'd glanced over at Silas more than once. What if it boiled down to pity? The brisket turned to concrete en route to his stomach.

Well, best get his surprise over with. The remodeling plans were underway. Now he'd found a solution for her late-night walks—if she'd accept the dog. Then he would have completed what he set out to do.

Why did it feel so bleak?

He stirred from the chair. "Ready to find out what the secret is?"

She nodded, but her eyes looked troubled. "I'm not good with surprises." Her bottom lip resembled raw meat where she'd chewed it. If only she'd let him kiss away whatever was bothering her. *Focus, dude.*

"I promise this one will be different." He stood, holding out his hand. She took it and stepped around the food tray, careful to avoid the used cups and plates.

He moved her in front of him and placed his hands on her shoulders, happy when she didn't object. "Your feet are jingling," he said playfully.

"Yeah, no sneaking around tonight. Where are we going?" She stared straight ahead.

He guided her to the hall. "Back of the house. Whichever room has the back door."

Her shoulders bunched under his hands, steps slow as molasses. "What's this about?"

Now she'd stopped altogether. Rory swiveled her around to face him. He couldn't let her renege when they were so close to a solution. "I need you to trust me."

Vi's eyes widened. "Trust isn't my strong suit."

"I know." Rory understood, even if the *why*-factor eluded him. "Please? I have your best interests at heart."

Her shoulders drooped even further. "Okay. Show me the

secret." Her lack of enthusiasm warred with her cheerful holiday outfit.

He took her hand, lest she bolt, and led her the rest of the way. Opening the door, he switched on the light and then guided her in. The kennel sat on the floor between the bed and the dresser. Letting go of Vi, he kneeled to unhook the latch. "Come, Cyrus."

The majestic dog unfolded himself. Cautiously, he slipped out the wire mesh door and stretched first one leg, then the other.

"Cyrus, meet Vi." Rory pointed to her.

The dog obediently padded over to where Vi stood. Rory's mouth turned up as astonishment leaked from every pore in her body.

He commanded in a low voice. "Sit." The dog sat. "Shake hands." Cyrus raised a paw.

With a hand over her mouth, Vi gently shook Cyrus's paw. She looked at Rory, a hundred questions in her eyes. "Wh-wh-what is this *dog* doing here?"

Rory's smile became a full-blown grin at her stammer. So un-Vi-ish. If nothing else, he'd managed the surprise part.

"Can I ... will he let me pet him?" Without waiting for an answer, she clumsily maneuvered her walking boot to the floor to sit next to the regal dog. Cyrus gazed at her, his golden-brown eyes sad.

Satisfied Vi was acting more herself, Rory said, "Lay down, Cyrus." The dog immediately lay on his belly.

Vi stroked his back, murmuring soothing words Rory couldn't quite make out. A negative sensation snaked through his insides.

Yeah. Okay. He was jealous of a four-legged animal. Rory arranged his leg to a more comfortable position. Once situated, he cleared his throat. "Cyrus belonged to Manny. He's trained to protect, but Rosa feared him. When I mentioned I might know a person who would use the dog, she begged me to take him." The way Vi gazed at him made his breath hitch. "Cyrus would solve your need for a walking buddy. He'll protect you with his life."

Vi inhaled sharply, her hand stilled on Cyrus. "You brought this dog back to be my bodyguard when I walk around the lake?" Her eyes pierced him.

Uh oh. Major backfire. Rory held his hands up. "If you hate the idea, I can take him to a K9 refuge in Houston …"

When she continued to stare at him, Rory looked away, disappointment biting hard.

Vi rose, knee-walking to where he sat. Her fingers grasped his chin as she turned his head to face her.

"Are you serious? This beautiful creature is mine to take on walks whenever I want?"

The hope in her eyes gave him courage. "Yes. Exactly."

Her mouth fell open. The next thing he knew, Vi tackled him in a ferocious hug. Rory wrapped his arms around her and held on, enjoying every second of her closeness. Finally, she pulled away with a dazed look.

"Sorry. I got carried away." The words were breathy. Her cheeks flamed. Backing up hastily, she sat by the dog.

"I'm not sorry at all," Rory reassured her. Her hug had made him a little woozy. His heart flopped, like a fish on the bottom of a boat.

With effort, he kept himself from grabbing her for another hug. "If you want to keep him, we'll have to work out the logistics."

"Okay." Her instant compliance boded well. "Let's get comfy." She scooted farther away.

He moved closer, but she shook her head. "The dog goes here." She patted the space between them. "Right now, he's most familiar with you. If we stick together, he'll get comfortable with me as well."

Her "together" reasoning suited him fine. "Cyrus, come." The dog's ears pricked, and he moved toward them. Rory pointed. "Lay down." He praised him when Cyrus did as he requested.

Rory looked at Vi. "He's heartbroken right now, missing Manny. He needs time to bond with you."

Vi's eyes were luminous as she stroked Cyrus's black fur. "I understand his grief."

CHAPTER EIGHTEEN

Vi would never again underrate a typical walking experience. The boot grouched, refusing to get on board with her urge to pirouette down the hallway. At least nature aligned with her mood as sunlight streamed through the windows, creating its flickering light dance.

Her mind had refused to accept any sleep last night until she had formed a plan to keep Cyrus. She still found it hard to believe Rory had given her a guard dog to keep her safe.

Nobody had ever cared about her well-being except Daddy.

Brimming with purpose, she rapped on the closed door. "Brenna, it's me, Vi."

A muffled voice bade her enter. Vi walked in, unable to hide her grin. Brenna sat in her desk chair, Santa hat tilted to perfection.

A lazy smile stretched across the slender brunette's face. "Well, look who decided to rise and shine after a late night. Dare I attribute your good humor to the cozy conversation I saw between you and Rory?"

Vi raised her shoulders an inch. She and Rory had talked

about Cyrus's needs for a long time. When they'd finally moved to the living room, the late hour had Vi yawning, but Rory had insisted on a snack and more time to catch up. Honestly, the man oozed charm. They'd eaten leftover pasta salad and chatted for another hour. Or two.

The whole evening remained a pleasant dream she wasn't ready to wake from. The moment Rory had walked in the door last night, a new vibe pulsed between them—the way they communicated, the level of physical touch. Very different from their previous encounters. Well, yeah, she'd been nervous when he appeared to be escorting her to a bedroom. Later, she realized old fears had gripped her, trying to gain a foothold. She and Rory weren't destined for a relationship. No way he could get around her past.

She swallowed past the lump in her throat, pressing on with her mission. "Got a question for you. If there's a reason it won't work, tell me."

Curiosity shone in Brenna's green eyes.

Vi took a deep breath and plunged in. "Big ask. Rory brought me a guard dog, but Paige needs a break from my ongoing menagerie. It is her house, after all. Thunder and the kittens are foster pets. Still, I'd rather re-home them than take them back to the pet adoption center. Do you think your mom would let your brother take the dog and maybe a kitten?"

Brenna's eyes were thoughtful as she twirled a strand of chestnut hair. "Theodore adores your sad-looking hound. I'll ask Mom while he's in school, or she'll have no peace. And one cat?"

"I have another idea about a home for the rest of them. Thunder loves the cats. If a kitten accompanies him, he might adjust easier to a new home."

"Ever the soft touch with animals." Another smile tweaked

Brenna's features. "Are you all right with giving Thunder to Theodore? He's gotten a lot more responsible …"

"Yes, if your mom's okay with it. Thunder is a great dog, but I think he's sensed I'm temporary. He needs his forever home." A grimace pulled her lips down. "Rory assures me I need Cyrus more." Out of habit, her fingers reached to smooth her braid. Would accepting Cyrus further complicate things between her and Rory?

Brenna's brows raised. "Cyrus is an answer to prayer for those of us who love you. Your late-night jaunts have always bothered me." She scribbled on a sticky note. "I'll give Mom a call this morning."

Vi's breath swooshed out in a huff. Wow. Cyrus thrilled her, but anxiety poked up its fierce little head, demanding access. Shifting away from the negative emotion, Vi pushed on with her plan. "Thanks. I need to talk to Jesse. Is he in?" Vi loathed contributing to the hordes of people tracking in and out of his office.

"Let me check." Brenna reached for her phone, then thumbed a quick text. "If he's in, I'm certain he'll see you."

Seconds later, she read the return text aloud. "Of course. Come right now."

"Thanks, Brenna." As she turned to leave, Brenna hurried around her desk and gave her a quick hug.

"Did you have fun last night?" Brenna's eyes were hopeful.

Vi's pulse raced. A shy smile emerged as she remembered the easy way she'd chatted with Rory. "Yes, only it's not what you're thinking."

"What am I thinking, Vi?" Brenna teased.

Vi ignored the innuendo, firmly shutting the door behind her.

Before she took two steps, Jesse stood in his doorway, rubbing a shoulder against the doorjamb. "Hey, Vi.

Appreciate the break. Gave me a chance to stretch. Come on in."

"I'm sorry for the loss of your friend, Jess," she murmured as she passed.

"Thanks." His tone sounded appreciative but didn't encourage small talk. All the better. Vi stunk at chit-chat—Rory knew how to talk to people. Pushing *that* thought away, she flicked her braid over one shoulder and slid into a guest chair.

Jesse's workspace overflowed with reports, manila folders, and yellow highlighters. He slipped behind his desk and sat. "Good to see you. What can I do for you?" His dark eyes could have pierced a hole in the wall.

Oh, here we go. Jesse had always been polite and gentlemanly with her. Still, his intensity made her want to catch a flight to Shangri-La. "I ... um ... need to ask ... a favor."

"Name it." He leaned forward on his elbows, interlocking his fingers.

Vi swallowed. "I need some time off."

Jesse's head tilted as if the news didn't surprise him. "I hoped you would ask for time off."

Vi's suspicions rose when he didn't elaborate. "Have you been talking to Rory?" If a certain attractive redhead had been blabbing her business ...

Jesse eyed her evenly. "The other night when you ate dinner with Brenna and me, you were dead on your feet. You're too valuable to burn out. Peeps needs you. How busy is your schedule this week?"

He'd noticed she'd had a tough day? Her respect for him rose yet another notch. "Heavy. Every slot full. And I need time to bond with Cyrus."

"The dog's a good option for you?"

"Yes!" Vi's euphoria over Cyrus gushed forth. "I plan to

keep him. It's a matter of figuring out the details." She clamped her mouth shut against the temptation of blabbing every jot and tittle of her plan.

A smile ghosted Jesse's lips. "And no M1 Abrams tank could stop you, I'm sure. Is it time to add another massage therapist to the mix?"

Vi nodded slowly once she absorbed the suggestion. "We all appreciate the extra hours …"

"I imagine it's taxing work." Jesse rubbed a scruffy jaw. "Do your hands hurt?"

The direct question caught her off guard, and her lips scrunched sideways. "It's not so bad in the morning, but … at night …" Not a soul knew about the uncontrollable shaking in her hands. Her insides quaked at his knowing look. An MT with twitchy fingers didn't bode well.

"Okay. How about you do mornings and leave at noon? I'll get on hiring another person." Jesse seemed to have given it thought already.

A breath escaped between her teeth. "It would be a big help. until I can—"

"You need a substantial break. Would it help if you only massaged women?" Jesse's eyes bored into her.

She stiffened. Jesse and Rory *had* talked. "No, I can handle the men …" she faltered, remembering Curtis.

Jesse's lips thinned. "Vi, your comfort level on the job is important, so I'll make this perfectly clear. You don't have to take any appointments you don't want." Irritation passed over his face. "If a jerk is stressing you out, he doesn't need a massage."

A shiver washed over her. Jesse's dark look could intimidate the hardest heart. Too bad she couldn't borrow it for certain clients.

Vi rose, digesting his words. Her insides slowly unclenched.

"Thanks. You're a peach, Jesse." Her cheeks flushed with warmth. She hadn't meant to call her boss a piece of fruit, even if he had offered an unprecedented level of support on her behalf.

His wry chuckle eased her embarrassment. "Better than other things I've been called. Vi, I'm serious about lightening your load. Mornings only this week. We'll talk again before you take on a full schedule."

Jess climbed out of his chair, rounded the desk, and walked her to the door. "Thanks for stopping by. We appreciate you around here." As ever, his professionalism stood staunchly in place, but his eyes had drifted next door.

Vi hid a grin. Brenna never had a chance with Jesse's office so close by. The man didn't know how to leave her alone. It reminded her of—oh dear. *God, help me.*

Forcing thoughts of Rory away, she clunked down the hall. Her feet itched to dance when she remembered Cyrus. She'd reschedule her afternoon massages, do the one scheduled for this morning, then zip back to Paige's. First, though, she had to track down Silas. His text said he would be at the gym.

Her phone chimed with an incoming text. Brenna's name flashed across the screen.

> Mom's okay with Theodore taking
> Thunder and a cat. Tonight, they're going
> to discuss Responsibility 101. I'm pretty
> sure it's a slam dunk. THIS IS AMAZING!

Vi grinned, agreeing with her. Two foster pets had found their forever home. Five felines to go. Surely a guy who loved cat videos deserved his own filming crew. Pitching to a soft spot never hurt anything—if the guy had one.

CHAPTER NINETEEN

In his parking space at Dad's building, Rory sat in the car after going over tomorrow's schedule with Paige. The day had proved a grueling round of catch-up with on-hold tasks and meetings. His leg was hassling him, but no rest would come until he saw the progress on Vi's house. Even better if Vi came too.

The sunset painted a vivid evening portrait. Neon pinks and oranges swelled through the furled clouds. The crisp, dry air provided a welcome contrast to the drizzle of the last two days. He popped two cinnamon mints in his mouth, letting them melt on his tongue. Hours ago, he'd wolfed down a sandwich between appointments. A cup of java would revive him.

Three texts later, Rory had promised to pick up coffee and meet Vi at the house. One side of his mouth tugged upward. Vi and Cyrus were already there. Win-wins were his favorite.

Vi's delight over the dog and last night's conversation had simmered in his mind throughout the day. Skitters wrapped around his spine. If only they could keep this lovely streak of harmony going.

Thirty minutes later, Rory drove into the dirt driveway next to Vi's yellow bug. He pulled out his phone, tempted to text. Save a few grueling steps. Nope. Not giving in. He grabbed the coffee cups and shoved one leg, then the prosthetic, out the car door. He bit off a yelp. Streaks of fire ran up his thigh.

Rory walked toward the lake, insisting the prosthetic keep pace. Once he cleared the shrubs surrounding the path, the pain fled for a moment. A pint-sized redhead strolled on the concrete sidewalk with an enormous black dog at her side. The wind whipped at her hair. Maybe she'd let him try a ponytail again. When Vi spied him, a grin enveloped her heart-shaped face, and she waved. Rory's good leg wobbled a bit, not from exertion.

Right, babe. This flimsy string tied between you and me? Let's make it stronger.

He held up one cup of coffee. Vi nodded, spoke to the dog, and they chugged up the path to him.

Vi jaunted the last few feet between them, taking the cup from Rory's outstretched hand. "Good thinking. It's breezy on the lake." She stood, both hands wrapped around the cup, and sipped. "Ah. Thank you." Cyrus sat at attention, his eyes watching Rory.

"I need to check the progress in the house. It might be a little warmer in there." Rory would prefer to stand there, drinking in her sweet presence. Instead, he veered back the way he came.

"Okay. You can show me, and I'll tell you about Cyrus." Vi sounded lighthearted and happy.

Rory needed to sit in the worst way. Placing his hand on her back, he helped her up the path. She glanced at him once, concern etched into every facial feature. Much as it galled him, he didn't object when her steps slowed.

They reached the porch steps. Vi reached for his hand, and they navigated their way between her walking boot and his weary nub. Once they walked into the house, she made her way to a stack of sheet rock and hoisted herself onto it.

"Let's sit."

Rory's teeth clenched. The opportunity to get the weight off his leg proved irresistible. He slid next to her, pleased when she didn't scoot away.

"At ease, Cyrus." The dog wandered over to a tarp and lay on it, his nose between his paws. Vi sipped her coffee. "Fill me in on what's happening."

Rory worked to control his breathing, wiping perspiration from his forehead. "Plumbing in the new bathroom and kitchen has begun, along with the electrical work and shorts in the wiring." He pointed. "The pink stuff in the walls is insulation—guaranteed to help with your electrical bill. It's in the attic too—helps in hot and cold weather."

"I'd forgotten about the attic. One of these days, I'll have to see what's up there." Hearing Vi's raspy answer, something niggled at the back of his mind.

"We need to make sure there's no rotten flooring up there, but since the guys were able to insulate, it's probably okay. We're sitting on the next step—sheetrock for the walls. Do you want to walk through, check it out?" He drained his coffee cup, setting it aside.

Vi sat quietly for a moment, chewing her bottom lip. Finally, she looked at him. Her jaw had a stubborn set. *Uh-oh*.

"No, I'm sure the house is fine." Her voice had become soft and breathy. "What I want to do is massage the muscles in your thigh. It's obviously killing you."

When she placed her small hand on his leg, it cooled the

raging fire, but Rory sucked air so fast, his throat constricted. He spoke past the tightness. "You let me sit close to you because you want to massage my leg?" His voice had risen to a shout. Cyrus scrambled to his feet, growling.

Vi stared at him, her blue eyes wide with shock.

Rory hopped up, grunting when his feet hit the concrete. "I'm fine the way I am, Vi. I don't need to be fixed." Despite the strong assertions, his confidence chipped into bits.

"Whoa, Rory! What happened?" She sneezed, then gasped for air.

Oh, no. Mentally smacking his forehead, Rory remembered too late. Vi and sheetrock dust didn't play well together. He hobbled to her. "C'mon. You've got to get out of here." He stretched out a hand, hoping she would take it after his outburst.

When she doubled over in a coughing fit, Rory circled his arm around her waist and held her. Once her coughs dwindled to dry rasps, he guided her to the door. Cyrus butted his way in between them as if to protect her from him. Great. A stiff breeze buffeted them as he led the way to her car. He opened the door, and Cyrus jumped across to the passenger seat.

"Got your inhaler?" When she nodded, he reminded her, "Two puffs. Steady breathing before you drive anywhere." Rory stayed close by to make sure she puffed twice. Once she gave him a thumbs up, he limped away, evading the hurt in her eyes. He'd contained the threat. Now, he had to maintain distance. By the time he got to the Lexus, his anger had faded to depression. He climbed in and pounded the steering wheel. They'd been having a great time. Why couldn't she back off?

The bigger question loomed a black cloud over his brain, refusing to go away.

Why *had* he gone off on her?

Vi pulled up alongside him, worrying her lip to shreds. The

steady rumbling of her vehicle played havoc with Rory's whacked-out emotions. Instead, he focused on her respiratory symptoms—the rise and fall of her chest had leveled out. Her color had returned to normal. He raised his hand in a curt wave, motioning for her to drive on. Punching his ignition button, he yanked at his tie. Only one of them should be in pain over his leg.

VI PICKED up Daddy's tablet off the nightstand. She'd gone through the motions of dinner with Paige and Brenna, relieved when they, too, seemed preoccupied with the events of the day. Clicking on a new document, she skimmed Daddy's brief note about how he had wrapped and stored her dollhouse in the attic. She'd wondered what had happened to it. Not sleepy, she clicked on another file.

Dearest Red,

In spite of the divorce and everything else that happened, I never stopped loving your mother. The short time we had together meant the world to me. Then she moved on. I'm at peace with it now. Love don't play fair, though. I'll love her 'til the day I die, but it's a different, better kind of love. I just want her to be happy. This guy Marshall seems a pretty good fella. He'll be good to her, treat her right.

I hope with all my heart you can let the past go. When bad things happen, they'll want to hang on and mess with you, but don't let 'em. Go ahead and get married. And don't be put off by the sorry example your mother and I set. Pick the right guy and have a whole passel of kids. You brought me so much joy, I'd hate for you to miss out.

I love you, Red. You go and have a great life.

Vi set the tablet aside. She stared at the wall as silent tears rolled down her cheeks. Relief and heartache mingled in her heart. Sadness that her parents never worked through their differences. Yet their mutual love for her had remained rock solid and provided her with a strong sense of identity

Snores came from the corner of her bedroom. A giggle forced its way up her throat. "Glad you're comfortable, buddy." Cyrus lay in his new dog bed, all four paws in the air, sound asleep. So far, Thunder and Cyrus pretended each other didn't exist. The cats were still hiding.

From the TV noise emanating from the living room, *It's a Wonderful Life* had reached the grand finale. Vi turned her light out with a sigh. Maybe a wonderful life for George Bailey, but not for her.

Would she ever find contentment? Or had she messed up so badly she'd lost her chance? Daddy's advice to move on and find joy seemed too much to hope for.

Her phone chimed. She dug around in the blankets until she found it, then clicked on the screen.

Are you awake?

Vi couldn't handle any more unpredictable behavior from Rory.

It depends.

She stretched, wiggling her toes.

Sorry I was a jerk this evening.

Vi stared at the screen. This Rory she recognized. The hard-edged, irrational person he'd morphed into this afternoon? Not so much. Her thumbs tapped the keys.

Can we talk about it?

She waited until her screen turned dark. Several minutes later, it chirped again.

I don't know if I can, Red.

She winced. *Ouch!* An unhealed wound.

I'm a safe place, Rory.

Silence.

CHAPTER TWENTY

Rory sat on the bottom bleacher at powerlifting practice, fingers smoothing the sides of his beard. He'd signed off as coach but promised Tavo he'd monitor a few sessions. Absently, he watched individuals go through their custom workouts. Rock music blasted from the speakers. The main event today was Tina. Barring no problems, she would achieve her latest weightlifting goal. Even now, she walked off excess energy, continually shaking her limbs to keep them loose. The vertical line between her brows creased with concentration.

He rubbed at the knot in his right thigh. His elementary attempts at self-massage, combined with more sitting, had eased the additional pain brought on by the airplane ride. No doubt Vi's hands could accomplish better results. If he could only get past someone seeing, much less touching, the scars covering his legs. How that translated into eventually getting married, he hadn't quite figured out. The right woman would love him, scars and all, right? It's what gave him the courage to end his relationship with Stella. He'd known from the beginning they weren't a good fit. Whenever he'd stepped back, though, she'd burrowed in deeper. Gradually, his life became an ongoing round of placation until God helped him find the fortitude to break off the relationship for good.

Procrastination wasn't helping his leg either. He needed to visit his doctor at the vet center in San Antonio, much as he dreaded it. This latest, greatest prosthetic won the bad fit award. Over the months, it had worn down faster than predicted, causing other problems. He muttered under his breath, "You promised to handle this with me, Lord. Sorry my attitude stinks."

The powerlifters went through their routines. Each person lifted a custom amount of weight from his or her station. The air buzzed as teammates called encouragement to one another. Tina provided an additional spark. She stood with her head down before a massive weight bar, no doubt praying for the strength to break her own record. Her shoulders bunched as she wrapped her hands around the bar, then raised it ever-so-slowly, eyes bulging, jaw gritted. She held, then let the deadlift bar drop with an exhale, equal parts grunt and snort. An intense beat pulsated through the atmosphere.

A few feet away, Tavo looked up from his stopwatch and gave her a thumbs up.

"A-ya-ya-ya-yala!" Tina's loud victory cry trilled through the gym. Her teammates cheered, gathering around her with arms raised. Rory clambered over the bleacher and engulfed her in a hug. At long last, she'd reached her goal of lifting twice her weight in hard cold metal, and then some. His respect knew no bounds.

Vi strode in wearing dark jeans, red boots, and a turquoise coat. Over Tina's shoulder, Rory feasted on Vi's perky beauty. His pulse ratcheted skyward, and he tried to disengage from the hug. Too late. When Tina spied Vi, she tightened her hold on him, then smacked a sweaty kiss on his cheek.

"Thanks, Tina," he said wryly. She swaggered over to her fan club, then glanced back, eyes full of mischief. Her teammates egged her on with hoots, knowing full well it was all an act. The woman doted on her husband and son.

He stepped away from the practice area and plopped next to Vi on the aluminum bleacher. Amid the ongoing clamor, he asked, "Did you and Cyrus have a pleasant afternoon?"

"We're making progress. He had a hard time resisting the goose. And talk about personality. I could have sworn he pouted when I yelled for him to stop chasing Harry."

"Poor Harry."

Vi's face scrunched into a comical frown. "Right. Poor Harry. I hope Cyrus sees the goose as a playmate."

"Instead of dinner?" When Vi smacked his arm, Rory yowled playfully. Grinning, he rubbed his arm for good measure.

Together, they watched the practice floor until Tavo's whistle shrilled. "Five minutes." He ambled over to Vi, wiping his neck with a white towel. "Hey, Magic Hands, whatcha up to?"

"Meeting with Rory after practice." She tilted her head his way.

"Now, what's a nice girl like you doing hangin' out with him?" Tavo's voice rumbled.

"He's fixin' up my house."

"If he messes with you, let me know. I'll conk him on the head." Tavo winked at her.

The way Vi's lips stretched could have split the sun. "You got it, Chief."

Rory rose clumsily from the bleacher. A rock-climbing

session hiked to the top of his to-do list. He stuck his hand out. "Good going, Coach."

Tavo arched a brow. "You need a massage, buddy?" He gestured with the towel to Vi, who had suddenly become interested in the gym floor. "She has the best hands on the planet."

Leave it to Tavo to ferret out what Rory was trying to ignore. He jerked his head in a decisive *no*.

Faint creases lined Tavo's forehead. "Now you're being stupid. I'd live in a world of hurt if it weren't for her." He shrugged moose-size shoulders. "If you wanna hurt, it's your business." He turned to address a team member.

Rory shook off Tavo's remarks, wishing the man would mind his own business. He leaned toward Vi. "Have you eaten?"

She swung her head sideways. "I can dash over to the deli before they close while you shower."

"That'd be great." If left up to Rory, he'd have pushed for a nicer place. *And she would have balked.*

His lips twitched as she ran out the door, her fiery mass of curls streaming behind her. When had watching the divine Miss Vi become more than a hobby? In truth, he'd been sneaking peeks at her for months. Even before his breakup with Stella.

Rory stretched, pinwheeling one arm, then the other as he headed to the men's dressing room. The upper body workout he'd done before practice found muscles he hadn't used in a while. He'd endure the stiffness because strong back muscles would help his gait.

The deli screen had been closed, and the lights were low when he arrived. Vi waited at a table with their food.

"How did you manage all this?" Rory's eyes rounded at the

various food choices as he slid into the seat across from Vi at the small table. He cherished the privacy the semi-darkness provided.

"I must have looked famished because the staff shared the leftovers."

He held out a hand. "Do you want to say grace?"

She nodded. Rory leaned forward to hear her soft words. When she finished, he squeezed her fingers, pleased when she returned the pressure.

Vi opened a cup of soup. Rich tomato broth steamed the air. "So, what's next with the house?"

"Sheetrock, then a fork in the road. But let's eat first." Rory unrolled the paper from a chicken wrap.

They finished eating in companionable silence. Afterward, they made drinks at the beverage bar and settled back at the small table. Tendrils of steam from Vi's hot tea wrapped around Rory, the fruity fragrance soothing his mind's frantic pace. A twilight sky gleamed from the frosted window.

Rory took a swallow of coffee, surprised to be so content. His never-ending task list vanished. He only wanted to revel in this moment with Vi. Well, maybe not all he wanted. He was dying to find out if the kiss they shared in the hospital had been a fluke. She seemed to enjoy it. He sat up straighter. Her attraction to him seemed obvious. If only he knew the reason she kept pushing him away.

"So, tell me about the fork in the road." Vi fiddled with her tea bag.

Wishes and unanswered questions aside, Rory focused on the remodel. "The finishing part of any house takes the longest. We can go one of two ways. We can visit a design center in San Antonio. It's a place where you can make most of the finishing decisions in one fell swoop. I know the folks there and have used their services. They'll do right by you and won't stop until you're satisfied, but we'd need to go this week. The other option means you shop here in Valiant and choose as needed."

A knuckle pressed against one cheek, Vi considered the options. She asked a few questions to clarify, listening carefully as he answered. Faint horizontal creases lined her forehead. "Will you be mad if I don't want to use the design center?"

Rory's brows jutted upward. This woman continually surprised him. He'd been certain she'd want to take advantage of the one-stop shopping the design center afforded. "If local is your thing, I'm good with it."

She shifted in her chair, clearly uncomfortable. "This is my first time to make these decisions, and I won't do it again for a long time. I'd prefer to take it step-by-step and savor the experience. Have fun with it, instead of a big rush. And since I'm in the process of being the owner of one pet instead of several, Paige won't mind if it takes longer."

Vi's logic poured oil over Rory's weary soul. He dealt with the ins and outs of construction daily. Maybe his attitude had become a tad jaded. Her pure, untainted outlook recreated the wonder of a new home. Even if the structure had pre-existed, the changes they planned would create a totally different place. He reached for her hand and cradled it between his. "I appreciate your approach, Vi. It's refreshing. If you need help with choices, I'm right here."

In the dim lighting, her lips twisted to one side. "Good grief, Rory. What do I know about picking out doorknobs or bathroom faucets?" An endearing little giggle escaped, spiking his adrenaline. "I'm countin' on you, bud."

She wiggled her fingers through one of his hands. "Deal?"

The scent of her hair floated toward him. Rory would forever associate the sweet floral aroma with her. She used no wiles, no entrapments, yet her raw authenticity intoxicated him.

How on earth could he handle the heady mix of sweetness and fire? Her words came back to him. *Step-by-step and savor the experience.*

Rory gripped her hand, even as his soul quaked. "Deal."

CHAPTER TWENTY-ONE

Silas's cramped signature curled across the time slot. Her onetime walking buddy signed up for a massage? Vi stared at the schedule book, then blew out a lengthy exhale. She should have had a text about this hours ago. Discovering an appointment on the books she hadn't known about messed with her day. Must be a new person at the front desk.

Vi's hands tingled as she focused on this latest twist. Silas didn't seem the type to have the wrong idea about an MT's job. Curtis's awful behavior was causing her to overreact. Guarding against unprofessional overtures remained her least favorite part of the job. Vi would keep it light and ask when Silas wanted to pick up the cats.

Still wearing the boot, Vi settled for a sedate stroll to the massage room, then changed sheets on the table. The front had blown in as predicted. Temps were cold enough for snowmen, warm fires, and hot chocolate. Mm.

Vi stepped into the small reception area. Silas sat in the chair she'd come to think of as Rory's. "Hey, bud." She stuck out her hand.

He gripped it loosely. "I've heard about your hands. Thought I'd check 'em out."

Silas's shaggy honey-blond hair needed a trim. His hazel eyes had lightened under the fluorescent lighting. Not tall, his frame bent toward the wiry side. He never said much and kept to himself.

Vi pointed to the room and explained the procedure. "I'll check your paperwork and return shortly."

Minutes later, she re-entered the low-lit room and set the playlist to soothing water and rain sounds. Once the atmosphere suited her, she explained how the massage would proceed. Silas's silence didn't affect her. Many of her clients gave no sign they'd heard the spiel.

Vi's hands glided across his shoulders, kneading the taut muscles. Her fingers discovered several pitted scars. Artillery wounds? Shrapnel? His skin resembled leather. Stiff at first, he slowly unwound under the pressure of her hands.

Satisfied he'd relaxed, Vi allowed happy images of Cyrus to fill her mind. The dog seemed to enjoy the lake outings as much as she did.

Silas jerked under her hands with a moan.

Her fingers stopped on the sensitive trigger point. "You need me to back off?"

"No."

"If I continue, the sore spot will loosen up and your back will feel much better when I'm done." She applied incremental pressure until the tightness melted.

When Vi finished, she gave Silas exit instructions. She took his groggy moan as proof he'd heard, then she left the room. A small half-smile formed as she looked forward to another blissful afternoon with Cyrus. The giant dog had utterly stolen her heart. He grew more familiar with her every day, and his misery had vanished. They'd needed the uninterrupted quiet times together. Vi wondered who was healing who. Grieving her dad's absence had dissipated into far more manageable levels.

She'd have to tell Rory about Cyrus's latest antic with the goose. Her phone vibrated. Mother. Glancing at the screen, Vi held in a sigh. She'd call later and tell her about Cyrus—omitting the part about the dog providing protection. Any hint of trouble would send Mom to Valiant faster than a snake after a chicken. Her appearance at the hospital proved it. A corner of Vi's mouth turned up. Granted, the kiss with Rory should never have happened. Given the circumstances, finishing the kiss would have been a lot more fun than listening to Mom fuss.

She wandered back into the reception area with an orange. A lemony tang hung in the air. Emilio and his ever-present cleaning cloth must have passed through.

Her thumbnail stuck in orange peel, she realized Rory stood to one side of the reception area with Silas. Her pulse zinged. How long had she been daydreaming not to have seen them? Uh-oh. Rory wore his irritated look—hair spikier than usual, eyes on the squinty side, jaw set.

Vi's stomach flipped as she stepped toward him. "Hey, long time, no-see." His eyes softened when he looked her way.

Throwing Rory a careless glance, Silas beelined straight for her. Startled, she glimpsed a smirk before he enveloped her in a crushing hug.

"Silas!" Vi struggled as he lifted her off the ground. Why had she let her guard down? Men were so unpredictable. She raised her face from the hollow of his shoulder and commanded, "Put me down."

Relieved when her feet touched the carpet, she backed away. "Not cool, Silas. Don't do it again." Panting, she drew a slow breath, willing her equilibrium to catch up.

His stance casual, Silas didn't seem put off by her warning.

Or Rory's furious glare. "I would *never* hurt you, Vi. It's true what they say. Your hands are to die for." Silas swiveled. "We'll talk later." Then he sauntered away as if nothing happened.

Vi stared after him. Any questions about the cats could wait. Slowly, she turned to Rory. Lips in a flat line, he held out the orange she'd dropped when Silas swept her up.

Her cheeks warmed. "I don't know what instigated the hug."

RORY SCHOOLED his features with effort. He knew why Silas had hugged, even if Vi didn't. He and Silas had hung out occasionally. It stopped about the time they both got interested in Vi. "I heard about the massage you gave him." His molars ground so hard his jaw ached.

"Yeah, the front desk messed up. MTs get twenty-four-hour notice of who's on the schedule." Vi concentrated on peeling the orange. "Last minute for me, but not a big deal. Silas was an easy client until ... the hug. I'm sure it won't happen again."

His disagreement must have shown on his face because Vi said, "There's not a problem here, Rory." She stood closer than usual.

Inwardly, he groaned. *Yes, there is. Please don't give Silas any more massages.*

Rory cleared his throat. "We're good. I ... um ... had fun last night."

"You did? When Tina laid the smooch of the century on you? Or when I bailed about using the design center?" The challenge lurking in the blue pools of her eyes knocked him off-kilter.

"Tina smacked me on the cheek because my eyes were on

you. Same reason Silas decided to play Tarzan." *Nice, dude. Totally eloquent.* When Vi's eyes widened, he stumbled to a different topic. "And I'm fine with how you want to handle the finishing choices." Blast it all. Vi burrowed under his skin with the tenacity of a chigger.

"You'll have to put up with me longer ..."

"I'm good with that too," he fired back.

"All right, then." She stepped into his space and held up a tiny orange slice. "Wanna bite?"

Rory opened his mouth and bit the slice she placed between his teeth. The sweetness burst on his tongue, but it wasn't enough.

Not nearly enough.

THREE DAYS UNTIL CHRISTMAS. Late afternoon at his office at Spence Enterprises, Rory sat with his phone glued to one ear, waiting on an investor. His fingers drummed the desk. The chair he occupied had better lumbar support. Swapping this chair for the one at his Peeps' office would help. Resting his leg for two days hadn't been horrible. The self-imposed discipline helped him catch up on paperwork, and he couldn't deny the improvement. Adjustments to the prosthetic life seemed never-ending.

The faint smell of Paige's classy perfume still lingered in the room. She used this desk more than he did. Paige epitomized class and style. Just not for him, though it relieved him to hear her say it. His thoughts drifted to Vi. Despite her size—good grief, the woman didn't top five feet—he'd classify her as an entire army, invading every inch of his mental space. The takeover had been so swift, he'd had no time to regroup, much less retreat.

Rory clicked the phone off. Holding for longer than five minutes galled him, no matter how bright the prospect. He gazed absently around his office, a replica of Dad's. The man himself walked through the adjoining door, rubbing his hands. Another reason Rory preferred his Peeps' domain—more privacy.

"Want to hear some good news?"

An affectionate smile parted Rory's lips. Dad's good news centered on business projects. "You closed a deal."

"Not any deal. I closed on the tract you and Jess want for Peeps' expansion." The older man's eyes twinkled.

Rory's grumpy attitude retreated. "You did?" He stood and closed the gap, hugging the older man. He stepped back, still gripping Dad's upper arms. "This is great news! Best Christmas present ever."

"What did you and Jess decide about the larger tract?"

Uh-oh. Rory had forgotten all about their plan to survey the other acreage. "We haven't made it out there yet, but if you think it's a good deal, I say go for it."

Dad studied him. "I'll get back to you about the offering price."

"In other words, pay up, boys." Rory's mouth stretched with humor.

Dad laughed, then broke off. His face turned a dusky shade. He moved out of Rory's grasp and doubled over, coughing.

Concern snaked up Rory's spine. "Hey! Are you all right?"

The older man gasped, then sputtered, "F-fine. Water."

Rory hurried to the side table, then poured water from a sweat-beaded carafe. Dad took the glass with shaky hands and drained it. The rosy hue receding, his breathing returned to normal.

"Are you okay? Need more?" This ... incident ... had become more than a coughing fit.

"I'm fine now." Other than a raspy voice, Dad seemed recovered.

"When was your last doctor's appointment?"

The older man looked away. "Becca keeps up with those."

At the first opportunity, Rory would ask. Dad notoriously skipped medical-related appointments. *Help me here, Lord.*

"What do you need? Dinner? We could celebrate your close on the land deal." Further discussion about Dad's health would be counterproductive.

"Naw, I'm headed home to put my feet up. Call Jess instead. The two of you forked over the money."

"Your expert broker skill made it happen." Rory wrapped an arm around Dad's shoulders. Had the man shrunk? He'd always seemed ten feet tall. "Thanks. I appreciate this."

Dad's eyes were moist. He reached up, placing his hand on Rory's. "Pure pleasure, son." He walked out of the room, slower than usual.

Rory turned back to his desk. He grabbed his phone but decided against calling Jesse. He and Brenna probably had plans. Did those two ever take a night off?

Dare he ask Vi? Her last no still reverberated. Rory picked up a pen and clicked the end cap. Open. Shut. She'd looked so cute in those plum-colored scrubs this morning. What he wouldn't give to see her all dressed up. Hmm. The gala loomed a little over a week away. Since Paige had declined, he'd better secure a date, or else he'd be fending off not-so-subtle advances all evening. His fingers punched her number though wisdom cautioned him otherwise.

CHAPTER TWENTY-TWO

"Hey, Rory." Vi's cheerful greeting gave him courage.

Rory pumped his fist, then switched to speaking mode. "Hey, yourself. Whatcha doing?"

"Cyrus and I are about to head home. Good training session today, but it's too cold outside. We're both shivering."

"I guess so. Hey, Dad closed a special deal. I want to tell you about it and celebrate. Have dinner with me?" He pulled more air into his lungs.

Vi's long pause didn't bode well. "We've talked about this, Rory."

Jaw clenching, his earlier grumpiness flared with a vengeance. "No, we haven't. You said no, and that was the end of it."

Silence.

"Talk to me, Vi."

"I need to go." She sounded upset. Saying no was tearing her heart out, only he didn't know why.

Before he could formulate a response, she whispered, "Bye, Rory."

When Rory realized she'd hung up, all self-control deserted him. Jumping from his chair, he aimed the phone at a soft couch pillow and fired. Then he yelled a word he hadn't uttered since Afghanistan. He paced, raking a hand through his hair.

"This woman is driving me crazy!" he gritted the words out between harsh breaths. "God, I need somebody to talk to." Movements jerky, he lowered to the couch and leaned forward, elbows on his thighs, head in his hands.

The building hushed. Outside noise faded. The pounding in his ears magnified.

You don't need her constant refusals. Find somebody else.

He didn't want anyone else. "I want Vi," he muttered against the rebellious thoughts.

No response. Only the empty room and the mindless purr of the ceiling fan.

Why did she keep turning him down?

Rory wanted to go to her. Sit with her. Beg her to confide in him.

You've already tried. She rejected you before. Now she's done it again.

His eyes squeezed shut. Talking would do no good. Not when she'd already dealt him two strikes.

The options without Vi were grim. An evening at home counted as a non-starter. Those ugly walls reminded him of another failure. He stretched one leg, then the other, as an idea wormed into his mind.

Rory ignored the small internal voice clamoring for attention. Instead, he strode to the coat tree by the office door. Rummaging through the pockets, he found a business card. *Melissa Strom.* He vaguely remembered her from a board meeting. Shoulder-length brownish hair and light brown eyes? Pretty in a made-up way. She'd flirted with him, pressing her business card in his hand when he left the meeting.

Up to this minute, Rory hadn't given her a single thought. Fingering the card, he retrieved his phone. He needed a break from the drama. A casual dinner, a change of pace. A way to get his mind off a tiny red-haired woman. He touched numbers on the screen, then cleared his throat.

RORY'S PHONE dinged the moment he stepped through his townhouse door. Jesse's name popped up. Well, crud. After his horrible evening, he hoped it would be Vi, however far-fetched the idea. As courteously as possible, he had cut the date short with Melissa, not confident he'd managed the courteous part. The evening morphed into a dreaded event the instant Melissa shrilled into a high-pitched titter before saying yes. Rory had forgotten that endearing detail. However, dread served as the appetizer—he'd gnawed on regret throughout their main course.

His ears bled from too much information. Chatty didn't begin to describe the sheer volume of words falling out of Melissa's mouth. His initial plan had existed as dinner. If it went well, maybe a stroll through the mall. It would be fun to have a woman's opinion on gift-giving. Those ideas bolted within the first five minutes. And her father was the bank president who loaned Spence Enterprises most of its capital. Rory wanted to kick himself all over the fair city of Valiant.

With a sinking feeling, Rory read Jesse's text.

Busy evening?

A few years ago, he'd thought up the brilliant notion of being accountability partners concerning the women in their lives with his best friend. Since Jesse couldn't know about his date with Melissa, this had to be about Vi. Well, Jesse could ask all night, but Rory had no answers.

Still grousing, he thumbed a response.

Fixing a pot of coffee. Want a cup?

He maneuvered his aching leg into the kitchen.

Moments later, a knock sounded on the door. Jesse strode in, wearing his game face.

Rory scowled back. "Are you determined to make this conversation as uncomfortable as possible?"

Jesse jabbed his hands on his hips. "You tell me."

"Let's get coffee." Rory relented.

They fixed their cups of coffee in silence, then settling on the couch with a mug, Rory inclined his head. "Fire away."

Sipping his coffee, Jesse wore another familiar expression. The one where he sized up his opponent. Rory's real foot tapped the floor double time. "Spill it, Jess."

Rather than spouting back a sarcastic response, Jesse's eyes appeared troubled. "I saw Vi tonight."

"You did?" The eagerness in Rory's voice sounded all too clear. "At Paige's?"

Jesse nodded. "Her tough-girl veneer had cracked. Puffy eyes. Cheeks all splotchy. I think she'd been crying. You know anything about that?"

Rory's defenses melted. He'd triggered the reaction. "Earlier this afternoon, I asked her out. She said no. Again."

Jesse wrapped his hands around his mug and waited.

"When she said we'd talked about this before, I got … upset. She may think we've talked about this, but we haven't." Rory focused on a dark speck in the vinyl floor pattern. "She hung up on me, and … I lost it." He exhaled heavily and gazed at Jesse. "I called another girl and took her to dinner."

Jesse's brows arched up his forehead. "That was stupid."

Irked beyond casual politeness, Rory blurted, "You know, I'm getting really tired of my *friends* telling me how stupid I am." His indignation mounted. "Tavo informed me I'm stupid for not getting a massage. Now you're saying the same thing. It's perfectly okay to go on a date, Jess."

"Not if you're in love with someone else."

Rory reeled as if Jesse had dealt him a blow. He set his coffee mug aside with trembling fingers. "Is this love?"

"What do you think?"

Rory steepled his fingers to his lips, wonder splashing over him. He hadn't considered love would feel this way. "Part of me is missing, and Vi is the only possible solution. I want her so badly, it's killing me." At Jesse's expression, he held up a hand. "I'm not talking physical—this is different. No other woman has affected me this way. Vi is … oxygen." Breath abandoned him as the truth revealed itself.

Jesse's jaw softened. "Sounds about right."

"But she's into Silas."

"What makes you say that?"

"You didn't see him hanging all over her this morning."

A frown thinned Jesse's lip. "Emilio informed me about the inappropriate hug, but I stopped by Paige's to see Brenna when Silas came by to pick up the cats. I wondered why Vi seemed more distant than usual. Opposite reaction from the tension arcing between you two at the Christmas party."

"What are you talking about?" Rory scratched one side of his mustache.

Jesse slapped his leg, shooting Rory a look of disbelief. "Oh, c'mon. If Tavo had flicked a lighter, Paige's house would have burst into flames."

"How would you know?" Rory demanded. "You were busy with Brenna."

"Ro, kissing my girl tops the chart for favorite things to do, but nothing's wrong with my brain … or my vision."

"I don't know what to do, Jess." Rory stood, then paced. "She won't go on a date with me."

Jesse crossed one leg over the other. "I'm hearing you loud and clear. Seems to me she's not on the same page yet. Slow your roll, bud. Give her time to catch up."

As Rory chewed on this new perspective, Jesse leaned forward. "You better tell her about the date. She won't be thrilled, but far better she hears it from you than anyone else." He rose. "You'll figure this out. Soon, I hope. Peeps' best MT needs her peace of mind." He took his mug to the kitchen and headed to the door. "How'd the date go?"

"Horrid." Rory smacked his head. "Jess! I forgot until this second. Dad closed the deal on the eight-acre tract next to Peeps."

A canyon-sized grin covered Jesse's face. "Yeah?"

"Yeah. Dad told me this afternoon. It's a good way to start our expansion plans even if it's small. We still haven't checked out the other tract, but I gave him the go-ahead. He knows what we need and how to proceed."

"Super news." Jesse started for the door, then turned back with a smirk. "Serves you right about the date." Still grinning, he left.

Rory rose and set his mug on the kitchen counter. He turned off the coffee machine and got ready to sleep. Fat chance.

His head nestled the pillow as he studied the phone screen. Sighing, he tapped a text.

Are you awake?

Long silence. His legs thrashed the sheets. Vi was asleep or not speaking. A message dinged.

Only if you're nice.

I'm nice.

Cyrus snorted at you.

He thumbed back.

I did a stupid thing.

We all do stupid things.

Can we talk about why you won't
date me?

Silence. His brain recited all the possible reasons she hadn't answered. Thankfully, he dozed off, then jerked awake at the buzz of his phone. Peering at the white screen, he read the message.

It's hard.

Still in a twilight sleep, he typed,

I know.

Nite, Rory.

I love you, Red. Delete.
He typed it again.

I love you, Red.

Holding his breath, he pressed SEND.

CHAPTER TWENTY-THREE

Vi glanced around the quiet lobby, a far cry from the usual hustle-bustle. Upstairs, the thud of a single weight hitting the floor sounded lonesome. Strategically placed diffusers wafted festive oil through the area. Foot traffic had slowed, the regular schedule bumped for holiday hours, but Vi wouldn't complain. She'd relished her easy schedule this week and had completed her last massage before the holiday. Now all she needed was an extra dose of courage to buy Rory's Christmas gift. A practical item since she couldn't imagine giving him anything personal. She hoped he would receive it with grace.

The massage door shut, and Vi's last client strode toward her. "Merry Christmas, Mrs. Richter. You have family coming in?"

"Lord, yes. I'm off to the store for cookie ingredients." The tall, friendly woman clucked and patted her salon-style do. "It'll be a madhouse, I'm sure. You have a delightful holiday, dearie." When the woman extended her arms, Vi leaned into her grandmotherly hug with a bittersweet ache. Her grandmother had never been the cookie-baking type. Nor did she give hugs.

Vi disengaged gently. Mischief glinted in Mrs. Richter's eyes. "Thanks to my favorite MT, I'm in tip-top shape to deal with my family. Bless their sweet little hearts."

Mrs. Richter's gracious manner soothed like expensive oil. Her cheeriness made Vi think her own life might not be a total train wreck. She moved to the reception area and lowered into a chair. A few relaxing moments before heading out into the shivery-cold weather would help the sting in her hands. Finding her gloves gained top priority. She dug in her pockets, found an orange, and began to peel it.

A deep forest scent filled her nostrils when a person sat in the other chair. "Hey, Vi." Rory's deep voice blanketed her from the inside out.

She didn't dare look at him but kept peeling the orange. "Hey, Red." Shifting in the chair, she winced. Red was *her* nickname. Rattled much?

"Got plans for Christmas?"

"Going to Mom's for the day. You?" She chewed an orange slice.

"I'll be at Dad's. Mark will make an appearance. We'll order takeout, and I'll make mashed potatoes. The usual football games." His fingers drummed a chaotic rhythm on the chair arm.

Vi held half of the orange in his direction. Their fingers brushed when he took it. They shared the fruit in silence. Had last night's text affected him the way it was affecting her? She couldn't think of anything else. Soft holiday music piped from the speakers.

"You'll be here Christmas Eve?" He stretched his leg, shifting in the chair.

"Jesse agreed to host the party to give Paige a break. A few appetizers, hot cocoa. Gift exchange."

"If I come to the party, will you stay?" Strain whickered through his voice.

The *yes* her heart trilled should be a definite *no*. So totally no. "Sure. Everybody will be there." Maybe he hadn't heard her ambivalence. Or the deflection.

"I'm not coming to see everybody. I only want to see you."

Alrighty, then. A smile played about Vi's lips despite the warning bells sounding off in her head.

He scooched the chair closer. His warm, citrusy breath tickled her ear. "Will you look at me?"

And drown in his soft gray eyes? No thanks. Searching for a compromise that wouldn't completely undo her, she focused on a razor nick on his neck. A powerlifter heaving weight had nothing on her thumping heart.

His fingers nudged her chin upward. "I meant what I said in the text last night. I love you, Red." He placed a chaste kiss on her forehead. "And I'm not going anywhere."

His slate eyes riveted her in place. Her gaze drifted back to his throat, and her forefinger touched the nick where a tiny spot of blood had hardened. His large hand covered hers.

"You cut yourself." Inane, but any sensible thought had airlifted to parts unknown. His nearness magnetized her. Heady stuff for a girl who hadn't had a date in years.

Her hand slid to cradle his jaw. She relished the wiry texture of his carefully trimmed beard. He groaned, shutting his eyes for an instant. Then he kissed her knuckles and rose. "I'll see you on Christmas Eve." He slipped away as quietly as he'd come. His gait seemed much improved.

She sat in the chair for a long time. Christmas music continued to float around the room. Members strolled in, toting bags of clothes and gear. Others left in a fast clip, while

Vi felt detached—life as usual seemed light-years away. Her world had eclipsed to a single stand-alone truth. No way she could misconstrue his words.

Rory loved her.

What a precious gift.

Minutes or hours later, Vi gathered her purse and tote. Cyrus would be restless. She stopped at the front desk to purchase Rory's gift on her way out.

ANTSY, Vi scraped the last spoonful of a dark goopy concoction from the slow cooker onto parchment paper. She needed a breather before Rory showed. Brenna arranged crackers around a pecan-covered cheese ball. Paige opened a drawer, moving items around.

"I forgot to bring plastic wrap and can't find any." Paige stared at the kitchen cabinets as if it would magically appear.

"Rory might have a roll." Brenna reached for another box of crackers.

Paige whipped out her phone, thumbed a few keys, then moved to the counter and slid a pan of bacon-wrapped jalapenos into the oven. The rich scent of chocolate wrapped around the room. Cyrus stretched under the table, eyes trained on Vi.

"What's the agenda tonight?" Vi squirted dishwashing soap into the ceramic pot.

"Besides eating?" Brenna nibbled a cracker. "Food, gift-opening, maybe sing Christmas songs. An informal get-together before we go our separate ways."

"Rory's bringing over the wrap." Paige set her phone aside and peered into the oven.

Vi tapped a piece of the cooling candy—still too tacky to

move. "Cyrus, come." The dog obediently rose and came to her. "I'm going to take Cyrus for a walk before everybody gets here. He'll behave better."

"Don't be gone too long." Paige's eyes drilled into her. A wave of cheesy bacon flavor rose into the air.

Vi gave her a weak thumbs up. They both knew she was avoiding Rory.

By the time she buttoned her coat and donned gloves, Cyrus pranced about, his huge paws barely missing her feet. "Cyrus, down." She gave him a wry look when he instantly became a statue. "Good boy. Let's walk."

Tail wagging, the dog didn't seem to mind the chill as they crossed to a neighboring street. Cyrus sniffed at various smells along the curb. The wonder she'd felt at Rory's confession had evaporated, leaving her a jittery mess.

Sighing, Vi looked heavenward. "God, I should have come to You first instead of stewing. You've already promised to help without fussing." She trundled along on the sidewalk. Small white clouds puffed the air when she exhaled. "So, I'm taking You at Your word."

"Rory says he loves me, but I don't know how to respond. What's *my* next step?" Her breath caught. The truth dampened the joy and lightheartedness she'd felt with his pronouncement. The streetlights beamed haloes of white into the darkness. Shadowy lawns brightened with manger scenes and Santa sleighs. No humans were around to poke fun, and Cyrus paid no attention to her musings. Finally, she murmured, "The last thing I want is to hurt him, so ... I'm asking You what to do."

Stilling her mind, she pressed forward as if to hear when a phrase popped into her consciousness.

Open your heart.

Her walking boot snagged on an uneven crack. Vi

staggered, then righted herself. Cyrus whirled, tilting his canine head at her as if to ask, *Are you all right?*

"I'm fine, bud." She reassured him as he trotted back to sniff at her boot. "Walk, Cyrus." At her command, he moved forward again, careful not to rush. As if he sensed the boot slowed her down.

Vi's gaze shot upward. Even though logic insisted she was tumbling down a rabbit hole, a deep peace settled over her. The phrase echoing through her with such clarity revealed what lay hidden for years. Fear lay at the root of her refusal to go out with Rory. The idea of allowing a man access to her heart petrified her. She'd vowed never again after the disaster with her first and only boyfriend.

She bowed her head. "Confronting the fear is pretty scary, but I guess it's the whole point." The wind rustling through the trees seemed to agree.

* * *

BY THE TIME Rory arrived at Jesse's, Vi had disappeared. He shoved away discouragement, busying himself with plating the candy. A swallow of hot chocolate scalded his throat when he spied her on Jesse's loveseat. He finished the candy plate in record time.

On his way to the living area, cup in hand, Rory directed Paige's siblings to the kitchen for an early start on snacks. By the hearth, Tavo unlatched his guitar case. Heads together, Brenna and Jesse bent over a tubular object on a shelf behind Vi, and then Jesse asked it a question. Rory frowned. What on earth were they doing?

Confidence, dude. He'd worn himself to a frazzle, wondering how Vi would respond to his confession of love. Attempting a casual air, he made his way over and sat beside her, close enough that their legs touched. She'd gazed at him briefly, then got lost in tying her scarf. Reaching down, Rory stroked Cyrus. The dog's coat felt cool to the touch from outside. Rory cautiously took another sip of chocolate.

He eased against the loveseat, unable to read Vi's mood. Their comfort level still hovered on the awkward side, yet something seemed different tonight. The sharp angles of her face had softened.

The murmuring behind the loveseat grew louder. "Ask Alexa another question, Jess," Brenna's husky voice instructed.

"What do I ask?"

Rory traded a knowing look with Vi. As one, they leaned back to eavesdrop on the conversation. The loveseat prevented them from seeing, but listening worked too.

"Anything. Weather report, playlist, ballgame score."

Vi's pink lips turned up when Jesse grumbled about talking to an inanimate object. In a commanding voice, Jesse said, "*Alexis*, tell me the weather."

Prolonged silence. Then he said, "Nothing happened."

A decidedly feminine huff came from Brenna. "Well, of course not, Jess. You have to call her by the right name. It's Alexa. And ask, don't bark."

Vi giggled. She leaned into Rory, whispering, "She's determined to bring him into the twenty-first century."

Rory touched his forehead to hers. "Here's hoping." They jumped when Alexa blared a brief weather report.

Tavo strummed his guitar. "Anyone up for Christmas carols?" He winked at Rory, playing the opening chords of "Jingle Bells."

The siblings wandered in and sang along, laughing when they flubbed the lyrics, and finished loudly, as if volume would cover any mistakes. Jesse sat in his recliner with Brenna perched on the side arm. A smile curved Rory's lip. His buddy would have her snuggled next to him in no time. When Tavo motioned Paige to a folding chair beside him, Rory's inner antenna quirked again. Vi's arched brow signaled she'd seen it too.

Tavo played as the group stumbled through different songs until Brenna suggested "Jingle Bell Rock." Tavo shook his head, "Don't know it."

Brenna wasn't having it. "I bet Alexa does—Alexa, play 'Jingle Bell Rock.'" After a slight pause, the jazzy tune floated from the speaker. She pulled Jesse from the chair. Hips and legs gyrating, he danced with her, shaking his head *no* the entire time. The small gathering erupted into catcalls and cheers.

"Not bad, Jess. Haven't seen those moves since high school," Rory called.

When the song ended, Paige raised her voice over the commotion. "Can we end on a good one before we eat?"

"That was good!" Jesse's protest made everyone laugh again.

Goose bumps pricked Rory's arms when Vi's small hand found his.

Much too soon, Brenna announced, "Appetizer break. Then we open presents."

Rory didn't want to leave their private world or let go of Vi's hand. Breathing in courage, he motioned to Vi's cup. "You need a refill?"

"Yes, and a piece of chocolate." Vi snuggled into the cushions.

"Don't go anywhere." He looked at Cyrus. "Keep her here, buddy."

"Why can't I go anywhere?" The confusion marring her pretty features had Rory's heart banging all around his chest.

Rory bent down until his face rested inches from Vi's. "'Cause I want to hold hands with you again."

CHAPTER TWENTY-FOUR

Vi's irises darkened to violet. Desire crowded Rory's brain. Grabbing their cups, he headed to the kitchen before he kissed her into next week.

Jesse cast him a side eye as they stood at the candy dish. "Vi seems better tonight."

"She is, but we've got a ways to go. I appreciate your prayers."

"You got it."

Rory plunked candy on a napkin, eager not to lose precious time with Vi, and hustled back to the living room. Settling in next to her again, he placed the napkin with the candy on the coffee table. Vi asked, her tone dry, "Did you leave any on the tray?"

He stared at the mound of chocolate and grinned. "I'm hoarding."

She chose a piece, then glanced at Cyrus, whose golden eyes followed the candy. "No chocolate for you, Cy."

Rory took a bite of his piece, then closed his eyes. "I

remember these from Thanksgiving. Paige said you made them."

"Yes. That batch disappeared while I was busy falling down a hole." She smiled, choosing another piece.

Flutters chased around Rory's stomach. "Glad I followed my gut, Red." Her poor response to the Epi-pen still haunted him.

She gently jostled his shoulder. "I'm glad you were there too. And I'm fine, Rory. Really."

Rory gripped her hand and didn't let go, not caring how it looked or who saw them. Having her beside him calmed his fear of losing her. He ignored the thought she wasn't his to lose.

Paige moved to the coffee table, picking up a gift. She waved it aloft in a wide arc. "Who is this one for?" When a sibling claimed it, she handed the bag over and reached for another gift.

A few gifts later, Paige picked up another gaily wrapped gift bag. Vi elbowed him. Must be his turn. Rory accepted the present, but the glint in Vi's eyes suggested …

Self-conscious, Rory dug through the tissue to a cardholder and fumbled it open. A gift card to Peeps? Not comprehending, he stared at her.

Then Tavo guffawed, and the room seemed to shake. "Aww. Ro, it's priceless. You're too stubborn to get a massage with Magic Hands, so she bought you one!" He smacked his leg and hooted. "We should all be so lucky." He dissolved into another fit of laughter.

As the meaning of Vi's gift sunk in, Rory glanced around the room. Brenna had clapped a hand over her mouth, and Jesse gave him a crooked smile. Even Paige looked amused.

Rory swung back to Vi. Her eyes sparked with challenge. "Gotcha."

Any self-control he had snapped at her smirk. If she wanted to do *this*—in front of everybody, he would too. He rounded on her. "It's double or nothing, Red. You get your scary little hands on me, I get a date!" He glowered, refusing to break eye contact.

Her mouth fell open.

The lively animation faded into a hush. At Rory's raised voice, Cyrus scrambled to his feet and growled a warning.

Rory's back stiffened. He refused to let her off the hook. They were going to settle this right now. "What's it going to be, Vi? Do I get a date?"

Jaw flexed, she asked, "Will you get a massage?" Cyrus wedged his big dog self in front of Vi, on high alert.

Rory glared at her. Vi glared back, not willing to give in. Cyrus barked. Vi shushed him, her blue eyes still piercing Rory's.

"For a date, yes." His molars ground together.

Her eyes softened. "All right then." A collective sigh whooshed around the room, followed by boisterous clapping.

Cyrus relaxed and laid back on the floor at Vi's command, but Rory hadn't finished. No way he'd let her back out. As she resettled on the loveseat, he slid an arm around her, gently anchoring her in place. He squeezed her shoulder and whispered into her ear, "I'm serious about the date. Are you?" Belatedly, he realized the party chatter had stopped.

"A deal is a deal. I'm good for it. Are you?" At his nod, she gave him a brief hug. Too brief. He withdrew his arm and threaded his fingers through hers, savoring her closeness.

In unspoken agreement, Rory and Vi acted as if nothing had transpired until Jesse gave a loud, dramatic sigh. "Good going, guys. Thanks for not burning down my house."

The whistles and applause started up again. Vi's face turned red as one of the twinkle lights on the Christmas tree.

Rory wanted to kiss her so badly, he swiveled his head the other way. If he ever got to kiss Vi again, it would *not* be in a roomful of people. Finally, the merrymaking died down.

Paige continued the gift exchange until only a gold bag with drawstrings remained on the table. She held it aloft. "Who does this belong to?

Rory nudged Vi.

Quiet fell over the room. Murmurs mounted. People scraped their chairs around for a better view. Great. An audience had worked to Rory's advantage moments ago, but now it might have the opposite effect.

Giving him a deer-in-the-headlights look, Vi reached for the bag. She undid the drawstrings and pulled out a small box. An eerie quiet descended.

She opened it, then put her hand over her mouth. "Rory, they're beautiful." The silence broke as oohs and ahs thrummed the air.

Vi held aloft a pair of gold hoop earrings. A strip of tiny diamonds marched down the middle, with a rich leopard print encasing each side. "Hold my hair so I can put them on?"

As if he needed a reason.

She unhooked the earrings and turned her back to him. Rory's knees weakened at the sight of those fiery tresses tumbling down her back. He carefully scooped the mass away from her ears, then reluctantly released it when she turned to show him the earrings.

A smile softened his frayed nerves. He'd shopped an entire afternoon, determined to find the perfect match for Vi's personality. Timeless. Elegant. Streaks of wild.

"Nice going, Ro. Those sparkly baubles deserve another date. Maybe two." The dimples on either side of Tavo's grin creased.

Rory raised his arm in victory as the rest of the group chimed in to support more dates.

When Vi's brows lifted, he smiled. "Gotcha back."

Tavo strummed "O Come All Ye Faithful." Paige picked up cups and plates. Others helped her. Vi moved to join them until Rory tugged her back down beside him. "Barely room for two in Paige's kitchen. Wanna go to my place for a last round of coffee?"

Fear darted across her countenance, so fleetingly, he could have imagined it. "I'm safe, Red. Coffee and a visit. Cyrus can supervise."

A corner of her mouth turned up, and the guarded look receded. "Okay. But no more caffeine for me. I'll grab a cup of wassail."

Rory allowed her plenty of space as they left and walked to his townhouse next door. As he inserted the key, the reality of what she'd see in his living room nearly changed his mind. Stella's ugly color scheme and atrocious furniture would, no doubt, cast him as a real sicko.

"You and Cyrus settle while I make coffee." He hurried into the kitchen. Grabbing his favorite brew and a new filter, he set the pot to fill with water. As the coffee percolated, the rich smell filled his nostrils. Tension drained from his shoulders.

VI CLIMBED on a barstool with her cup of wassail, fingering an earring. She watched Rory pour a cup of coffee as if he'd done it a thousand times. The crease between his eyebrows had faded.

"Let's move to the living room. It's ugly, but more comfortable than a bar stool." Ever the gentleman, he waited for her to go first.

Trying not to gape at the unsightly décor, Vi headed to the friendliest piece of furniture in the room—an old glider with worn maroon cushions. A Bible lay on the end table next to it. "Is this your favorite chair?" She hesitated, not wanting to claim it if he had a preference.

"Guests usually sit there. At least the ones I like." Rory grinned and sat on a dreadful gray couch.

Vi sat in the comfy chair. Cyrus lay next to her, and Vi swallowed more of the warm drink. The spicy scent soothed her jarred emotions. The décor, however, rattled her brain. Nothing about Rory suggested this horrible taste in furnishings.

"So, what will you do tomorrow?"

She looked back at him, warmth creeping up her neck. He'd caught her rubbernecking. Her need to know rose a notch, but it could wait. "Oh, I'll spend the day at Mom's. There'll be a literal feast. We'll visit a bit, and I'll work at playing nice."

He frowned. "It sounds ... strained."

"Mom and I are ..." Vi searched for the right words. "Very different people. We're not close." She stared into her empty cup, wishing for more of the yummy brew. Shaking off the gloom, she attempted a smile. "What about your day?"

"We'll do Christmas at Dad's. For years, it's been an all-male get-together." Wistfulness laced his words. "Not too exciting."

The conversation flowed into the latest Peeps news, and then Rory lined out the next phase in remodeling her house. Vi savored the easy back and forth, though her emotions were free-falling. His heated jab about her hands bothered her. Taking a deep breath, she dove in. "Nobody has ever said my hands were scary." She searched his face for a clue. "What are you afraid of?"

Rory looked away, then back at her. "What are *you* afraid of, Vi? And I'm not talking about a massage."

Their questions hung in the air. The coffeemaker hissed. Cyrus rumbled, rearranging his bulk near Vi's feet. Rory had been a sweetheart the entire evening—even if he got pushy about a date. Hadn't she been guilty too, forcing the massage issue with a gift card?

His steady gaze scared her.

The idea of going out with him ... his presence had a disconcerting way of sailing past her carefully constructed walls. Even now, she desired to snuggle next to him again, as if they were still at the party. She'd initiated the hand-holding because she loved the feel of his hand wrapped around hers. Had she also hoped it would replace repugnant memories? Thoughts of Rory had a way of relieving her pain. Imagining a happily ever after for their relationship had become easy. Vi scrambled out of the chair. The fairy tale had to stop.

Rory set his coffee cup aside. Her sudden departure didn't seem to faze him, but the brief glimpse of longing tracking his features matched her own feelings.

"Cyrus, come," she said needlessly. The big dog had already moved to her. She carried her cup to the wastebasket in the kitchen.

Rory waited for her at the door, hands in his pockets.

Slowing her exit enough to be courteous, Vi said, "Thanks. I enjoyed this."

Surely, his molten eyes could see every single insecurity. He held his arms open. "May I have a hug? It's Christmas Eve."

She should resist, but her willpower faltered, then crashed in a heap. Her legs turned to jelly, even as she walked straight into his amazing arms and laid her head on his chest. The steady rhythm of his heart allayed her fear. When he cocooned her in a hug, her arms slid around his waist. His warm lips kissed the top of her head. The sharp, arresting scent of his cologne surrounded her. She felt secure. Protected. They stayed wrapped together for no short amount of time.

When she stirred, his arms loosened from around her, then he grasped her hands. "Truce?"

She shivered at the word, but he continued to hold her hands in a light grip.

"Truce," she whispered, hurrying out the door.

A few more seconds, and she would have kissed him. Not on the cheek.

CHAPTER TWENTY-FIVE

"Violet, dear, your prospects would be so much better here in Houston. You should consider the idea of moving back. I don't expect you to live with us. You'll need your own place." Vi, Mom, and her third husband, Rodney Marshall, sat in cumbersome dining chairs with gold brocade cushions. The table groaning under a traditional buffet could have fed a small village.

Vi forced her face into a mask as she gazed at the petite, well-dressed woman. On Christmas day, staying polite came with the territory. "Mom, you know it's not going to happen. I'm having the house in Valiant remodeled and plan to live there." She didn't mention sheetrock allergies, illegal squatters, or safety issues.

"You could easily live here while it's being done. High time you put that old wreck on the market." Mom dabbed her lips with a cloth napkin costing more than Vi's hourly massage rate.

Vi blew out a sigh, her patience level dipping into reserve.

Did Mom ever hear anything aside from her own wishes? With effort, she staved off the anger itching to ignite.

Rodney, who had been quiet up to this point, intervened when Mom opened her mouth again. "It's not what Vi wants, Tru. All your pushing isn't going to change her mind." He swallowed the last of his iced tea and pushed back his chair.

Vi shot him a grateful look. They'd never been close, but she appreciated the help. Rodney possessed a mind of his own, steering clear of Mom's manipulation tactics. "I'm off to watch the football games in the downstairs den. I promise to answer questions requiring yes or no." He turned to Vi's mom, eyeing her with affection. "Excellent dinner, love. You have the best taste in cooks of anyone I know."

Vi hid a smile as he left the room. She'd forgotten about Rodney's superb sense of humor. A handy trait when living with Mom.

Mom's smile thinned. "Why don't we retire to a sitting room? I could use a cup of coffee, and you need to open your Christmas gift."

Vi groaned inwardly. She hadn't heard the last of moving to Houston, but Vi had zero interest in being Mom's shiny new toy to show off at parties. Or the endless array of "nice men" she would arrange for Vi to meet.

She wove shaky fingers through her hair, casting about for a diversion. Cyrus needed a walk—a long one. Guilt burrowed deeper, remembering Mom's less-than-enthusiastic reaction to the dog. Everything Vi did only created more tension. Knowing it would be this way, she had arrived at dinnertime and planned to beg off early.

"One cup of coffee, Mom. Then Cyrus gets a walk." Vi glanced down at her one red boot and black broom skirt. A white blouse with long puffy sleeves and Rory's earrings completed her ensemble. She traced a finger around one hoop. Her tight jaw relaxed, knowing a tiny part of him was with her.

Vi followed Mom to another richly furnished room, only this one had more comfortable furniture. A quaint place to talk. Or hide. Vi sat in an ornate upholstered chair, sinking deep into the cushions.

"This is pleasant, Mom. Do you come here often?"

The older woman pulled out her phone, sent a text, then set it aside. "It's one of our favorite rooms. Rodney and I often sit in here in the evening and visit about our day." A manicured hand smoothed her stylish coif.

Vi reluctantly engaged in small talk, nearly cheering when the maid entered with a full coffee service. The rich aroma mingled with a cinnamon Christmas scent. Unbidden, Rory stole into Vi's thoughts again. She poured, then flavored her coffee, hoping Rory's family day was smoother than hers. Briefly, she wished he were here. Vi envied the ease with which he'd handled Mom in the hospital.

Mom's agenda seemed on hold, at least for the moment, while she tsked over Vi's boot. Vi admitted to leaving it off in the evenings to build up her ankle. The constant ache had mostly subsided, depending on her level of activity.

"Ah, I almost forgot." Mom reached into the end table drawer next to her. She pulled out a thick red envelope and held it out to Vi. "Merry Christmas, Violet."

Vi eyed the envelope with suspicion. She'd bet the house and all its contents that Mom had this moment planned for weeks. Summoning courage, Vi took the envelope. She slid her thumb under the seal, then pulled out several pages of a legal-sized document. Her heart sank as she scanned the contents. A contract of sorts. "What's this?"

"The lease to your very own apartment here in Houston."

Mom beamed as if she'd presented Vi with a winning lottery ticket.

Vi stared at her. "Mom, I'm not living in Houston."

Mom's bright smile faltered a tad. "Well, of course not. You've said it often enough. Think of it as a weekend getaway. Goodness knows there's entertainment galore here in the metroplex."

"I'm not moving here, Mom." Vi stuffed the lease agreement back into the envelope and placed it on the coffee table. The idea suffocated her. The testy attitude she had tamped down all morning roared in protest over Mom's latest ploy. *Choose love, Vi.* She steeled herself with a deep breath. A minute spark of hope chased through her weary mind and guided the way. If Vi mentioned Dad's letters, maybe the conversation would drift in a different direction. At the very least, maybe they wouldn't argue over Vi's non-existent move to Houston.

"Mom, I have a question, but Cyrus needs a walk. You're welcome to come with me, or we can talk when we're done. Your call."

Mom stared at Vi as if an enormous pimple had sprouted on her nose. "Did you invite me to do something with you?"

Vi winced at her mother's incredulous tone.

The older woman stood so fast coffee sloshed out of her china cup. Mom hastily dabbed at the rug, then glanced down at her formal pantsuit. "Let me put on a pair of boots and get my coat." She strode from the room, mumbling about a shopping trip for outdoor clothes.

Vi's head spun at the turnaround. What if she embraced Mom instead of constantly pushing her away? Her stomach tightened at the red envelope on the coffee table. No embracing yet.

Cyrus wanted more than a sedate stroll. When they

stepped off the portico into the chilly day, he tugged at the leash as they wandered the grounds. Vi issued sharp commands, which he responded to, though his golden eyes pleaded for freedom. "You can let off steam on the way back," she promised with a smile. It required all her willpower to rein him in. Mom kept up, sidestepping muddy spots. This stroll would ruin her soft-looking boots, but she didn't seem to care.

Vi stopped to admire a grove of gnarly mesquite trees, their bare branches a mass of tangles. The heaviest limbs drooped and lay on the ground, sucker branches still spiraling upward. Christmas lights from the front eaves of the house sparkled through the spidery boughs. Two white rocking chairs sat on the front porch. The enormous dwelling had a graceful, old-money air—a living, breathing embodiment of Rodney. She could grow fond of this.

As the wind grew fierce, they hurried back and huddled in the rockers. Vi let Cyrus off the leash. He capered about, nose poking into the shrubbery. Weak sunlight helped to dispel the chill. The wind whistled with the fragrance of rain. She wouldn't get a better opportunity.

Vi swallowed an icy breath. "Mom, during the demo stage of the remodel, Rory, my contractor, found Dad's electronic tablet wedged between couch cushions. It had a few documents on it—letters Dad wrote to me. I'll give you copies if you want."

Mom's rocker stilled. "I'd like that." The wistfulness in her words pierced Vi's heart.

Vi's throat closed, but she forced out what she'd wanted to ask since she'd read the letter with Dad's version of Mom's second marriage. "What happened with Wa-Wallace?" Vi could barely utter the man's name. Mom had never talked about him or their marriage, as if he'd never existed. Vi knew better. She had the scars to prove it.

Mom's eyes held a deep well of sadness. *Oh, no.*

To Vi's amazement, two fat tears rolled down her mother's cheeks. She turned aside to peer out at the expansive lawn. Minutes passed. Vi opened her mouth to apologize.

Then Mom's lips parted, and the air puffed white. "It was such a difficult time. Looking back, I made mistakes I'll regret for the rest of my life." She exhaled another frosty puff. "You and your dad always loved that old house, but I hated it. *And* living in the sticks." Her glassy eyes were far away. "I was so unhappy, it made listening to Mother easy. She painted such a wonderful picture of our lives if only I moved back home. Away from Thomas." An unladylike snort bubbled from her lips. "Mother detested him." Mom's fists tightened in her lap.

"So, I divorced Thomas and moved the two of us to Houston. Mom and I argued constantly. I've never cared for Valiant, but I missed your dad. When Wallace came along, I married him quickly. Too late, I figured out his true nature."

Her hard gaze razored into Vi. "I drank to numb the pain. I couldn't see, or didn't want to see, what Wallace did—to you." She blinked and took a shuddery breath. "Your dad confronted me. Thomas let me believe if I didn't straighten up, he would take you away from me." Her eyes misted.

Vi tore her eyes away to gather her thoughts. Cyrus was happily digging holes in a patch of expensive amaryllis. "I remember how unhappy you were. How did the divorce happen?"

Mom flicked her carefully arranged hair with pink-tipped fingers. "I can tell you what I think took place, though neither your dad nor Wallace would ever admit to anything."

Tru looked around the expansive property, then sighed ruefully. "I believe Thomas found Wallace after one of his gambling stints or he might have been with another woman." One delicate brow lifted. "Wallace's vices outnumbered his good traits." Stark misery filled her eyes as she looked at Vi.

Vi raised her chin, then looked away.

Mom sniffed, her mouth turning up on one side. "He came home after one of his all-nighters looking worse than usual and kept yelling about my 'crazy ex-husband.' I think your dad found him and beat the daylights out of him." Tru tugged one end of her scarf and shrugged. "Oh, I suppose it wasn't right in the eyes of the law, but knowing Thomas still cared gave me the gumption to stand up to Wallace. After the divorce, Thomas helped me get back on my feet again, this time without Mother."

Vi found her voice through the bricks lodged in her throat. "Did y'all ever try to get back together?"

Mom offered a tired smile. "We talked about it. But

Thomas didn't want to live in Houston, and I couldn't abide Valiant. Neither of us was interested in a long-distance relationship. When Thomas said all or nothing, I agreed."

Somehow, it didn't surprise Vi. She knew how stubborn her parents could get. The coldness from Vi's icy feet crept up her legs. "Mama, Daddy loved you to the end."

Mom dipped her chin. "I never quit loving him either. We'd settled into a stalemate—one of the few things we did well—when I met Rodney. He loves me, Vi." Her next words were soft. "You've probably been afraid to ask, given my history, but I love him too. Differences of opinion are inevitable, but we keep it civil." A sad chuckle left her lips. "Thomas and I didn't know how to fight fair."

"Emotionally, I'm in a better place now." She waved around the lawn and house. "And, of course, financially stable, but that doesn't mean I haven't wanted a do-over where you're concerned." She snuggled her hands into her coat. "Surprised?"

Mom's transparency stole Vi's breath away and upended years of preconceived notions. She deliberately inhaled through her nose, then exhaled.

Mom frowned at Cyrus, then continued, "I've made horrendous mistakes. We've both paid the price. Especially you. If I were in your place, I wouldn't want anything to do with me either, but I do love you." Her mouth tweaked in a wry grin. "Our mutual love for you was the only thing your dad and I agreed on without question."

Vi swallowed hard. Rory had pegged it right. Mom loved her. Another jagged edge of her soul wove together in a seamless stitch. "Thanks for telling me ... everything." However welcome the news, she didn't want Mom to assume anything. "I'm still not living in Houston."

Mom's nose wrinkled. "First your father, now you. Well,

maybe I'll drive to Valiant more often. I hear they have a stellar gym with a to-die-for massage therapist. And who is this Rory who's remodeling the house?"

Vi shot her a warning look. "You know perfectly well who Rory is, Mom."

"Those earrings you're wearing. Did he pick them out?"

"Mom!" Vi stood, stamping her feet to revive circulation.

"It's time we went inside, Violet. I'm freezing." Chin high, Mom brushed past her to the front door. "The man appears to have excellent taste—in jewelry ... and women." Laughter lurked in the depths of her blue eyes.

RORY COULDN'T LET Christmas pass without a word from Vi.

Are you home? Awake?

His fingers had itched to text her all day. Not knowing her circumstances, he'd held back, though it had required monumental effort.

Yes and yes. Too much coffee.

How did your day go?

Part aggravation. Part healing. And yours?

Mostly boring. I've been thinking about our date.

No response.

He might as well share his idea.

What if we have a prequel first?

What's a prequel?

His thumbs flowed over the keys.

A little pre-date.

Cyrus is snorting at you again.

This Wed. evening. A prequel.

Nite, Rory.

At least she didn't say no.

I'm missing you, Red.

CHAPTER TWENTY-SEVEN

"How do I look?" Vi stood in the kitchen doorway. She'd dressed for a casual date, and even applied makeup. Glancing down at her black jeans and cable-knit sweater, she touched her matching tam. Would her outfit please Rory? Should she even care?

"Where are you off to?" Brenna paused from slicing tomatoes at the counter.

"Rory said to dress warm and meet him at my house. I guess we'll go from there." Vi wound a lock of hair around her fingers.

"Is this the big date?" Paige asked as she tore lettuce leaves into bite-sized chunks.

Vi mustered a shy smile. "No, he's calling this the prequel. A little pre-date." She was babbling.

Paige and Brenna exchanged knowing looks. Vi tugged at her sweater collar. "Well?"

"Nice shade of lipstick. All the better to pucker with." Mischief leaked from Brenna's green eyes.

Vi's entire face flamed. "Uh, no. He told me he wouldn't

initiate any more kisses." She winced. Could she chop her tongue off?

Brenna's mouth gaped open. "Any *more* kisses? What haven't you told us, girl?"

Vi scrunched her lips to one side, determined not to talk about their moment at the hospital. Their perfect kiss. "He's kissed me on the forehead since then, so I don't know what to think. I want to trust him ..." Her eyes narrowed. "I could use a little help here."

"*Mija*, in Rory's mind, a kiss on the cheek or the forehead wouldn't count as a real kiss." Paige gave her an encouraging smile. "You can trust him."

"Unless he finds you so irresistible, he can't help himself," Brenna smirked.

Paige rolled her eyes and snapped a towel at Brenna. "Vi, you look stunning. Have a great time."

ON THE DRIVE OVER, Vi had worried her bottom lip until the carefully applied lipstick had disappeared. She shouldn't be gritting her teeth, antsy to get this over with—dates were supposed to be fun. The boot dragging, she climbed out of her car, grateful for her sweater and thick socks. Rory waved from the balcony.

A chill frosted the air. White clouds puffed a frothy tide against a deep sapphire sky. An enticing aroma Vi couldn't identify emanated from the house.

Rory met her at the door in a navy sweater that accentuated his sculpted shoulders and trim waist. She found his wind-tousled hair utterly charming. As if the man needed more charisma.

"For you, pretty lady." He bowed, holding out an

environmental mask. "I plan to take your breath away but refuse to compete with sheetrock dust and paint fumes."

Giggling, Vi took the mask. "Is this where the prequel happens?" He continually surprised her.

"Allow me, please." Rory's slender fingers navigated around her hair and the tam, gently securing the strings behind her ears. "We're going to the upstairs balcony. You should be in the clear, allergy-wise, but let's not risk it."

Once they'd climbed the stairs and crossed a carpeted floor, he said, "Close your eyes."

A shiver encased her spine. She could trust him, couldn't she?

Her eyes fluttered shut. She inhaled the sharp scent of his pine cologne as he guided her forward.

"Okay. You can open them now."

Vi blinked. And blinked again at the transformed balcony. Last she saw, the neglected mess of odds and ends required a firm hand and plenty of time. Now the wooden flooring and rails were spic and span. Two new chairs with colorful cushions and a matching chaise lounge replaced dilapidated lawn furniture. A smoking hibachi squatted on a small table. Dead plants and pots had disappeared, and a small Christmas tree glimmered from one corner. Holiday music played from an unseen source.

Still staring, she tugged the mask down. "You did this?"

"A house-staging seminar I took came in handy. And Paige tutored me through a menu and grocery list." White teeth flashed between his mustache and beard.

"This is the prequel?" Vi searched his face. His gray eyes had warmed to pewter. "Yes, ma'am. Dinner at your place. A walk around the lake. You leave when you're ready to go. No pressure."

Vi sagged against the door frame. She could do this.

Without conscious thought, she stood on tiptoes and kissed him on the cheek. "Thank you." Oh, mercy, his mouth was much too close. *Refocus, girl.*

His lips tilted up before she looked away. Had he taken a seminar in mind-reading too?

As Vi turned to the coolers, heat infused her body, despite the nippy air. "Let's see what's for supper."

RORY'S INSIDES sailed over the bar. Vi had almost kissed him. Not an aren't-you-sweet kiss either. His mouth went dry when he glimpsed the passion flaring in the depths of her eyes. For a second or so, anyway.

She visibly relaxed at the prospect of dinner and a walk. Rory had observed enough of her responses to know she'd be skittish, but he didn't understand why. She needed to trust him enough to tell him. It had become his priority. *God, please help me here.* If only one of her tight layers loosened tonight, he'd consider it a win.

Rory opened a cooler and pointed to foil-wrapped packages. "A little bird told me shrimp is one of your favorites, so I tapped Tavo's brain for grilling instructions. Spiced shrimp in one. Garlic bread in the other."

"Salad, dressing, and what's this?" Vi pulled out a carton of store-bought lemon bars. "Oh, yum! My favorite. A little bird knows me well." She hugged the box. "Can we eat one now?"

Rory rubbed his hands together. A kid on Christmas morning had nothing on Vi. "By all means. Want hot chocolate to go with it?"

"Yes!" She plunked into a chair, wrestling with plastic tabs while he poured the creamy liquid into sturdy paper cups. Vi handed him a lemon bar, then licked the sugar off her fingers.

Rory's pulse spiked. She didn't possess an ounce of the artificiality he saw in so many women.

He checked the grill. "Let me get the shrimp started. While it cooks, you can tell me about your day."

Vi melted into the chair with a broad grin. Ankles crossed, her feet swung back and forth, not quite touching the ground. Rory's heart nearly hammered out of his chest. A real, live doll, this one.

Once they'd stuffed themselves on grilled shrimp, bread, and salad, the temperature had dropped. Vi's comfort level rose like mercury, making Rory's chest puff with satisfaction. They'd chatted throughout the meal, and they now sat in companionable silence.

The buttery shrimp smell hung in the air. Golden light glimmered from the setting sun, and the north star peeked out of a darkening sky.

"Wanna go for a walk?" Rory asked.

CHAPTER TWENTY-EIGHT

"A walk sounds great. You outdid yourself, Red." Vi seemed reluctant to move. Instead, she stretched her legs, a bottle of water clasped in her hands.

Rory adored it when Vi called him Red. She never did it on purpose—it slipped out and sounded absolutely perfect.

She straightened, shaking her flaming hair off her shoulders. Rory tore his eyes away. Her resemblance to a doll crashed to a halt with her jeans curving in all the right places.

They leisurely wound their way to the lake, holding hands. The goose honked from a distance.

Vi's steps slowed. "Cyrus would have loved this."

"How's he doing?" Rory steered her around an intrusive branch.

"We're good. I'm thankful to have him, Rory."

"Has he alerted out here?"

"*Mm-hmm*. A few times. He growls at the bushes. I think it's four-legged critters he senses."

"I'm confident he'll protect you, but you still need to be careful."

"I am. Every so often, Cyrus will need a practice session to keep his protection skills sharp, but having him gives me the freedom to roam." She stopped, her gaze serious. "I can't put a price on it, and our bond has helped both of us with the grieving process."

Rory moved behind her, putting his hands on her waist. She leaned into his chest, looking out at the lake. Harry honked from a distance. Moonlight outlined the trees, giving them a spooky appearance.

"Rory?" She turned a bit, then resumed staring at the water. "I, um, need to tell you something ... difficult." She bit her lip. "Then it's your turn. I want to know who decorated your townhouse."

Wow. Rory swallowed hard. He'd wanted deep conversation, but her directness took him off guard. "Yours sounds a lot more important." He faced her.

Vi gazed at the inky water directly below them. A turtle's head poked the surface, creating small ripples. "You won't want to hear this."

"Tell me anyway." A foreboding chill streaked down his flesh and blood leg.

Her forehead creased, and she took a deep breath. "Mom and Dad divorced the year I turned six, and Mom got custody of me." In the darkness, only the barest hint of her eye color showed. "She remarried quickly to a man she hardly knew. It was a terrible mistake—her words. I missed Daddy terribly and despised her new husband. I acted out all the time. Hateful to his face. Disrespectful."

Rory's heart quaked. *Oh, Vi.*

"As it turned out, our feelings were mutual." She took another deep breath. "The physical abuse started in small ways. Whenever I misbehaved, it escalated."

A tear glistened on her cheek, but her voice remained low

and steady. "At first, he beat me into submission." Her shoulders rose and dropped. "Then, after I became truly afraid of him, he did ... other things." The last words came out in a whisper. She was trembling all over.

Rory spoke through a closed throat. "Sexually?" When her eyes confirmed it, a dagger lodged in his chest. "He ... raped you?"

"Back then, I didn't know it had a name." Vi dropped her head.

Rory had never felt the murderous rage Jesse had often spoken of. Now he understood. White-hot heat coursed through his body. His hands shook with the desire to hurt the man who'd done unspeakable things to an innocent child.

Clenching his fists, he gulped a ragged breath. *Help me, Lord.* Gradually, his thoughts reordered into protection mode. Her abuser was completely out of reach. But Vi was here. With scars. She'd moved away as if to brace herself.

Rory opened his arms, willing any harshness out of his features. What happened had never been her fault. As she searched his face, the tension in her stance crumbled. She came to him, pressing her face against his chest.

He stroked her hair as she sobbed. Sniffing, he wiped his own eyes, not knowing when the tears fell. Her jumpy behavior made sense now—the trust issues, the hesitancy, the fear.

Harry waddled closer, greeting them with a raspy screech.

Rory raised her chin so he could look at her. "Thank you for telling me. I'm a safe place, Red."

She murmured so low, he bent to hear. "My heart knows, but my head gets in the way."

He hugged her again, resting his chin on her head. He longed to kiss her but didn't dare. Her trust level survived as a vulnerable baby bird learning how to fly.

"Oww, Harry!" Rory disengaged from Vi to rub his leg. "The

goose pecked me! Too bad he didn't get a beak full of prosthetic."

Vi grabbed his hand. "Let's go before he tries it again." They quickly outdistanced the goose, headed to the house, and climbed the stairs to the balcony. A light breeze rustled through the trees. An owl hooted close by. Rory's thoughts still tumbled at Vi's revelation.

Leftover shrimp had turned the air fishy. Rory flicked the lighter to chase away the odor while Vi wrapped the leftovers and stashed them in the cooler.

"There's more hot chocolate and coffee. And lemon bars." His fingers longed to trace her face, erase the bruised look. The telling had cost her.

"Okay. I'd better switch to coffee. And I want to try out the chaise lounge …" She held up a finger. "The bathroom upstairs still works?"

Rory chuckled. "Can't vouch for its cleanliness. Do you need the mask?" He glanced around for it.

"Nope. The fumes aren't strong up here. Be right back."

"I'm keeping tabs on your breathing," he said as she retreated.

"I'm fine, Red," she called back.

When she returned, he handed her a cup of coffee. She situated herself with the awkward boot into the lounger, then scooted over, patting the space next to her. "There's room for you."

Eyebrows raised, he slid next to her, balancing his cup of coffee. "Mm. Perfect." Her pinched look had eased a bit. Rory marveled at her ability to adjust. He doubted Paige or Brenna knew what she'd revealed to him. A significant step forward.

They sipped in silence for a bit, then she stirred. "Moving on to part two. Tell me about your townhouse."

What? Rory had forgotten all about part two. He nudged her shoulder. "You're sneaky."

She gave him a side-eye. "I'm in splendid company, Mr. Avoid-the-Subject. If I can spill my guts, you can too."

Much as Rory hated talking about his ex, Vi deserved the same transparency she'd given him. He blew out a long sigh and sipped his coffee. "Jess and I hadn't lived in the townhouses long when I met Stella. At the time, I found her ... extremely attractive. All too soon, she convinced me my place needed a facelift. In retrospect, that should have been a red flag. Nevertheless, I moved in with Jesse for a couple of months so she could have full rein." He scowled. "I gave her my credit card to redecorate, but she insisted I wait to see the finished product."

He swallowed more coffee. "Stella dressed smart, so I assumed she'd make the same thing happen with my living quarters. We dated while she 'performed her magic.'" He air-quoted the words. "It took me a while to figure out her agenda. She used me to finance her latest career whim. She also wanted my lifestyle."

Vi set her coffee cup aside, then intertwined her fingers in his hand.

"Looking back, we argued—a lot. Stella hated Jess. She wanted me to quit coaching the power team because heavy lifting didn't count as a cool sport. My townhouse was the last straw. I broke it off for good. She, um, didn't take it well."

The breakup had happened months ago, but Stella's accusations still reverberated.

"She was a fool," Vi muttered under her breath.

"No more so than I." Rory shrugged, slipping an arm around her. Vi snuggled closer. He sensed no pity, only bone-deep empathy.

Stars blinked in a hazy sky. Rory saw a spire of smoke curling from the scrub brush, not close, but still on the property. He rose and went to the railing, then joined her again. "I think your uninvited guests are back. I'll let Tavo know."

"How aggravating." Vi blew out a breath. "Good thing I have Cyrus."

Rory nodded. Cyrus afforded him peace of mind too. He sat up straighter. "Hey, I almost forgot. Are you up for a big ask?"

The faint line between her brows deepened into a rut. "Ask away." Caution wound through the simple words.

"The whopping big deal of charity fundraisers happens on New Year's Eve. I go for business because it's hard to beat the networking opportunities." He turned to face her. "I hope you'll go with me as my date."

Vi made a face. "I've heard Paige talk about this fundraiser. It's one of those high society dress-to-the-hilt deals, isn't it?"

"All that and a box of chocolates. I will enjoy the evening far more if you're with me."

A frown twisted her lips. "I don't know, Rory."

"You don't have to decide tonight, but I won't be asking anyone else." His breath hitched. "I'm done being stupid." He still hadn't told her about his horrible date with Melissa. With what had transpired tonight, however—another instance of his foolishness could wait.

"Let me think about it. It's a hard one." Her eyes looked far away.

"Why? There's more to it than the event."

The light in her eyes had vanquished. "Rory, most people have more than one skeleton in the closet." She rose from the chaise. "I need to go. Thank you. This has been ... lovely." Her voice broke on the last word.

Only he'd spoiled it, but he didn't know how. "Are we good?" he asked softly, trying to repair the damage.

In the yellow light, her eyes gentled into two violet stars. "You're fabulous, Red. Walk me to my car?"

On lunch break, Vi peered in Paige's fridge. Ham and cheese or PBJ? Gala or no gala? She opted for ham and cheese and pulled out the ingredients. As she assembled a sandwich, Rory's request came to mind.

Paige strode in. "Hey, *mija*. How did the *prequel* go last night?" The dark-haired woman said the word playfully. She peered at Vi's sandwich and began to make her own.

Vi chuckled. "Surprisingly fun. You're the little bird who helped him put it together?" She took a crunchy bite. Cyrus's wolfish eyes pleaded for a snack.

"So, I'm a little bird now, huh? Glad you had a good time. Goodness knows, he worried about it enough." Paige finished with the mayo and pressed the top layer of bread into the meat and cheese.

Vi took another bite of the sandwich and chewed. "Paige …"

Paige placed her plate and sandwich on the table. She opened a cabinet, found a bag of chips, then sat. "What, *mija*?" Her brown eyes pierced Vi.

"I, uh ... Rory asked me to be his date to the gala." Vi toyed with a crust of bread. "I told him I'd think about it."

"Well, you need to think fast, because the gala is this Saturday night." Paige's brisk tone left no wiggle room.

Vi reached for the chips. "He said it's a whopping big deal."

Paige snorted. "Dead-on. The gala is the front-runner with no competition for charity events. Rory's participation is crucial. And he needs a date. Besides—" Her eyes danced. "Rory in a tux is a sight not to be missed."

Chips forgotten, Vi took a deep, slow breath. "Okay. Take me to gala school."

Paige's eyes flashed. "He'll be thrilled." She retrieved a memo pad from the fridge and handed it to her. "Make a list. The first thing you need is the right dress."

"Don't you have a dress I can use?"

The other woman frowned as if Vi had suggested going in dirty scrubs. "*Mija.* No one wears borrowed attire to the gala. First impressions for everyone else, but you need to knock Rory's socks off."

Vi's jaw slacked. "How?"

Paige's scrutinizing look made Vi squirm. Then her friend flashed her trademark smile. "I'll help. And Rory will love every second of it."

BACK GLUED TO THE BENCH, Rory pumped iron. When his upper body muscles performed up to par, it helped distribute his weight and evened out the pressure on his legs. No stopping until the limp disappeared. If only exercise would satiate his need to see Vi again.

He had sailed through his day with superpower strength. Overall, his pre-date idea had been a success. His heart still ached over Vi's admission, but her resiliency had impressed him. Then he'd smacked headlong into another hidden reef, all sharp and prickly. Her positive response about the evening had given him hope. He needed more time to get through the other hurdles, and the gala would be the perfect way to make it happen.

He'd hung out most of the day at Peeps, doing paperwork and inventing errands near the massage area. The glimpses he'd managed were mostly the back of her head. He needed another face-to-face to plead his case for the gala. If Vi wouldn't go with him, he'd have to strategize how to stay away from the man-hunters. And the cougars. He groaned. Dare she blame him for not wanting to ring in the new year holed up in the men's bathroom?

Finishing the last reps, he toweled off before hitting the shower. Jesse strode toward him with an enigmatic smile. "How was your date last night?"

Rory lifted a brow. News traveled fast. "Low-key. Sweet. Hard."

Jesse's grin widened. "You're learning."

"What am I learning, dude?"

"About the kind of girl you've got. Brenna's not a party girl, and Vi doesn't strike me as the type either."

"You got it right. I've asked her to be my date for the gala this weekend, but she hasn't given me an answer yet."

"Mm. Have you seen her today?" Jesse knew the event ranked high for future expansion contacts.

"No, though not for lack of trying."

Jesse scrubbed his jaw. "I'm going to Paige's tonight to see Brenna. They'll cook dinner. We'll visit and probably watch a movie. Doesn't matter. I just want to unwind with my girl." He looked at Rory. "Why don't you come with me? Same low-key atmosphere. Hang out for a while. Not a date."

Rory brightened at the thought. "I'll text. She's not much on surprises. I'm heading out to watch the team do a prowler push. Wanna go with me?" He grasped his phone with trepidation. Deep down, fear planted the unwelcome thought Vi wouldn't want to see him. The gala had been too much to ask. And her relationship with him didn't extend past the house remodel.

When Jesse nodded, Rory said, "You go on ahead. I'll text and catch up." Better to find out sooner than later. He pulled out his phone and thumbed a message.

Okay if I drop by after practice?

His throat went dry, but he pressed SEND.

He trailed Jesse to the bleachers. The gym echoed loudly as teammates yelled encouragement, and weights thudded on the wooden floor. Tavo's leadership had upped the productivity level. A half smile crossed Rory's lips. Not a minute had passed when his phone chirped.

> Yes. Dinner included if you help me take
> down the Christmas tree.

A pleasant warmth invaded him over her simple, uncomplicated invitation. He tried to swallow past the brick in his throat. He'd fallen deep in a hole over this woman. If their relationship didn't work out, lost wouldn't begin to describe his state of mind, emotional health, ... or any other status he possessed.

He and Jesse stood on the sidelines, watching in silence as the team took turns pushing the heavy iron machines designed to build strength and test limits. Tavo joined them, arms crossed, eyes not missing a beat. Finally, he blew a blast on the whistle.

Rory strolled over to him. "Excellent practice. You got this."

They exchanged more powerlifting talk until Tavo's drawn countenance caught Rory's attention. The guy had exhaustion written all over him. Rory wound down the conversation and said, "FYI—the squatters are back at Vi's. I saw campfire smoke last night."

A faint horizontal line creased Tavo's forehead. "I'll get a patrol out there again. We need to figure out a way to make the place unfriendly." He eyed Rory. "Signed up for your massage yet?"

Rory looked away. The transparency of a massage unnerved him.

She was transparent with you.

Tavo gave an exasperated sniff, then lumbered after the other powerlifters.

PURE AGONY. Brenna tortured Vi's hair into a deceptively casual French braid as Paige looked on. They'd pored through online videos, searching for a style that would satisfy Vi's need for simplicity and Paige's insistence on elegance. Vi's teeth clamped on her lower lip as yet another pin jabbed her tender scalp. She owed Brenna for watching countless videos to make it happen. A fussy salon would have only increased Vi's stress level.

Vi couldn't believe she'd agreed to attend the gala. After she and Rory had taken down the Christmas tree the other night, he'd snuggled next to her on the sofa and asked again. His slate eyes had looked so hopeful, she couldn't bear to say no. He'd stayed close the rest of the evening, as if afraid she'd change her mind. She'd thoroughly enjoyed the attention.

"Don't bite your lip, *mija*." Paige smiled. "A sore, mushy lip won't do at all."

Vi glanced in the mirror. Thank goodness Mother had tutored her in the art of makeup. She didn't wear it much, but she could apply it with the best of them. Her skin felt heavy beneath the extra cosmetic layers.

If only the dress would arrive. The shoes had come this morning, a pair of strappy black stilettos. The gorgeous heels wouldn't do her ankle any favors. Dressing up without the boot for an evening would be worth it.

"This do is perfect on you, Vi. You're the real, live version of a fairy tale princess." Brenna stood back to examine her handiwork, then tugged at the large braid. The loose, thick weave swept up on the sides and trailed down her back into a minute pearl barrette.

"Let me use spray to hold it." Brenna held the bottle, aimed and ready.

"As long as it stays soft—no metal hair." Vi rearranged a curly tendril around her face.

Once the mist had cleared, Brenna leaned next to Vi's ear. "Are you going to kiss him tonight?"

The roots of her hair tingled. "Thinking about it."

Paige smirked. "You ought to lay one on him, *mija*. The poor man hasn't had a good kiss on New Year's Eve in years."

"Poor Rory." Sarcasm threaded Vi's tone.

Brenna put her hand to her mouth to hide her smile.

"Any new tracking info on the dress?" Vi's foot jiggled nonstop. "What if there's a glitch?"

"No glitch. The dress will be here any minute." Paige studied her phone screen, then looked at Vi. "I've cut the timing closer with shipping. The gala doesn't start for another hour. We've got plenty of time."

"What if it doesn't fit or looks terrible?" Vi's voice rose. Her matching fingers and toenails twinkled with pizzazz.

According to Paige, fire engine red was rated as the only accessory color that mattered.

The doorbell rang. Cyrus scrambled from under the vanity, barking ferociously.

"The dress!" Brenna ran to the door.

CHAPTER THIRTY

Rory tugged on his collar an hour into the gala and stifled the urge to check his phone. Vi had texted eons ago to say she was running late. A business acquaintance standing next to him continued his spiel. Nodding at intervals, Rory had no clue as to what the man said. The collective gala mindset lived for appearances and laying down sizeable sums of money. His private mission, however, consisted of enjoying the evening with Vi.

He asked for seltzer water when a server slid by with a tray of champagne flutes. The server inclined his head a fraction, then headed back to the kitchen.

Richly decorated in red and gold, the enormous room sprawled with round tables strategically placed for mingling. Black drapes billowed from the floor-to-ceiling windows. Soft strains of a band warming up drifted through the opulent atmosphere. An appetizer buffet boasting fresh garlicky shrimp brought back memories of his prequel date with Vi. Rory wished for another evening at her place, eating on the balcony, or walking around the lake together. Even sharing difficult parts about their pasts had been beautiful. In an impossibly short time, Vi had become vital to his well-being. He'd survived without a leg. She was his heart and his lungs—no chance of survival without her. He glanced toward the entry doors for the zillionth time.

Giddy laughter nearby turned his veins to ice.

Melissa.

She flounced his way as the band struck up a country-western love song. He gazed at the black toe of his polished dress shoe. *Please hurry, Vi.*

The man he'd talked to had disappeared. Melissa took his place, chattering in her high-pitched voice. He grudgingly conceded the woman looked pretty in a fluffy pink concoction, even if her hair was scooped to one side in a weird pile. If only she would zip the lip. The glass of seltzer water at his elbow provided a much-needed distraction. The acidic liquid burned his parched throat.

"Now, look what you've done. Your bowtie's askew. Let me fix it." Melissa fussed over his tie, hen-like and cluckish.

He attempted to remove her hands. "Thanks, Melissa."

Anticipation buzzed around Rory, and the ocean of people parted. His breath swooshed out.

Vi had arrived.

She appeared oblivious to the curious stares, gliding toward him in an off-the-shoulder purple dress. The ever-sophisticated cocktail crowd gawked over her newcomer status. The band's melody filled the sudden hush.

As Vi drew near, her pink lips tipped in a mysterious smile. Dazzled right down to his toes, Rory couldn't take his eyes off her. The wild elegance of her swept-up braid did funny things to his brain. The dress cast her eyes in the violet hue he loved.

"Glad you made it, babe." He managed, his voice husky. Melissa huffed and stalked out of his space. Vi kissed him on the cheek, then spoke in a low, just-for-him voice, "Sorry you had to wait."

Chest swelling, he threaded his fingers through hers. "Would you care to dance?" He set his glass on the tray of a server passing by.

She squeezed his hand. "Yes, please."

He nudged her toward the dance floor, pulse racing. Trisha Yearwood's song "How Do I Live" floated through the air. His fingers meshed at the small of her back. "Impeccable timing. My well of polite chit-chat had run dry."

Her let-me-get-my-bearings air captivated him. Content at last, he drank in her appearance. The earrings he'd given her were the only jewelry she wore. His knees turned to putty as they stepped and swayed to the music. When the song ended, he whispered, "You look enchanting tonight."

"Thanks," she murmured dryly. "I had hordes of help."

He touched her hair. "I love it."

"A princess cartoon inspired it." Her smile turned impish. "You're quite dashing yourself. Glad I didn't miss this."

When her hands encircled his waist, he couldn't resist touching her bare shoulders, then rested his hands on the little pretend sleeves. Soft, shimmery fabric snugged around her hourglass figure. A woman stood before him tonight, not a shade of dollish girl anywhere.

Her perfume wafted over him. She swayed in rhythm with him, as if they'd danced together for years.

He peered around the swishy skirt to her feet. "I spy high heels and pretty toes. Where's the boot?"

Vi lifted a delicate shoulder. "It didn't go with the dress."

Rory mustered a serious look. "You know what no-boot means, don't you?"

"No. Tell me."

"You'll have to hang on to me for support all evening long."

"That's my plan." Her eyes twinkled. "I came for one reason, Rory."

The song had ended, but he enjoyed holding her too much to let go. "I know. And I appreciate it." He brushed his lips across her forehead.

As Rory guided her off the dance floor, she lifted the snazzy braid off her neck. What? A hummingbird tattoo peeked at him from between her shoulders. Small. Colorful. A dash of sass, reminiscent of its owner. Bubbles of laughter rose in his throat, rolling out into a grin.

Then a chill darted up his spine along with the feeling of being watched. Glancing around the room, he found the source and nearly stumbled.

Stella.

Dressed in a flashy black gown with bright red lipstick, she looked straight out of a fairy tale cartoon herself—only he'd cast her as a villain. Malice vibrated off every cold feature as she stared at him. Rory spared her a curt nod, then led Vi to his table.

Placing an arm around Vi's shoulders, Rory introduced her to his business acquaintances. Vindication replaced the emptiness Stella had left as Vi shook hands and accepted hugs from strangers. Respect for her puffed his chest. He alone knew she was light years out of her comfort zone.

The evening evolved into a charming routine. Rory networked and traded business cards while Vi chatted with wives, girlfriends, and female business owners. He heard her describe Peeps in glowing terms more than once, inviting women to sign up for massages. When her smile grew tight, he'd usher her away to sit for a while. Or they would escape to the dance floor.

Pure heaven—if not for Stella glowering at him. Rory sloughed off her murderous looks. He moved from side to side with Vi as the band played another lazy love song. Her head on his shoulder, her scent ... slow dances were the best. "How's the ankle?"

"It's giving out," she admitted. "As long as you hold me, I'm good." Her smile etched into his heart, an echo of the achingly sweet music.

He tightened his arms around her. "Not a problem, because I'm never letting go."

She looked beyond him. "All the tables along the walls—are those the charities?"

"Yep. I usually do a sweep after the speeches. You up for it?"

"If it means I can talk to real people, then by all means." She grinned wickedly.

Rory grinned back. "No promises, Red."

At long last, the host announced dinner. As they ate pecan-crusted chicken and steak, Rory didn't snub his tablemates, but neither did he feel obligated to take part in any of their conversations. Call him partial, but he preferred quietly chatting with Vi. His chest buoyed with lightness. Her presence brought a peace he'd never experienced with a woman.

After dinner, Rory slid his hand into Vi's and pretended to listen to the speeches. His side peeks at the fascinating woman beside him only justified his decision. Her facial expressions provided more entertainment than what anyone had to say.

Finally, the band began a new set. Rory murmured, "You ready for another round?"

Her stifled yawn charmed him. "I'm game."

However, once he helped her up, Melissa stood in their path, a bright pink spot on each cheek. Reeking of alcohol, she peered at him with unfocused eyes. "You owe me a dance." She poked him in the chest, then spun toward Vi, slurring loudly, "We had a date, you know."

Vi shot Rory a sharp look. Before he could react, she stepped up to Melissa and whispered in her ear. When the taller woman gave her a befuddled stare, Vi angled her head, raising one strawberry brow toward the door. Melissa's lower lip protruded as if she didn't care for what she'd heard. Vi never broke eye contact. Finally, the woman wobbled away on unsteady legs. Even her bouncy skirt seemed deflated.

Rory let out the breath he'd held, crooking his elbow. Vi plunked her arm through his, and they made their way to the dance floor. He relished her closeness as they moved in sync. "Dare I ask what you said to her?"

Vi's lovely features hardened. "I told her sharing's not my thing." She watched him closely. "You told me you had done something stupid. When she said the two of you had a date, I knew what stupid meant." One hand knotted into a fist against his shoulder. "What were you thinking, Rory?"

The brick in Rory's throat enlarged by the second. "I was mad and upset because you wouldn't go out with me."

Her stiff posture relented as his words sank in. To his utter relief, she rested her head on his shoulder. "Okay," she murmured, "Point taken."

"Are you mad at me?"

"No," she drew the word out slowly. "Don't push it, though." Her blue eyes drilled into him.

Rory kissed the top of her head. "I won't."

CHAPTER THIRTY-ONE

Taking a deep breath, Vi blinked back tears. She gazed into a mirror in the ladies' room and wove a wayward strand of hair back into the braid. When she and Rory had made their way around the non-profit booths, he stopped to chat with the mayor. After he'd introduced Vi, she'd wandered over to the Adopt-A-Pet table. Their enthusiastic response to her story about fostering Thunder had almost convinced her the gala was fun. Until she spied the banner for Valiant's maternity home for teens. The onslaught of memories had caught her off guard. Now she'd all but locked herself in the bathroom, desperately trying to hold together for Rory's sake.

Suddenly, a woman stood behind Vi, gazing into the same mirror. "So, are you having a good time?" Her smoky eyes simmered with anger.

Vi's sense of being caught in a time warp receded as she faced this very present challenge. "Do I know you?" The woman had been staring at them throughout the evening.

The woman moved to the next mirror and pretended to arrange her hair. Her lack of answer didn't fool Vi. The only way to handle these mean-girl types was to scoot out of target range. Vi would leave—on her own terms.

Painting on a bright smile, Vi said, "Marvelous evening. I've had such a wonderful time." Stepping around the woman, Vi reached the door and then turned back. "And my date ... well, Rory is the absolute best."

When she emerged from the ladies' room, Rory stepped close. "I lost track of time and hoped you might be here." The line between his brows deepened. "What happened?"

The adrenaline rush that carried Vi through the last bit left her lightheaded. She managed a shaky smile. "I'm fine."

Concern streaked through his eyes. "Do you need to sit?" He glanced at her feet and held out his arm. "The shoes—they're killing you."

Vi concentrated on putting one stiletto heel in front of the other. The mere act of walking had morphed into torment. Back at their table, she unobtrusively slipped them off and massaged feeling back into her feet. She glanced around, hoping Mean Girl hadn't chosen to retaliate. Why *had* Vi gushed? She'd always disdained the sorority-girl vibe.

Because you want Rory for yourself. The words mocked her. She pinched her big toe until it hurt.

Close to midnight. The clamor had increased throughout the evening. A few revelers seemed on the verge of hysteria, while others looked sleepy. A countdown started. Gala-goers chanted, "Five, four, three, two, one!" Boom. The bass drum struck midnight. Stirred by the band, the crowd sang "Auld Lang Syne." Rory snatched two flutes of champagne from a serving tray, handing one to her. The bubbles tickled her nose.

Vi gazed at Rory, knowing the protocol for welcoming in the New Year meant a kiss. Or two. He intercepted her look with dark gray eyes, then he squeezed her hand and held it. She was relieved, yet disappointed when the moment passed.

He'd wanted to kiss her, and the idea of kissing him had tugged at her all evening—okay, for days.

Could she trust him?

He leaned over and tapped her nose as if he'd read her thoughts. "Stay right here while I close this shindig."

Hustling to the stage, Rory pulled a notecard from his pocket. Twice, in his brief closing speech, he forgot who to thank for the event. When he put the notecard in a different pocket and couldn't find it again, he held up his hands in a classic where-did-it-go pose. Charmed, the remaining gala participants applauded. Vi shook her head, clapping along.

Her heart flipped when he zipped down the steps as if he had two normal feet. When she rose, he touched her lips with an index finger. "Let me check with the closing crew, and then" —he pecked her cheek—"we're out of here."

Minutes later, he steered her to the exit.

Yellow light from the tall parking lamps beamed through the darkness. Recent rain hung heavy in the air. Not looking forward to the trek to her car, Vi scowled at her feet.

"Need assistance?" Rory slipped an arm behind her knees, swinging her into his chest. His beard rubbed her cheek. He stepped from the curb as if she weighed nothing.

Vi relaxed and inhaled his scent as he carried her to the car. Tears prickled behind her eyes. She'd miss his strong arms. He set her feet on the ground, steadying her with such care she choked back a sob. This relationship she wanted so badly could never work.

"What's going on, Vi?"

Her mind shrouded in despair, she couldn't utter a word, fixating on his once-shiny shoes, now rain-splashed from puddles. Vi rubbed her bare arms in the chilly breeze.

Rory bent close to her ear. "It's been a long evening. All you have to do is get in your car and drive to Paige's. I'll be right behind you all the way."

When he walked away, steps firm and purposeful, she put her forehead on the steering wheel. Probably better they hadn't kissed tonight. It had been hard enough to forget their kiss in the hospital. Keeping her distance had succumbed to the sheer joy of having him in her life. Until the maternity home banner, she hadn't even remembered why staying away mattered.

At Paige's, she hobbled up the veranda steps and into the house with Rory's help. Cyrus bustled out with a woof, wriggling with pleasure at her appearance. At this hour, she assumed Paige and Brenna were asleep.

Rory leaned into her. "Is it okay if I wind down here? A cup of coffee sounds wonderful."

She held onto his arm for balance and lost no time taking off the weaponized heels. She should end this now. "Perfect. I'll have hot chocolate."

"Of course." Rory gazed at her as if he was sealing away the memory in a vault. "I adore the dress. But if you want to change into more comfortable clothes, I'm fine with it."

She frowned. "What about you?"

A snicker bubbled up her throat when he shrugged his I'm-the-boss shoulders out of his tux jacket. "Minus the coat and bowtie, I'm a new man." Her insides swooned at his rakish grin.

It should be a crime for a man to be so handsome after midnight. His dusky red hair glowed in the low lighting, nickel-colored eyes entirely too alert. He was such glorious fun. Precisely the reason it had become a herculean effort to let go.

She scampered into the bedroom, delighted over liberation from all things gala. A little more time with him ...

RORY PULLED out two cups and grabbed the carafe of cold coffee. He poured a cup and stuck it in the microwave, treasuring the memory of the way Vi had looked tonight. The hair, her dress. He smiled, remembering how she leaned on him for support as the evening wore on. Grateful for spiky heels—though he hoped her ankle hadn't suffered a setback. He tore a packet of chocolate open, sprinkling it into a cup. He hurried to fix their beverages. The sofa would be a more comfortable place to talk.

He'd settled in, and Vi joined him. Her eyes drooped. She'd been awake too long, and her hair had come undone. She stilled when he tucked a strand back into the ropy braid, then sat close enough so their shoulders touched. Cyrus padded over and lay down, covering her bare feet, as if he knew they hurt. As they sipped their drinks, the clock on the mantle chimed 1 a.m.

"So, what did you think of the grand gala?" Rory set his mug aside, then laced his fingers through hers.

Vi swallowed the last of her chocolate. "No exaggeration with the grand. It exceeded my expectations, but I enjoyed it." She gazed at him. "Because of you." Leaning down, she petted Cyrus.

Warmth radiated through Rory's body. "I think you two have bonded." He wished it had happened with him, but the dog was enough for now.

Her eyes wouldn't meet his.

Inwardly, he sighed. He needed to address the elephant in the room. No way she would ever talk about it otherwise. He gently gripped her hand. "Red, we need to talk."

She shrank into the sofa.

Tell her.

Okay. I'm praying you have my back here, Lord. You're the only one who knows what's going on in her sweet little head.

Rory plunged into deep waters. "Vi, you know I want to kiss you."

Longing passed over her delicate features for the barest instant, and then confusion set in. "You said you wouldn't initiate any more kisses."

He stroked his beard, thinking how best to answer. "It needed saying—I stepped over the line when I kissed you at the hospital, and you deserved the assurance I wouldn't do it again. But it *doesn't* mean I don't want to."

Her eyes lit with understanding as the meaning of his words sank in.

Doggedly, Rory continued, "Here's the deal. However much I want to kiss you, you need to be okay with it. So, I'm going to ask"—he put his other hand on hers—"because it's not in my heart to take something you don't want to give."

At her sharp intake of breath, he frantically retracted. "Honey, I'm only talking about hugs and kisses. Nothing else is on the table. I won't ever push for more."

Vi dropped her head. Why? Shame? Embarrassment? Those emotions weren't his goal at all.

Rory lifted her chin and gazed into her wet eyes. Black trails of mascara streaked down her cheeks. Fishing in a pocket, he offered her a handkerchief.

Blotting her face, she gave him a watery smile. "Thank you."

When she seemed at a loss, he said, "So, I'll ask for a kiss now and then, but it's okay to say no. And if *you* want a kiss, Red"—he couldn't keep from grinning—"I can deliver."

Her shoulders heaved.

Oh, dear. What had he done? Much as he wanted to scoop

her into his arms, he reached for her hand. Massaging her fingers, he asked, "You're in pain. How can I help?"

When she curled into a ball, and the silence lengthened, he said, "I'm a safe place, Red. You want to talk, I'm here. You need a hug—"

Rory barely heard the whispered words. "Hold me."

Oh, he could do that.

He shifted to face her and opened his arms. "Come here."

As if a small child, she cuddled into his chest. He wrapped his arms around her, certain she could hear his heart pounding. Her trust soothed any fear of having said the wrong thing.

The braid trailed down her back in a river of red gold.

He whispered, "May I touch your hair?"

She rose from his chest and gazed at him with red-rimmed eyes. "When I didn't want to go to bed, it's how Daddy would get me to sleep." Her energy seemed to fade with each word. She melted against him. "If you're okay with it ..."

Rory held her, stroking her back until her tense muscles relented. He slowly wound his fingers through the braid, gently removing the pins until a curtain of flame draped her back. The silky texture between his fingers provided a measure of contentment he hadn't known existed.

Sure enough, Vi fell asleep. Minutes ago, her breathing had evened out. The desire to stay all night with her in his arms was tempting.

With a sigh, Rory eased her off his chest. Limp as a ragdoll, she never stirred when he laid her on the sofa. The overhead ceiling fan blew cool air down. He stretched, then retrieved his jacket and covered her.

Slipping out the front door, he spied a police car driving slowly by the house. Tavo came to a stop, giving Rory a hard stare. "Sup, bro?"

Oh, great. Tavo's job required him to pay attention to questionable situations. He'd definitely question the late hour if nothing else. "I took Vi to the New Year's Eve gala. Then a late-night chat." He gave Tavo an even look.

"Okay. I hear you." Amusement replaced the edge in his voice. "Was this the big date that ramped both of you into a tailspin?"

"Yes," Rory couldn't resist crowing a little. "Things are progressing quite well."

A smile played about Tavo's lips. "Glad to hear it. Guess the massage helped, huh?"

Anger flared, closing Rory's throat. The anger he hadn't known existed. Of all the busybody things to say. "Stay in your lane, dude," he said through tight lips.

Tavo merely gazed at him, not budging. Finally, he turned, throwing the words over his shoulder as he headed back to the patrol car. "If you want to keep this gal, you need to keep your word."

Seated across from Jesse, Vi tried not to fidget. He'd sent a text earlier asking her to stop by. She hoped the meeting classified as a follow-up about her schedule. Or had he decided to let her go? An MT with hands not up to par wasn't good for business. What if she couldn't work full-time? Would he still want her on staff? *Breathe.* The windowless room frayed every nerve ending she possessed.

Jesse turned from his computer screen. Black wavy hair curled beneath a red Peeps' baseball cap. His dark eyes pierced hers. Many Peeps' employees feared him. His intensity could be a bit much, yet he'd never been moody with her.

"Have you enjoyed your time off?" Jesse arrowed straight to the point. One thing she appreciated about him. Usually.

Vi crossed her legs, then crossed them the other way. "Yes. Thank you. I needed it."

"Are you ready to take on afternoons again?"

"I can." *Oh, dear. Not what she wanted to say.*

"But deep down, you don't want to." Jesse supplied what Vi couldn't bring herself to admit. No wonder people were afraid of him. She silently chalked one up for his mind-reading skills. Scrubbing his jaw, he gazed at her.

Her feet wiggled, making her insides do a shake, rattle, and roll number.

"I have an idea. If you hate it, I need you to say so," Jesse said.

Vi bit her lip. He'd decided to let her go.

"What if you continue to do morning massages, but spend your afternoons teaching and training others to do massage?"

As Vi's mind wrapped around his words, calm invaded her body. She quit toying with her braid and leaned forward. "How so?"

Jesse's eyes gleamed. "We grow and develop a massage school on the premises. The teaching angle would bring in new members, and we'd get to cherry-pick the best MT candidates. The numbers look promising. We have the room, and Peeps would gain regional exposure."

Vi's brows knit as she considered his proposal. Future MTs could train at Peeps and then take their skills back to smaller towns. Contrary to cutting her loose, he was giving her a new direction. "I love the idea, Jess."

"Okay. How about you investigate what courses you'll need to become a licensed instructor and bring me a cost breakdown? We'll discuss salary too. If you're serious about taking it on, credentials matter." He eyed her carefully. "How are your hands?"

Vi flexed her fingers. "They're doing so much better, I forgot they hurt." Oops. TMI.

"Good. It's what I hoped would happen." He chuckled. "If I could clone you … For now, keep your afternoon schedule divvied up between the other MTs and continue with mornings only. I have a new hire or two lined up to keep from being spread too thin. In a couple of weeks, I want you to present cost info and a working schematic."

"I'll have it ready." This fresh spin on massage excited her. "Thanks, Jesse."

IN THE DELI, Rory's lips twitched. Vi flipped her thick braid over her shoulder, punctuating the air with her hands. He drank in her enthusiasm about the meeting with Jesse. He'd set up this working date because he missed her, not because he had major house-related business to discuss. His breathing hitched as she wound her purple shawl around her shoulders. The day she fell into the cistern, they had let Thunder sniff the shawl, hoping Vi's scent would lead them to her whereabouts.

The day Rory's world narrowed into one desire—Vi.

He focused on her words. "How could Jesse have known? I didn't know myself. A nameless dread circled whenever I considered a full massage schedule." Her pretty face clouded. "You didn't talk to him, did you?"

Rory held up his hands. "Nothing from me."

The yeasty aroma of fresh bread drifted toward them. A group of women attired in workout gear chattered as they waited in the deli line.

Vi stared at him a moment longer, her bottom lip poking out. "Okay. Where's this list I need to look at?" An orange appeared from her pocket, and her thumb pierced the stem end.

Rory handed her a folder. Vi absently held a piece of orange toward him as she perused the list, then scrunched her face. "So far, I can't make heads or tails of it. Help?"

He took the slice and turned the paper sideways. "This column is what you need to pick out." He pointed down the line and explained the construction terms. "Valiant carries a decent selection of everything on the list except for granite. Unfortunately, our one granite store is way too proud of its stock. You can get it for less and better variety in San Antonio." He popped the orange offering in his mouth.

Vi's eyes trained on him. "Granite. We're talking kitchen and bathroom counters?" She nodded, proud of her newfound knowledge. "It's an important item. I'm up for a trip to San Antonio. How about you?"

Rory blinked. "Today?" He did a quick mental review of his tasks. "Let me check with Paige." It only took a minute to verify. Nothing that couldn't wait until tomorrow. "Are you game for a day trip on such short notice?"

"I'll need to stop by the house and take Cyrus for a walk before we go, but I'm done for the morning. When will we get back?"

"Couple hours over and back. An hour at the granite store." An idea occurred to him. "We could have dinner on the Riverwalk." He held his breath.

An emotion Rory couldn't define lurked in the depths of Vi's eyes. A country-western love song floated from the speakers upstairs, reminiscent of the music they'd danced to at the gala. When Vi had melted against his shoulder. She wore the same intoxicating perfume today. His senses bulged from overload. He hoped their togetherness affected her the way it did him.

"I'd love it." He barely heard the soft words. She stacked the lists together and rallied. "We'd better get cracking if we want to get back at a decent hour. Meet you at Paige's?"

They set a time, and Rory watched her retreat. Her curvy little figure raised the hair on his arms. Much as he appreciated her sweet physical attributes, his desire entailed a much deeper connection. He wanted to belong to this woman for the rest of his life.

Vi's forlorn behavior after the gala suggested something else threatened future progress. Rory intended to find out what it was.

A COLD FRONT MOVED IN, transforming the blue sky into ominous gray clouds. Not a great day for an outside jaunt, but Vi didn't care. She shivered and stuffed her hands into her coat pockets, glad she'd grabbed the matching turquoise tam. Rory trailed behind her, looking dapper in a heavy coat and scarf. He gazed at the showcase of huge vertical slabs of granite resting in sturdy racks.

Fighting the blustery wind, she quickly passed the two-tone pieces. Too drab. Spotting a multicolored slab on the far end, she stumped to the end of the row. The open-ended boot turned her toes into ice cubes. She chewed her lip, studying the gray and orange blend with speckles of black and swathes of pink. It would work well in her new kitchen. The smooth surface glittered with a golden sheen.

"Is this one in my price range?"

Rory leaned between the slabs to cipher notations at the top right corner. "I think so. We can double-check at the desk." He flashed her a smile. "Vivid colors."

"Let me do one last look-through." She toured the yard, scurrying past the remaining rows. An especially heavy gust impeded her progress. She held onto her hat and circled back to Rory. "Nope. The vivid one wins."

His wide-eyed look of surprise pleased her. Vi smugly took his arm. "Let's go inside. I'm getting blown away."

Once Rory confirmed the price and discussed the details with the store rep, they hastened back to the car. He pushed the ignition button, allowing warm air to blow through the vents. "I wish all my clients made up their minds as fast as you do."

"The color palette talked to me." Vi lifted a shoulder as if her quick choice had been easy. "Several ways to go with decorating schemes. Besides, it's cold out there." She held her hands to the vents. Sensation slowly returned to her fingers.

Rory blew on his hands. "You still up for the Riverwalk? It'll be chilly, but it's sheltered from the worst of the wind. We can eat inside."

"Yes. We can snuggle like lovers do." She gasped. Why did *those* words pop out of her mouth?

Rory's eyebrows climbed up his forehead, and a smile played about his lips. "Are we lovers, Red?"

She pressed her fingers to her mouth. "That came out wrong." Her skin prickled with too much heat.

Grinning broadly, he leaned over, planting a smooch on her forehead. "You're adorable."

Rory listened to his phone's GPS navigate directions as he drove to the Riverwalk. Vi peered at the assortment of tall buildings from the freeways. Brick office buildings nestled side-by-side with sleek black ones, all grand and imposing. Fatigue would be her constant companion if she lived amid such congestion—no place for her soul to find rest.

Vi stifled a giggle when Rory argued with the GPS and missed a turn. They eventually arrived at their destination and parked in a vast garage. Traffic noise decreased as they wound down the stairs to the river. The wind died to a whisper.

The dark, mysterious river snaked through the heart of the city. Sidewalks with colorful cafes lined the green water. Gnarly oaks formed picturesque rest stations. Wide, flat boats with rails and seating glided both ways. Bundled passengers gazed at the sights.

Rory checked his phone. "It's a little early for dinner. Want to take a stroll or do a boat tour?"

Mesmerized by the quaint setting, she murmured, "Let's walk."

She slid her arm through the crook of his elbow, and they strolled along the uneven sidewalks. Small bands played music, and restaurant vendors called out their daily specials. Diverse cuisine aromas woke her stomach.

Vi's grip loosened on the problems surrounding a relationship with Rory. Couldn't she enjoy his company while it lasted? Her internal alarms should have been clamoring loudly over how much she cared for this man. Instead, she was sliding right into the flame, not caring if she got burned.

CHAPTER THIRTY-THREE

Noise from the streets above dwindled to mere echoes as Rory and Vi meandered into an underground tunnel. Light appeared on either end, but it was deserted.

They slowly drifted to one side of the tunnel, their compass a hair off course. When her shoulder brushed the stone wall, Rory stopped, mischief streaking across his features. "This is the scene where lovers kiss."

Vi couldn't quite manage the fierce frown she intended. "What's it got to do with us?"

His eyes twinkled. "Kiss me?" He stood with his hands in his pockets, impossibly good-looking. A foresty scent emanated from him. Sharp. Fresh. Enticing.

"Are you asking?" she teased, remembering their conversation from before. She traced her fingers down the chevron pattern on the twin columns of his scarf, wrapped her hands around the fabric, and pulled. The gentle pressure on his neck forced him a tad closer.

Rory's gaze stayed on her. Flickers of longing pooled in the depths of his eyes. "Are you saying yes?"

Indecisiveness tore at Vi. Her deep, ongoing ache of regret had receded. She was only conscious of Rory. His sweetness. Still mute, she rolled her hands again around the scarf ends, tugging him closer. He put his hands on her waist and snugged her to him. She closed her eyes as his lips met hers. In no hurry, he kissed her thoroughly. His gentle touch made her feel safe and cherished. Finally, he pulled away and took a deep breath. She tingled with warmth.

"I can't get enough of you, Red."

Well, that makes two of us. She nuzzled his beard, planting a tiny kiss on his throat. His soft groan vibrated under her lips. Rory tucked her into his chest and hugged her until the fear nipping at her soul slunk away. Slate eyes soft, he kissed the tip of her nose, then sighed. "Are you hungry? If we stick around here, I'm going to eat you for dinner." He held her slightly away from him. "We'd better walk and talk about restaurants."

In a daze, Vi took the hand Rory offered, and he led her back the way they came. When she could talk again, they narrowed the myriad of culinary options to Italian.

The bright room had sketches of the Old Country scattered about the red brick walls.

Seated in a corner booth, Rory paused in giving their food order to the server and asked, "I recommend the house tea. Want to try a glass?"

"Is the tea flavor super-strong?" Vi didn't usually care for tea.

"More fruity. And I chase everything with coffee."

Her lips twisted to one side. "Okay. I'll try it ... once."

When the server departed, Rory smiled at her. "You chose a beautiful slab of granite."

Vi's thoughts slowly came around to the present. "Thank you for helping me find a good price. What do you recommend for cabinet colors?"

He didn't hesitate. "White paint and stained wood are the classics. Black and gray are trending. Other colors come and go."

When the server brought their drinks, Vi tested hers with a tiny sip. "Oh, it's good. Sweet."

"Trust me, Vi. I make it my business to know your preferences." Rory waggled his eyebrows.

Did he, now? She giggled. "What am I going to do with you?"

His gaze bored into her. "Keep me."

The air crackled with tension at the serious turn his words had taken. An imp of fear scurried back into Vi's heart. A tray clattered in the kitchen, and laughter rang out from a large table in the corner.

As she rubbed at a water spot on the table, Rory covered her hand with his. "Tell me more about Jesse's massage school idea."

Vi launched into the subject, relieved to set aside the status of their relationship. Once she wound down, he asked questions, confirming he cared about her opinion.

"Haven't you and Jesse discussed this before?" She drew a finger down the condensation on the glass. It seemed odd he would hear it from her and not from Jesse.

"Not yet. We meet officially once a month to discuss new projects, but Jesse's a whiz at expanding day-to-day operations. When members into elite performance needed their own space, he researched the idea and had me draw up plans to make it happen

"Besides, he wants to protect an important asset." Rory gave her a droll look. "You are the asset, Vi. He knows I'll go along with whatever will make your massage world easier."

"Not working every afternoon helps my hands and my comfort level."

Rory pierced her with a look. "If I had my way, Vi, you would only massage women."

She frowned. "Why?"

His eyes turned to gray chips. "I know how guys think."

"Yeah." She drew the word out as Curtis's vulgar suggestions flashed through her mind. "Most come in for pain relief. Tavo is a prime example. He's asleep within the first ten minutes."

The hard set of Rory's face cleared. "Okay. Chief is all about not hurting." Then he scowled. "What about Silas?"

Vi didn't care for where this was headed. "The jury's still out on Silas. What about *your* massage? We had a deal."

"I'm good with that," he snapped.

She gazed at him evenly. "I keep hitting a nerve here. Want to tell me why?"

Rory didn't look at her. The silence broke when a server set a tray next to them. Another person lowered steaming dishes onto the table.

Vi didn't realize how hungry she was until the fragrance of chicken parm tickled her nose. The cheesy chicken scent made her mouth water.

Rory gazed at his pizza with appreciation and took her hand. "Let's pray."

After saying grace, Vi forked a bite of chicken and shut her eyes, savoring the warmth and flavor of the blended ingredients.

The subject of massage didn't come up again.

After dinner, Rory took a swallow of coffee, made a face, then called for the ticket. They shrugged into their coats and carried boxes of leftovers.

"You ready to brave the wind?" Rory held her hand as they climbed the stairs to the street.

Sleepy from the cold weather, Vi dozed on the way back to

Valiant. The bittersweet refrain of Trisha Yearwood's "How Do I Live" woke her. The same song they had danced to at the gala.

Rory's hand stole over hers. "You recognize it too? They're playing our song."

Not wanting to think about "their" song, she sat up, attempting to smooth her rumpled tam and sweater.

"Where are we?" The take-home boxes still whispered the ambiance of their time together. She tucked away the lovely memories of their stroll and dinner. The steady hum of tires whooshed on the highway.

Eyes on the road, Rory squeezed her hand. "Almost home. Not long now."

Thirty minutes later, they pulled into the townhouse drive. Vi couldn't believe he'd talked her into coffee at his place, but he'd promised to behave and not hound her for any more kisses. His words.

A cup of his cinnamon brew would be a pleasant way to end their perfect day. Maybe she could get him to open up about the massage issue.

The wind brisk, they wasted no time gathering food cartons and getting to the door.

"Maybe one smooch." Rory teased, his hand on the small of her back.

"Rory, your kisses are to die for, but you said—" Vi stepped inside, then sputtered to a stop.

"Babe, we don't have to kiss if—" He bumped into her.

An apparition floated up from Rory's terrible couch. Vi stared at her. Medium height with a mass of tousled hair, her outfit accentuated every curve. Full red lips pouted. The mean girl from the gala.

"What are you doing here, Stella?" Rory sounded strangled.

"This place is as much mine as it is yours, Rory." Stella's low, sultry words aired a challenge.

"No. It's. Not. You need to leave."

Vi's mouth hung open. She'd never heard him use such a harsh, uncompromising tone. Not when Silas hugged her. Not when a team member pressed his alpha button at powerlifting practice. An army of fears slammed into her gut.

Rory's face flushed cherry red. "This is not how she's making it look, Vi."

"Of course it is!" Stella's face flared with anger, then her features smoothed as if nothing had happened. A short dry bark issued from her throat. "I can see you're in play mode." She tossed a haughty glance toward Vi. "A redheaded *girl?* How ... high schoolish."

"Out, Stella. Now." Rory gritted out each word.

Stella sashayed around the coffee table, hip-action on full display. Vi didn't miss the look of contempt directed at her.

"Don't believe a word he says, dear. He does this ... often." She slithered to the door. Vi could have sworn she heard a hiss.

RORY WANTED TO KICK SOMETHING. Vi looked shell-shocked. The foam carton crumpled under the pressure of his hand. He set it aside. On auto-pilot, he removed his coat and scarf.

He turned to Vi and took her carton, stacking it next to his. Marinara sauce dribbled onto the counter.

Ignoring it, he led Vi to the couch and helped her out of her coat. She sat, still looking dazed.

Troubled blue eyes riveted on him. "What was she doing here, Rory?"

He heaved a weary sigh and sat next to her. "I don't know. She showed up at the gala, but we didn't speak. Before then, I hadn't seen her since we broke up."

"How did she get into your house?" Her hollow voice tore at him.

Rory savagely rubbed his beard. "She must have a key I didn't know about. I'll have to get the locks changed. I had no idea ..."

"She did this?" Vi motioned around the room.

"Yes. Let me make coffee. Ask me anything you want. Anything."

He hurried into the kitchen and grabbed the coffee package and filter. Twinges of pain fluttered around his head from lack of caffeine. His leg throbbed from the cold weather. Worst of all, his heart ached. Why had Stella chosen this night to make her vitriolic presence known?

Months had passed since their breakup. Rory had dared to hope she'd moved on. He should have guessed she wouldn't let it go—especially after the cutthroat glares she'd given him at the gala. When the aromatic brew dripped, he inhaled a calming breath.

Vi wandered in, stashing the food cartons in his fridge. She found paper towels and cleaned up the counter spill, then retreated to the living area again.

His foot tapped with the quick drip of coffee into the pot. As soon as humanly possible, he fixed two cups and returned to the couch where Vi sat with a glum expression. She accepted a cup, blowing on the hot liquid before taking a sip. They sat in silence, processing what had happened.

Swiveling to face him, Vi grimaced. "What made her think she could simply walk in?"

Rory circled the rim of his cup with a finger, choosing his words carefully. "I have never said anything to make it okay. I made it crystal-clear we were done, and now she's—" The idea that she'd come back made his head hurt. He willed Vi to understand. "The breakup wasn't her idea. The only thing she hates more is not getting her way."

"Were you intimate?"

The swallow of coffee Rory had taken threatened to come back up. Vi's bluntness astonished him. "No. I'd moved in with Jesse while she decimated this place." His brows raised at her look of relief. "I knew it would break Jesse's trust if I didn't stay straight." He gazed at her miserably. "I don't deserve any gold stars, Vi. If not for Jesse's tough questions, it could have easily gone the other way."

Vi's sapphire eyes never wavered. "Stella knows it."

She placed her coffee mug on the table. "I get you didn't see this coming, but I'm fresh out of sympathy. I need space. Please take me home."

Words of protest formed on Rory's tongue. He wanted Vi to stay, but her response wasn't surprising. A month ago, she would have bolted without bothering to hear an explanation. The tiny bit of progress brought a pea-sized glimmer of encouragement.

Stella had left a sour taste in both their mouths.

HOURS LATER, Rory couldn't get comfortable. His mattress resembled a bag of rocks. A sigh escaped. The bed had nothing to do with it.

Earlier, when he'd walked Vi to the door, she'd submitted to his hug with the emotion of a board. Their warm, vibrant afternoon had been replaced with distance and preoccupation. She'd effectively shut him out. How could he mend this rift?

He gripped his phone and texted.

Are you awake?

His screen eventually shut off.

CHAPTER THIRTY-FOUR

"Cyrus, down!" Vi issued a sharp command as they prepped for the next phase of an assailant scenario. Bright sunshine tamed the nippy lake air.

The dog rumbled a protest as he sat.

Vi handed the leash to Silas, then he walked with Cyrus to the boardwalk. Another person, a K9 officer dressed in protective gear, hid behind the broad trunk of an oak tree. Luis had instructed them through the drill. Now they would practice in earnest.

Vi felt eyes watching her ever since the night Rory pulled a gun on the strange men in her house. When she'd mentioned it to Silas, he'd insisted on calling a friend from the police force. She'd rather have run her concerns by Rory. However, it was safer for her heart not to have him around so much.

Silas lifted his arm, signaling they were ready to begin. Luis stealthily zigzagged through scraggly bushes, then darted toward Vi on the bridge. Cyrus barked, lunging on the leash, though Luis elicited little noise. Silas released the leash. The dog bounded onto the bridge, snarling with menace. Luis reached to grab Vi. Cyrus bared his teeth and attacked, clamping onto the protective gear. Luis danced about, trying to disengage the large black dog. Straining, he lifted the dog in the air, but Cyrus refused to back off.

"Cyrus, down!" Vi issued a sharp command. The dog obeyed most unhappily.

Luis stood with a hand on his hip, breathing hard.

Vi retrieved a small treat from her jacket pocket and offered it to Cyrus. "Good boy."

They did another couple of rounds, and then Silas crossed the bridge to meet them. The wind whipped his shaggy blonde hair. "He knows what to do, Vi."

Luis nodded. "You've got a great dog there, ma'am. Whoever trained him knew what they were doing. You have every right to feel safe when he's with you. Feel free to call the next time he needs practice. Or Silas can borrow my gear—we'll let him be the bite target next time." Luis grinned, adjusting his baseball cap over a high-tight military cut. "I've got to get back." He shucked off the heavy jacket and pivoted toward the house.

Cyrus uttered a low growl.

"That's enough, Cyrus. Thanks, Luis." Vi shaded her eyes as the man jogged to his green pickup in the parking area. Rory had promised to fix the crumbly concrete and weed patches into a smooth driveway the day they'd pored over spreadsheets and schematics. It seemed eons ago.

Silas was staring at her when she looked back. "You good?"

"Yeah. I feel better now. Cyrus's teeth are nothing to mess with." She ruffled the fur between the dog's ears, then headed to the house.

Silas fell in step with her. Harry the goose honked but kept to the other side of the lake. Vi's lips curved. Ever since Cyrus came on the scene, Harry had kept his distance.

Green turtles sunned on the bank in a cluster. An azure sky peeked between puffy white clouds. The splendid day, time with Cyrus, the massage project—if only she could concentrate on her blessings. Instead, thoughts of leaving Valiant bombarded her mind, stealing any measure of peace.

She spied Silas's curious look at the house. "Do you want to see the inside? I think we can tiptoe around the painters."

He nodded. "Been a while since I've seen a remodel."

Vi opened the door and sniffed tentatively. Her nose and throat preferred the fresh paint smell over chalky sheetrock. "Come see. Rory designed a bigger kitchen with an island. It's my favorite part." She traipsed around the scaffolding. The painters were in the backyard, washing their equipment.

"You enjoy cooking?" Silas gazed around the new construction.

Her bottom lip stuck out. "At times. A beautiful kitchen helps."

"Nice. I'm glad you have this place."

Boots tromped on the porch. Cyrus dropped his toy, barking savagely. Rory stood in the doorway, a thunderstorm brewing on his face.

"Hey, Spence. Checking out your handiwork," Silas said easily. An invisible charge zinged around the room.

Rory's chin lifted. "Didn't know you were interested—in kitchens." Silas didn't respond but wandered next to the sinks, peering at the newly installed granite.

Vi tamped down the baffling little dance her pulse did at the sight of Rory. He wouldn't agree with her decision, but she simply had to get away from Valiant to sort out her feelings. This house used to be her happy place, only now everything reminded her of Rory. He said he loved her. She wasn't convinced her heart could take the risk. Between the date with Melissa and his ex-girlfriend, Vi didn't know where she fit.

Despite all his talk about being a safe place, the man wouldn't even commit to a simple massage.

Once Silas strolled down the hall, Rory turned to her. "What's he doing here?"

"I invited him." Vi's temper started to rise. Why did it have to be this way? She could hang out all day long with Silas and feel nothing. Rory had her stirred up and aggravated in under five minutes.

His eyes sparked. "You're avoiding me."

Cyrus growled at the challenge in Rory's voice.

"Down, Cyrus." Rory didn't pose a physical danger. *Only to her heart.* "I told you I needed space." She shivered in the cold air.

"Three days ago." He stepped closer, running his hands down her arms. Warmth flowed from his fingers. "Talk to me, Red."

She dared not look at him until he lifted her chin with his thumb. One brief glimpse at those inviting lips, and she squeezed her eyes shut.

"Nothing wrong with wanting a kiss, Vi." Rory's breath puffed onto her cheeks.

She turned her head. The chilly air snaked around her, gripping her tight. "I'm, uh, going to Houston."

He stood so close she felt him stiffen. "For how long? Why are you acting this way? Is it Stella?"

Vi looked back at him, unable to say a word. She hadn't been kidding with her "not good at sharing" line to Melissa. The Stella encounter had whipped her into a lather of jealousy and distrust. From there, doubt had gained a stronghold. If Vi told him about her past, he'd freak for sure. She couldn't bear being on the receiving end of the reaction Rory had to Stella.

Vi took a step back. Better to stay out of reach. His powerful arms and fiery lips would only ignite a desire for more.

More had never been the long-term option. Not with all her baggage. Vi wished they'd never kissed. Then she wouldn't miss it.

"You'll lock up?" Without waiting for an answer, she said, "Cyrus, come." Vi forced her feet to move. When the dog rose and shook, the residue clinging to him flew everywhere.

AFTER VI LEFT, Rory adjusted his weight on an upturned paint bucket. Uncomfortable, but his legs thanked him. Regular stretching only provided short-term relief. He needed a new solution. Frigid air penetrated his body, trailing down his limbs. Was Vi still upset about Stella? This seemed deeper. Whatever the issue, her going to Houston wouldn't help. His one experience with Tru Marshall had made it clear she'd tuck Vi under her wing in a heartbeat, but it would be more for herself than for Vi.

A casual whistle came from the hallway, then Silas appeared. A dark look lined his craggy features. Rory had forgotten all about the guy.

Rory rose, ignoring the ache in his leg. "You done looking? I need to lock up."

"You need to lock up, all right." Silas's shoulders were bunched with tension.

"What does that mean?" Rory asked. Silas's interference aggravated him.

His eyes mere slits, Silas observed him for a long moment before he spoke. "She's a sweet little gal. You better quit bumbling around before—"

"Before what?" Rory gave back a hard stare.

"Before I step in and fix it." Silas moved to the door without a sound.

A white ball of anger shot through Rory. "You leave Vi alone!"

BACK AT HIS TOWNHOUSE, Rory swung the fridge door shut with more force than necessary. No food. Unless leftovers from the Italian place counted, but he couldn't bring himself to revisit their magical day. He'd break a tooth on the rock-hard pizza crust.

He pulled his phone out and texted Jesse.

You got anything to eat?

Seconds later, his phone dinged.

You're in luck. Mac and cheese on the stove.

Rory stared at his phone. Hunger warred with his desire to avoid any updates Jesse would demand. One petite redhead remained a particularly sore spot.

No way he could dodge. Jesse knew him too well.

Hunger won. Minutes later, he stood at Jesse's stove, dishing up a bowl of creamy pasta. His mouth watered at the golden sauce. "Why aren't you with Brenna?"

Jesse poured a glass of chocolate milk. "Want one?" Without waiting for an answer, he retrieved another glass from the cabinet. "Brenna took her brother to a movie. I got an invite but passed so they could have sibling time."

They moved to the living area with their food and drink. Jesse chose the large recliner, so Rory kicked back on the couch. Jesse offered a blessing, and they ate in silence.

Setting his empty bowl on the coffee table, Rory stretched. "Your mac and cheese always hits the spot."

"One of my few cooking accomplishments. What's bugging you?"

Rory wasn't ready to talk about it. "Why aren't you and Brenna married yet?"

Jesse gazed at him, then shrugged. "Once I proposed, we talked about setting a date. I preferred the ASAP option, but she insisted we wait."

"Well, that begs the question." Rory leaned forward, fingers steepled, and rubbed his thumbs.

Jesse made a noise between a chuckle and a huff. "*Mm-hmm*. The woman of my dreams claimed I had a horrible temper."

Despite his anguish, Rory grinned broadly. "Kudos for her."

"Oh, it gets better." Jesse's mouth quirked. "Apparently, my mood fluctuations made me a miserable person to work for. She said I was incredible, but the big green guy had to go. Thankfully, she gave me time *and* the incentive to learn other responses besides anger."

"Bet you loved the incentive part."

"Ya think?" Jesse's lifted brow raised Rory's spirits. "She was so darn cute about the whole thing, and I'm nuts about her, so ... easy choice. A corner of his mouth tilted up. Your hounding paid off. The counseling sessions with Pastor Mike have been a key component. He helped me see the years of pent-up anger had formed a default button in my psyche. He assured me I could reprogram with God's help. Once I learned change was possible, I've been in overhaul mode ever since."

"So, you're on track to get married?" Rory pressed. Normally, he'd know these things. He pushed down the jealousy twinging for attention. He missed the camaraderie since Brenna came on the scene, knowing full well, he'd act the same if he had a girlfriend.

"Yep. I'm vastly improved—Brenna's words. We plan to tie

the knot in July. The first anniversary of her dumping salad on me at Cowpokes." His white teeth flashed in a grin.

Rory raised his hand for a high five. "Ecstatic for you, bud." Jesse slapped his hand. They gathered their bowls and took them to the kitchen.

Jesse spoke over the clatter of putting dishes in the dishwasher. "You didn't answer my question. What's bugging you?"

CHAPTER THIRTY-FIVE

Jesse left the kitchen and sat back down. Rory reluctantly followed. Dread over what he had to say stirred about the room. Jesse gazed at him steadily as if he had all night. Might as well get it over with. "Vi's avoiding me, and now she's taking off for Houston." He laid his head against the couch for support. "The day Vi and I went to San Antonio, Stella let herself into my townhouse. When we walked in, there she was, decking the halls in an outfit that looked like sexy pajamas."

"Ouch." Jesse's grimace would have been comical under different circumstances.

"Yeah. Vintage Stella. I had to flat-out demand she leave. Eventually, she did—but not before spewing pure fiction about our time together."

"And Vi heard it all." Jesse's eyes glimmered with sympathy. "Small wonder she's avoiding you."

Rory winced at the blunt assessment. "Vi understood I got blindsided. We talked about it"—He held his thumb and index finger a hairsbreadth apart—"this much. Then she shut down and wanted me to take her home. We had such a fantastic day, but now she's running."

"Do you blame her?" Jesse's tone suggested he didn't. "Stella's a hard pill to swallow. Vi needs time."

"It's been three days. I went by Vi's house this afternoon to check on the painters. She was giving Silas a tour. Once she left, the guy had the gall to say he'd take over if I don't fix things. We used to hang out. Now he's a real jerk."

A knowing look passed over Jesse's features. "Silas wants to get a rise out of you."

Rory's mind kept circling back. "Jess, our pre-date, and the charity gala were great. And we had an awesome time in San Antonio. Vi's idea. She won't let me love her."

Jesse's eyes narrowed with suspicion. "Have you signed up for the massage she bought for you?"

"I've been busy." The idea of going through the torture of a massage still rankled.

"And you can't figure out what's wrong?"

"Jess, a massage will not fix everything."

"It'd be a good start. I heard what transpired on Christmas Eve. She agreed to a date, and you agreed to a massage. You got your sweet end of the deal and more, but what about Vi?"

Rory blinked. It couldn't be that simple.

"And I'll bet you haven't told her one iota about your life-changing accident." Jesse's eyes pressured him.

"Why does it matter?"

"Dude!" Jesse shook his head in disbelief. "She wants to know all about you. If Brenna asks me about Afghanistan or anything else, I tell her. Most of the time, I leave out the brutal details, but she gets the gist. She says it helps her understand why I overreact." His jaw flexed.

"Transparency is overrated." Rory brushed the idea aside. "What I know is Vi won't let me love her."

Jesse's posture morphed from relaxed to ramrod straight. "She's always been standoffish. You won't let *her* love you either." He held up a finger. "You say you're too busy for a massage, but we both know that's bull." He added another finger. "She's probably clueless why you don't have a foot because you ignore all inquiries on the subject. Vi is *not* the only one who doesn't let people get close."

Desperately wanting to argue, Rory rolled his head from side to side. Jesse's observations couldn't be accurate. Could they?

Jesse headed to the kitchen. "Wanna stay and watch a movie? I need more time to knock sense into your thick skull."

Rory's options had vanished. His lonely townhouse held no appeal.

He sauntered into the kitchen after Jesse. "Okay, but no more talk about a massage. And I'm picking the movie."

Jesse's face could have carved stone. "How about *Apollo 13*? Because if Vi goes to Houston, *we* have a problem."

VI SAT on a wrought-iron bench on the estate where Mom and Rodney lived, facing a beautiful rose garden. Roses in every hue rioted over the mounds, filling the air with a sweet, flowery fragrance. Daddy's tablet lay in her lap. The winding path around the beds reminded her of home. Home, Vi thought dully. The place Rory had filled with his magnetic presence. Cyrus loped up with a stick between his teeth. She took it from him and tossed it again. Streaky white clouds dotted the sky. She scrunched her nose, peering at the ladybug on her sleeve.

Jesse needed a text from her. He wouldn't have a problem with her taking vacation time—she had accrued tons of it. Then what? Leaving Valiant hadn't helped her think more clearly. If anything, depression was gaining the upper hand. She shook her head, trying to clear the haze in her mind.

Paige deserved an update as well, though she'd been kind about not asking questions. Waving the tiny red bug away, Vi twisted her hair into a long coil, securing it with a grimace. The makeshift do imitated her emotional state. Both could unravel at any moment. Her universe had tilted, and she couldn't find her balance.

Vi had dreamed about Daddy last night, the first time since he'd passed. He'd sported a red and black checkered shirt and his favorite pair of jeans, worn to threads at the knees. Black cowboy boots. And his pipe. The smell of tobacco still lingered in her mind—or would it be her nose? Could you dream a smell? She didn't know.

Cyrus bounded back, and she lobbed the stick again. At least the dog had energy. Vi's movements were languid. Daddy talked to her in the dream. Earnestly. His lips moved, and his expressive eyes conveyed the importance of his message, but she couldn't hear him.

If only Daddy could tell her what to do. "Lord, help me. I can't see my way to Valiant—not with Rory everywhere I go. But I can't stay here either. Can I? Could I make any kind of life for myself here—apart from Mother?"

She expelled a deep breath and opened the tablet. Her lovely dates with Rory had distracted her from Dad's letters. No, she corrected herself. Rory was a fun, hunky distraction all by himself. He occupied every moment of her thought life, her carefully arranged schedule, and even her sleep.

A few clicks later, she pulled up a file.

Dearest Red,

This is another hard one. We've never talked about it, but I need to get it off my chest. You were so lost in grief, you couldn't make much sense of things at the time. Talking about it then wouldn't have helped.

In high school, you went through a hard spell. The hurt over that sorry-no-good's abuse spilled out, and you were mad at the whole world. It didn't make me love you less though—if anything, I loved you more.

Vi looked away from the screen into the bright sunlight, her eyes already moist. Daddy hadn't been joking about this letter being a hard one.

I'd hoped you could keep your baby, but your mom wouldn't budge. To this day, I don't know what we could have done different. You were so sick and grieving so bad, I thought we were going to lose you. Finally, Tru let you come live with me. You had a lot of nightmares. When you were little, I'd rub your back until you calmed down. Once you were asleep, I'd go out on the porch and cry. I begged God over and over to fix what had been broken inside you. One night I got real upset. You were having a rough time of it, and I went down the lake so's you wouldn't hear me. I ain't no preacher—ain't got no spiritual guns. I just loved you so much, it made me spittin' mad. I started yelling and told the devil he couldn't have you. All night long, I hollered at him to stand down. Then I told God He had to save you and heal your broken heart, cause I couldn't do it.

I remember walking up to the house. The sky had pinked, and I was pretty worn out and sleepy.

Afterward, though, the nightmares stopped, and health-

wise, you turned a corner. When you'd gotten over the worst part, your mom came and took you back to Houston. I had no say in the matter.

I learned an important lesson that night. All the fancy prayers in the world don't amount to a hill of beans if you don't have love. I ain't bragging on myself. I loved you enough to fight about it, and I'm hoping it was enough.

Vi drew in a shuddery breath and gazed into the sky. Memories moved into her present circumstances. The reason she felt so drawn to massage—Daddy's touch had calmed and healed her. She'd wanted to die, but he'd loved her enough to fight the unseen forces swirling around her during those dark, terrible days. Now she understood why she got better.

Daddy had done what she couldn't do for herself.

CHAPTER THIRTY-SIX

Rory stood at the front door of the imposing house and rang the bell. No exaggeration when Vi said her mom had married into money. These types of houses sold in the upper millions. Suddenly, he missed his three-piece suit and tie. The gray hoodie and jeans he wore shouted country bumpkin in this opulent setting.

The door opened. Once again, the resemblance between Vi and her mother struck Rory as ironic. Eerily similar in looks. Polar opposites in their approach to life. Even now, Tru's chin had a proud lift, and her blue eyes snapped with impatience.

"Hello, Tru. It's good to see you again." Rory extended his hand.

Her eyes shot skyward, but she reluctantly took his hand. Rory hid a grin. Mama had made sure his manners could rival Emily Post's—a part of her legacy he appreciated with all his heart. He had no doubt she'd known women like Tru.

Without a word, Tru turned, her shoes clicking on the tile entry floor. Rory followed. Once they reached one of the living areas, she faced him, all claws and wary feline. "You've come to take Violet back to that godforsaken place."

Rory stared at her evenly. "God hasn't forsaken Valiant. Yes, I want Vi to come home, but it's her decision." He stuck his hands in his pockets, affecting a non-threatening air since he stood a foot taller.

Not that Tru Marshall was easily intimidated.

Tru gave him a long look, then expelled a breath in a most unladylike fashion. "Well, you showing up may be a good thing. Vi said she came to visit, but it hasn't happened. She's been far too distracted." She leveled another hard look at him, crossing her arms. "I suspect you know why."

Rory's focus had been off the last few days too. "I need to talk to her … *if* she'll see me," he finished, his heart in his throat.

"I see you know my daughter." Grudging respect laced her tone.

A tall man with a receding hairline and eyes lit with humor joined Tru, holding out a hand. "Rodney Marshall."

Glad for the reprieve, Rory shook it firmly. "Rory Spence."

Awkwardness ensued. Tru's stiff posture relented a gnat's whisker. "All right, Vi is down by the rose garden." She waved toward a large picture window that looked out on the beautiful grounds. "She's not eating. Probably not sleeping. She stares at the flowers and walks that dog." Her lip curled with distaste. "I suppose you're here to fix everything." The accusatory tone had returned.

"Tru, I'm certain these young folks can work it out." Rodney winked at Rory, much to his wife's consternation.

Rory nodded, then looked back at Tru. "I love your daughter, Mrs. Marshall."

For the briefest moment, joy crinkled her eyes before a

pouty expression took over. "All in good time, young man. I have plans ..."

Behind his wife, Rodney pointed to a side door.

Lips pressed in a line, Rory strode out the door. One problem at a time. *Lord, you haven't forsaken me either.*

THE SUN WARMED Vi's back. Cyrus barked joyously, thrusting a proverbial stick into her gloom. Strange. The dog had not yet warmed to anyone in this household unless she counted Rodney, who fed him snacks on the sly. But Rodney wouldn't seek Vi out. She swiveled on the bench, putting her hands over her brows to stave off the bright sun.

Rory.

Vi's heart raced. She'd know his gait anywhere. Now with a slight twist to one side. She could fix it. As he grew closer, she recognized the raised chin, mouth hidden between the mustache and beard. His determined look burned into her soul.

Without a word, Rory eased himself onto the bench next to her, his hands buried in the wide front hoodie pocket. He'd worn it on Thanksgiving Day—when she ran from him and fell in a hole.

Moisture filmed her eyes. She'd run away again—and he'd come after her.

He pulled a tiny orange from his pocket and offered it to her. Slowly, she took it and peeled the tough outer layer. Cyrus chased a butterfly, his shiny black coat glistening in the sunlight. Birds rustled and flew from a mesquite tree on the lake's edge. The dog chased after them. The pungent scent of citrus rubbed off on her hands.

She hesitated, then held up a quarter of the orange. Rory

accepted it without a word. When she bit into her slice, the sweet juice woke her taste buds. Suddenly ravenous, she ate the remaining slices in quick succession.

"I brought more," Rory said dryly. He pulled two more oranges out of his pocket and placed them on the bench between them.

A giggle escaped before Vi could rein it in.

"You're as beautiful as ever, Vi." Rory angled to face her. "Tell me what went wrong."

Direct as ever. She slumped and held up a hand. "I don't think talking about it will do any good."

Rory gently clasped her raised hand with one of his, then caught a tendril of hair flying across her face with his other hand and tucked it behind her ear. "You need to set aside the knee-jerk reaction. The one where you shut me out. I love you, Vi. You don't have anything to fear from me." His calm, reasonable voice steadied her, though her mind insisted on reciting the reasons she left.

Tears filled her eyes, and her breaths were shallow. This Rory guided her through the house remodel. Caring. Tender.

"Is it Stella?" His eyes searched hers. "Because I've told you any relationship we had is completely in the past. Do you believe me?"

"Yes," she said in a low voice. His reaction had made it clear enough, but the thought of him with another woman ate her insides out. The termite issue she'd paid big bucks to get rid of had nothing on her jangled emotions.

Rory continued as if not sure he believed her. "Stella and I should never have dated. I knew it, but I enjoyed the attention. It was wrong and short-sighted on my part, but I've repented. God's forgiven me. Can you? I'm not excusing my behavior." Pain lurked in the set of his jaw, his tight lips, and the crease in his forehead. "It messes with me that maybe I won't get a chance with you because of past mistakes."

Past mistakes. The words hit her with such blinding clarity she gasped. Rory reached for her hand. Weren't past mistakes the reason she kept holding him at arm's length? The reason she wouldn't date him? Because of *her* past mistakes? His relationship with Stella made her jealous. She wanted Rory so badly it scared her. Fear had caused the conflict within her heart. She had rejected him before he rejected her. Fear had driven her ill-timed trip to Houston.

She met his eyes. Those gorgeous gray eyes. "Rory, I have to tell you something." He released the light hold on her hand, and she crossed her arms. No matter what, he needed to know.

"You know I'm a safe place, Vi." The steady, encouraging words made her want to fall into his arms. If only.

Vi gulped a breath of air, then hurried to say it before she lost her nerve. "I had a baby when I was sixteen." She flushed, struggling to maintain focus.

Rory's eyes rounded with a flash of surprise, then quickly evened out again. He pried Vi's hand from her arm and held it again. "Tell me about it. I'm not going anywhere." No outrage. No accusation. Only concern and his calm presence.

Vi's back pressed against the bench. She motioned to the tablet next to her. "I read one of Daddy's letters this morning. I've always wished I could have a do-over, but his letter brought it right here." She held one hand an inch away from her face. "The abuse made me angry and rebellious. On prom night, I ... um ... made the poor decision to sleep with my boyfriend." She dispelled a breath. "Probably the reason I don't care for fancy, overblown events."

Rory rubbed her hand.

She wiped away tears. "Sorry. This subject sends me on a

crying jag. When I figured out I was pregnant and told Mom, she wanted me to have an abortion—"

A grimace shone on his features.

Vi nodded at what he didn't say. "I refused. It got so bad, I moved out and lived with my boyfriend for a few weeks." She sighed, remembering, then forced more explanation. "Another terrible decision. When I went back home, Mom insisted I give the baby up for adoption. I had pre-eclampsia—"

"What's pre—?"

"A serious condition with uncontrolled high blood pressure. Add anemia and depression to the list, and I was a mess. I wanted to keep him, only I didn't have the strength to fight Mother." She choked out the last words.

"A boy? You have a son?" Rory almost sounded excited.

Vi shook her head. "*Had* a son. I got to hold him. Then his adoptive parents took him, and I never saw him again." She met Rory's eyes, and a side of her mouth raised without mirth. "He had a chock of red hair."

In one fluid movement, Rory closed the gap, wrapping his arms around her. "Come here."

A bird sang in a nearby tree as she gripped the front of his shirt and sobbed. Even after all these years, the pain still reverberated.

"I'm sorry, Red. So sorry," he murmured into her hair. His arms comforted her. She dabbed at her eyes, trying to gain composure.

Rory released her one centimeter at a time. Sniffing, he scrubbed a hand down his face and beard.

What Vi had to do next would break her heart. She scooted away, trying to breathe around the brick in her chest. "I needed to explain so you could understand why I don't, why I don't date or do relationships. Why we can't ..." Vi fiddled with an errant curl, twisting and untwisting it around her fingers.

"You're right. I don't understand." Rory's tone could have flattened a tire. "You told me the night of our prequel date there was more to the story. I'm so glad you finally shared it." He gazed at her, eyes unwavering. "Knowing this only makes me love you more."

"How can you love me? I had a baby and gave him up for adoption. What kind of person gives her baby away?" Vi's voice rose.

Rory's eyes were soft with compassion. "Vi, my mom died when I was in high school. I was so angry and missed her so much I willingly took whatever a girl wanted to give me. But I'm not that guy anymore. And you're not a confused sixteen-year-old girl." He squinted at her through the sunlight. "How is saving your baby's life a bad thing?"

"It's not. But I wanted him and still miss him." She wiped her eyes. "I do realize at sixteen I wouldn't have been a good mother."

Rory snorted. "At sixteen, being a dad meant nothing. Not even on my radar. I would have mangled fatherhood. You were young and hurting. Sounds to me like you did the most loving thing possible. And I've been telling you six ways to Sunday I love you. You having a son doesn't change anything for me."

Vi pinched her shoulders to ease the tension in her neck. "Rory, I did everything wrong."

His head rocked from side to side. "It doesn't matter. I was doing everything right the day my foot got crushed. The only thing that makes sense is grace. God has long since covered all our sins. We don't deserve the freedom we have from past mistakes, poor decisions, and tragic accidents. You simply accept it and get on with living your life."

Shocked, she stared at him. "Daddy used to tell me the same thing. He's the one who got me to church—so I could learn about Jesus's sacrifice and how He forgave me. But the past is still a club beating me over the head whenever I think about the future."

His shoulders lifted easily. "I've been there. It gets better, but you have to fight for every inch."

For the first time in years, hope sprouted in her heart. She took a breath, surprised at the lightness of her chest. In wonder, she opened her mouth, eager to share what was happening on the inside. Then a thought occurred to her, and she closed it. Swallowing hard, she asked, "So what about us?"

There was no hesitation in Rory's answer. "You don't belong here, Vi. You need to come back to Valiant, to your house. I can't finish it without you."

Vi bit her lip. "Only the house?"

Eyes twinkling, he cupped her chin, tipping it inches away from his lips. "I need a massage too. And more hugs and kisses."

She raised a brow, forcing herself to look away from those enticing lips. "I'd almost given up on the massage. And you'll follow through?"

Rory whispered, "Not a thing wrong with my follow-through. You want a kiss?"

She shouldn't. Once Rory had time to digest what she'd told him, he would feel differently. Instead, she inclined her head the merest fraction and let his mouth claim hers. The tension plaguing her since she'd come to Houston evaporated like raindrops on a sunny day.

CHAPTER THIRTY-SEVEN

Vi's jaw dropped as she perused her schedule. Rory's signature scrawled a red-hot laser across her 11:00 slot. Oh, my. She wasn't ready for this. Only yesterday they had been in Houston. Last night he'd driven behind her all the way back to Valiant. They'd texted late into the evening, exchanging pictures of faucets, cabinets, and knobs, but he hadn't mentioned the massage again.

The texting, along with his hugs and kisses, had eased her stress about their pasts. Did Rory really love her? As if he knew the doubt would return, he'd kept her mind crammed full of accessory options ... and other things.

Now this. Her bottom lip resembled pulp. A mix of elation and dread filled her when she saw his signature on the schedule. Fixing the twist in his gait shaped up as the easy part. Far more difficult would be him under her hands for an hour. The man made her feel as if she'd only had the slightest nibble of a divine chocolate bar. Her insides were free-falling.

Stay professional. He's just a massage client.

If only.

———

RORY FIDGETED in a chair in the reception area, every fiber in his body clamoring to escape. Scribbling his name on the massage schedule proved easy-peasy compared to showing up. Never a fan of his hairy red legs to begin with, the heavy scarring raised his embarrassment to new levels. He hadn't worn a pair of shorts since he'd left the rehab facility.

Good grief, he'd have to perform gymnastics to get on the table. Would she want the prosthetic off? Sweat formed on his brow. Great. Any freshness from the shower he'd taken this morning had taken a hike. No way he could do this.

Rory rose to leave as Vi came out of the massage room.

Her steps quickened as if she'd read his thoughts, and she gripped his clammy hand.

"Glad you're here, Red." Her low, familiar voice ratcheted the anxiety down a notch.

He allowed her to lead him into the room. Now he stood way too close to her petite form. The sweet soft smell he associated with her permeated the air. The low lighting and sound of rushing water soothed him. Had he expected otherwise? Vi belonged to this world.

"Change into your shorts and ... um ... take off the prosthetic and slide under the sheets. Stay on your back. I'll return once you're comfortable." Vi slipped from the room, leaving him alone with his thoughts.

Rory's hands shook as he donned the shorts. He unfastened the artificial limb and set it aside. She'd touch and feel the thick scars covering his legs. The ugly nub. All of it. And whatever relationship they had would poof into thin air.

The façade he presented to the world was only a mask to protect himself. When people saw what lay underneath, they turned away in revulsion.

This is what you wanted, Vi.

He maneuvered onto the table and lay down. A tear rolled into his hairline.

God, help me get through this.

Vi re-entered the room. Rory barely heard her over the roar in his head.

Her upper torso barely rose above the table, but her tone was all business. "I'm going to lift the sheet from your right calf and shine my phone light on it. I'm checking for scrapes and sore spots, so I don't accidentally gouge one."

Rory managed a grunt. Vi moved slowly and lifted the sheet. She studied his leg with rapt attention. Instead of the pity he expected, thoughtfulness arrested her features. With a feathery touch, she examined the worst sore spot. "Mm. This has to hurt." Next, she moved to the nub, the premature end to his leg and foot. "Do you experience phantom pain?"

"At times." His voice croaked with emotion.

"Okay. Now I know what I'm dealing with." Her matter-of-fact attitude helped him breathe. She covered his leg. "Let's get you loosened up. Red, I need you to close your eyes and relax. You're tight as a tick."

Obediently, he shut his eyes, and she chuckled. "Now it's my turn to say, 'I'm a safe place.'"

Rory stifled a groan. She had no idea.

AN HOUR LATER, Rory woke to the pleasant sensation of no pain. The massage had lulled him into a twilight sleep of sorts. Except Vi hadn't used any meds, only her hands. *Those hands.*

At one point, he remembered her close to his ear, her low voice telling him to turn over. He must have complied because he didn't begin this journey on his stomach. The tightness had disappeared, and the constant itching had vanished.

This lovely haze could go on forever. Rory couldn't remember a blessed thing about the massage except her tender encouragement and the exquisite feel of her hands.

He reattached the prosthetic and stretched. Oh, man. His range of motion had increased. Now he understood why clients tried to break the rules with gifts, tips, and favors. The same temptation coursed through his veins.

What if Vi didn't want anything more to do with him? She'd gotten what she wanted, Was this beautiful gift the end of a deeper relationship? The thought had him reeling backward.

It would be less awkward for them both if he slipped out the back way. Rory stepped into the reception area, and his breath stalled. Vi sat in his chair, peeling an orange. Her eyes were gentle as they met his. She patted the chair next to her. An invisible force pulled him forward, and he slid into the seat. She handed him half of the small orb.

She deserved so much more than mere thanks. "I'm a new man, Red. Sorry I was so stubborn." He popped a slice of orange in his mouth, too wound up to enjoy sharing it with her or the squirt of sweet juice on his tongue. "Are we square now?"

"In your dreams."

Her dry response made his lips twitch. "What's next?"

"For starters, it's lunchtime. I need a buddy to help me drink a chocolate-peanut butter smoothie."

The desire to take her in his arms chafed at him. "Happy to manage it, Magic Hands."

On the way to the deli, Rory stopped and stared at Vi. "My leg. It's tons better, as in the limp is almost history. What did you do?"

"Your good leg overcompensated because the prosthetic doesn't fit the way it needs to. Hence the limp. Things are back in alignment now. Your hip may ache for a day or so—it was pretty far out of whack."

"You know all this in one hour?"

"Yep. Aside from getting the prosthetic looked at, regular massages will help keep things in balance." A sly smile curved her lips. "Unless you prefer an off-kilter gait ..."

His chest swelled as he tucked her arm in the crook of his elbow. "Regular massages? We need to negotiate a deal. How about you go out with me—regularly?" He playfully emphasized the last word, hoping his words weren't too much too soon.

A deer-in-the-headlights look skimmed her face before she pasted on a smile. "Slow down, cowboy."

Whatever you want.

When they entered the deli, Jesse waved, and Brenna pointed to the two empty chairs at their table. Rory ordered their food, and they joined them.

"What's up, guys?" Jesse asked.

"I had a massage from the most gorgeous lady on the planet." Rory gave a smug grin.

Mischief lit Jesse's eyes. "Good goin' bud. You out of the doghouse?"

Rory stroked his beard, appearing to think. "She's already informed me we're not square yet."

"Oooh, you go, girl!" Brenna gave her a knowing look. "Seriously, I don't know what I'd do without Vi's hands. After several runs, my legs start following her around."

Vi smiled, sipping her smoothie. Rory resisted the urge to run his thumb across her bottom lip to catch a chocolate drip.

Jesse slid half of his second sandwich onto Brenna's plate. When she made a face, he whispered in her ear. She picked up the half Jesse had given her, a smile playing about her lips.

A look of satisfaction crossed Jesse's features, but he said nothing.

Rory observed the quiet exchange with interest. *Nice going, Jess.* He'd find out the details later. Maybe he could apply a nugget of wisdom to his relationship with Vi—instead of tripping into every pothole along the way.

They chatted until Brenna checked her phone. "Gotta run. Ha! Did everybody get the pun? Reports await me." She grinned. "My boss insists on absolute perfection."

A wry note arched Jesse's brow. "Peeps definitely has an on-site perfectionist." He looked at Rory and Vi and stage-whispered, "And it's not me. She's the one who obsesses over every little detail."

Brenna and Jesse left, laughing and poking each other.

Rory watched their retreat and turned to Vi. "I'm green with envy."

"Peanut-butter-and-jealous here too," Vi said, then swallowed the dregs from her cup.

Desire pinched past Rory's resolve to take it slow. He leaned close, inhaling the massage room fragrance still in her hair. "We could do the couple's thing."

"You're a marvelous elixir, Rory." Vi's brows almost joined. She didn't look at him. "Tiny sips of you are all I can handle, else I'll fall flat on my face."

Suspicion tumbled through his mind, an ember rolling away from cheerful fire. Was this her diplomatic way of letting him down easy? The shards in his throat made his voice thick. "Babe, I've been falling ever since they pulled you out of the cistern. If you don't catch me, I'll splatter."

Vi's weary half-smile severed any newfound optimism

about their future. What he feared had come to pass. His marred physical appearance disgusted her.

Adding to his consternation, she brushed a kiss on his forehead and left.

It felt like goodbye.

CHAPTER THIRTY-EIGHT

At the lake, an agitated screeching noise split the air. Vi held her hands to her forehead, peering at the boardwalk. Children on the bridge? Too far away to judge size or age. Cyrus looked at her, ears pricked. He barked, then loped ahead, looking back, as if to ask, *Are you coming?* Clambering off the picnic table, she followed the dog. On the bridge, kids were throwing rocks into the water. They'd scream, pointing at the muddy bank, then scamper off and return, throwing more rocks. Vi stumped along as fast as the walking boot would allow. Harry's honk had become a noise of distress instead of his usual cadence.

Cyrus's bark brimmed with menace, and the children dashed into the scrub brush.

When Vi reached the boardwalk, her eyes scanned the area. On the bank, Harry frantically beat his feathers, but a large rock had pinned one webbed foot to the ground. Amid Cyrus's frenzied barking, she picked her way through mud patches down to the bank.

"I'm here to help, Harry." Vi's best soothing voice did little to assuage the hysterical bird. He flapped his wings and arched his long neck, attempting to dislodge his foot.

Glancing around for a stout stick to leverage the stone, Vi found nothing. If she could free him, a peck or two would be worth it. Cautiously, she closed the distance and tried to reposition the rock, but it was too heavy. Harry struggled harder.

"Cyrus, hush!" The dog's commiseration with the goose made a huge racket. She fought to think clearly. *Lord, I can't move it by myself.*

Her fingers curled under the rock, then her hands, and she lifted. Miraculously, the exposed space was enough for Harry to slide his foot out. The goose stumbled and dragged his orange foot to the water's edge. He honked and swam toward the middle of the lake, not looking back.

Vi grabbed clumps of weeds and pulled her way back to the path. As soon as she freed the goose, Cyrus stopped barking. He sat on his haunches, eyes the color of maple syrup, and watched her. All her ruminations clicked into a sad, dreary place.

Since the massage, thoughts of Rory had consumed her. Images of her fingers kneading the thick scar tissue covering his legs. Her palms palpating softness back into the nub. Her hands plying the tension out of his muscular shoulders. She'd wanted to do it forever. And now, through massage, at long last, she'd grasped Rory's character—the person who hid behind an easy grin and flirty behavior. A living, breathing champion. Brave. Determined.

And so unbearably gentle, Vi had lost her heart.

She now understood many things. Rory didn't need her. Not one whit. By his own admission, he was slow to figure out peoples' true natures. When he eventually realized her wretched state, he would swim away, taking those beautiful scars with him. She'd always have the gift of having helped him, but her newly awakened love wouldn't matter at all.

Resigned, she rose and called Cyrus. With the kids around, she didn't want him wandering. They were trespassing, but she needed to keep the dog contained. He would scare them, and they'd already shown a mean streak. This latest prank might have turned deadly if she'd not been here. Tavo should know about this.

The squatters were becoming more and more of a problem.

RORY SIPPED his coffee as he waited for his weekly meeting with Dad. A gray tinge pressed through Dad's ruddy complexion as he paced behind his office desk, talking on the phone. Yet he seemed his persistent self. He told the person on the other end to get back with him ASAP. Pressing a button on his phone, he grimaced.

"What's got you riled, Dad?"

The older man stamped around the desk. "My contractor needs to do things on my timeline, not his." He poured himself a cup of brew from the carafe.

Rory squinted, slightly mystified. "You're talking about Howell? He's good about timelines, isn't he?"

"No, you'd think it's his first rodeo." The older man threw his hands in the air. "Can't find our agenda. Okay if we wing it?"

"We don't do a written agenda." A faint alarm sounded in Rory's spirit.

"Well, must be why I can't find one." Bafflement streaked across Dad's ashy complexion.

They discussed the subdivision, then Rory shared how he and Jesse wanted to expand Peeps with the tract Dad had recently brokered the deal on. All subject to change at this early stage, but Dad seemed slow to make connections. Rory shook off the dismaying thought.

Despite lingering confusion, Dad pressed on. "As for new business, I've started negotiations on the second, larger tract of land you and Jess want for the gym. The realtor is working on the preliminaries for an offer. You guys ready to ante up again?"

They had talked of expansion since day one of their gym ownership. For weeks, Jesse had Brenna crunch the numbers for every scenario. Now on the verge of fruition, Rory felt a strange detachment from their dream. "Keep me informed, Dad. We're all in."

Rory gulped the last of his coffee and rose. "Gotta run, Dad. Need to sit in on powerlifting practice." As they walked to the door, Rory hugged him, surprised when the older man took his time disengaging.

His father's red-rimmed eyes swam with emotion. "Son, you got one of your mom's endearing qualities. She gave the best hugs in the world. You're a close second." He made shooing motions toward the door. "Out. The world waits for no man."

<hr>

WITHOUT A SHRED OF CONCENTRATION, Rory observed Tavo patiently instruct Curtis, of all people, through the steps of a deadlift. The team seemed acclimated to Tavo's leadership, even though the practice lacked its usual zip. The trash talk-slash-encouragement going back and forth between teammates seemed stilted. Rory's thoughts darkened. Probably because of the new guy.

Rory's insides chilled when Vi had strolled in minutes ago,

looking bruised and vulnerable. She'd come to break things off. His predictions were further enforced when she sat with more distance than usual between them. He tried to shake off the foreboding. Vi wasn't the type to cozy up in public.

Minutes inched by on the clock. Finally, Tavo blew the whistle. Rory strode over to offer support.

"What would you think if Curtis joined the team?" Tavo swiped his beefy biceps with a towel.

Rory's neck muscles tightened. He hated the idea. "Your team now. Do what you think needs to happen."

"Not what I asked."

The last thing Rory wanted to discuss was Curtis. Vi's troubled look had seized his attention, but Tavo could be as persistent as a dog worrying a bone. "If Curtis's size matched his mouth, he might be an asset."

"The guy has nothing. Probably why he's so cocky."

"Or maybe nothing is what he deserves." Belatedly, Rory pressed his lips together.

"So, this is you walking the walk? You're always going on about grace, but I'm not seeing it here." Tavo's eyes had narrowed to slits.

Rory glared. In high school, Tavo had been the one who kept the guys in line. The sarcasm didn't fit.

Tavo shifted his feet. "Look. I get it. The guy's rough. He'll need extra monitoring. Curtis is a follower. Isn't he better off hanging with an improved caliber of people over his usual crowd? He's hungry to fit in. Why not here?"

The impact of Tavo's words hit Rory like a bar loaded with weights. He opened his mouth, then closed it.

Flipping the towel on his shoulder, Tavo looked at Vi. Discernment creased the dimples on either side of his face. Glancing back at Rory, Tavo said, "Never mind. I got this. Your little red bird needs TLC."

Tavo noticed Vi's downcast mien too. Rory walked to where Vi now stood, looking as if she wanted to flee. Another ominous wave rolled over him at the raw emotion on her face. He shoved it aside impatiently. If she rejected him, fine. No more wading in the shallows. If she didn't want a deeper relationship, he'd deal with his broken heart later.

"Grab a cup of coffee with me?"

She managed a small nod, but her expression said otherwise.

"Good. Meet me in the deli? Or would you rather go to your place?" Rory stepped into her space, placing a hand on her shoulder.

"The deli is fine." Her voice gave nothing away.

"Okay. I'll shower and meet you there." Rory nuzzled the top of her head, holding her with firmness. He wasn't sure he could live with her decision if it didn't include him.

SITTING across from Vi in the deli, Rory drained his coffee cup, then pulled up the dregs of his mettle. Vi sipped at her tea, avoiding looking at him. He blew out a hard exhale. "Whatever is going on in your sweet little head doesn't look good."

She swept a long tress of hair away from her face, still mute.

Okay. Time to press. "What gives, Vi?" Rory didn't want to drag it out of her, but if she wanted to end their relationship, better sooner than later.

"Rory, I'm no good for you." Vi slumped into the seat, wrapping her hands around the foam cup.

He straightened in the uncomfortable seat, surprise coloring his words. "Where is this coming from?"

"You know." Her low voice rattled him, and he grasped for the likeliest straw.

"Hon, if you're talking about your son, my position hasn't changed. I still love you."

A brief flicker of hope darted through her sad blue eyes. Everything inside Rory rose to meet it, and then reality set in. She'd purposely made this about her—so it wouldn't be about his amputation. "This isn't really about your baby being adopted, is it?"

"What?" A frown pressed Vi's lips into a line.

Rory jumped in, anxious to get it over with. "You saw my scarred legs this morning during the massage. Well, what's left of them. I'm not a whole man." He jammed his trembling hands together.

Vi sucked in a breath, swooshing it out again. "Not whole?" She seemed confused. "What are you talking about?"

Defeat snaked up his spine, spilling out. "I've found out the hard way women don't want a man with scarred legs and no foot."

Her cheeks flushed. "Is this about the massage? Rory, you've got more character than any man I know. And I didn't fall in love with your foot." Her mouth snapped shut as if she'd said too much.

Which didn't lessen his need to know. "Do you mean it?" The rawness of his voice unnerved him further.

Before he could respond, Vi stepped around the table, placing her hands on his shoulders. Her nearness proved his undoing. Still sitting, he lifted his face to hers, then slowly wound his arms around her waist. She cupped his chin, her eyes deep amethyst. When she ran her fingers through his beard, a different kind of shiver curled his spine. "I wouldn't say it if I didn't mean it. Let me show you exactly what I mean."

She entwined her arms around his neck, touching her lips to his. Vi initiating a kiss sent his world spinning. He pulled her to his chest, kissing her soundly. Completely. Without reserve. When she returned his passion, a bright healing flowed between them. It covered their scars and hurts from the past and created a new life. Together.

The overhead fluorescent lights switched on, illuminating the room. Their kiss ended on a startled note, leaving Rory hungry for more. He tucked her head into his chest, letting his eyes adjust to the sudden white glow. Emilio sauntered into the kitchen, whistling. A minute later, he left with a broom, leaving the lights on.

"Do you think he saw us?" Vi leaned away, running a hand through her loose hair.

"*Mm-hmm*. He did it on purpose." Rory reached for her hair, rolling the silky texture between his fingers.

His arms stayed around her, and she snuggled back into his chest. Her lavender scent wove around his unsettled emotions, holding him steady. She acted the same way she always did— no repulsion, no condescension, nothing but Vi.

When she exhaled a warm breath, he nudged her. "What are you thinking?"

An amused expression lit her face, and her eyes glowed with tenderness. "I think it's a good thing we met in the deli."

CHAPTER THIRTY-NINE

Rory slipped his phone into his pocket, puzzled as to why Dad needed to see him so soon. He had barely enough time to drop by the office before his first appointment.

As he passed Becca's office, she gave him a disgruntled look. "He's waitin' for you." Paige sat in a chair next to Becca's desk, a hint of mischief in her eyes.

Taking in the situation, one corner of Rory's lip lifted. Paige would hold her own in getting the info she needed. Probably the reason Becca looked as if she'd stapled her tongue. She'd been Dad's secretary for so long she'd grown quite possessive about Spence Enterprises.

Overhead, the fan blades turned steadily as Rory entered the office, blowing the scent of furniture polish around the room. "What's going on, Dad?" he asked.

The older man threw down a manila folder. "I don't know how many times Becca's given me the wrong folder. The woman's getting dementia. Did you hear me? Dementia." His face and neck had turned a radish-red color. He yanked on the collar of his white shirt.

Rory was aghast. Dad rarely said an unkind word about anyone. In the last conversation they'd had, though, Dad had been impatient with Howell. Rory didn't know how to navigate this version of his father.

"You took your time getting here." The older man grumped his way to the small seating area where they met. They both stood as if facing off. "I wanted to let you know I've got a man meeting with the owner of the other tract of land you want for the gym."

On any other day, Rory would consider this odd. "That happened fast. What's he going to offer?"

Dad kept talking as if Rory hadn't said anything. "It's one of those sweet deals. The estate's recently changed hands. Always an opportune time to propose a sale." His breath came in short bursts.

"Dad, are you alright?" Rory asked, his voice rising.

The older man plopped in a chair, waving him away. "I'm fine. It's hot in here is all." He picked up a brochure from the table and fanned himself. "Becca keeps this room a furnace."

Rory sat, observing him. This room stayed cool. Dad's coloring now had an ashy tinge.

Dad pulled his phone from his pocket. "Marvin sent me the info. He's going out there this morning to see if he can't rustle up business. He wanted to do the polite preliminary thing, but it takes too long. I told him to come back with an appointment. I'll meet with—confounded strange name. Oh, here it is. A woman. Violet Summers."

Rory's world unhinged and swung crazily. Only one person had that name. "No, Dad. I know her—she won't sell." His hands rubbed together hard enough to kindle a fire.

"What are you talking about? If you know her, it ought to make it easier." A sheen of perspiration covered Dad's face.

Rory jerked his head. "No! Not Vi. The deal's off, Dad. She

won't want to sell." Realization crashed through him. The land they wanted for Peeps belonged to Vi? He'd have known if he and Jesse had followed through and checked. It all made sense though—the drive to her place from the gym didn't take long. She'd inherited all the surrounding acreage, but this—she'd think he'd—he had to fix this. Immediately. He stood and paced.

"I have to stop Marvin. He's headed to her place?" Rory grabbed his phone, punched his contact list, and scanned the contents. "Why don't I have Marvin's number? I need his number right now. This meeting can't happen."

Again, Dad acted as if he hadn't heard. "How do you know if we don't ask? Up to this point, you were ready to fork over a large sum of money. What we're prepared to offer would ease any financial worries, maybe for the rest of her life."

Rory ran a hand through the spikes in his hair. "No!" The word shot out with the force of a bullet. "Dad, Vi and I are —Dad!"

The older man had slumped over in the chair. Rory rushed to his side. When he pushed Dad against the chair back, his head lolled to one side.

"Becca! Call nine-one-one!"

<hr>

THE JANUARY AIR had warmed to an audacious degree. Good thing. In her haste, Vi had forgotten a jacket. Eager to see the house updates Rory had talked about in such glowing terms, she'd no sooner emerged from her car when Rory's foreman barreled out the front door.

"Hey, Miss Vi." Oscar touched the bill of his baseball cap with respect. "Were you out here last night?"

"No, what is it?" His worried expression bothered her.

Oscar's lips twisted to one side. "A window got left open, and the worker's power tools are gone. Stolen."

A new-model red pickup truck hurtled down the lane, leaving a trail of dust clouds. Who could this be? Vi felt the beginnings of a headache.

She glanced back at Oscar. "I haven't been out here for a couple of days. What do you think happened?"

He shrugged a shoulder. "I've got a call in to Rory. There's smoke not too far away, and there've been kids running around."

Vi's stomach tightened. The illegal squatters. "Were the tools valuable?"

"Yes, ma'am. If we're lucky, they'll turn up at local pawnshops."

A man wearing dress slacks with a long-sleeved white shirt and tie had parked the truck and walked their way.

"Sorry to bother you, miss. We'll take care of it." Oscar turned, climbing the steps to the house.

"Hello. I'm looking for Violet Summers." The man seemed pleasant enough, but Vi's inner antenna hummed at the use of her full name. For a brief instant, she wished Oscar had stayed.

"I'm Vi Summers." Her chin lifted.

He held out his hand. "Marvin. I work for Spence Enterprises."

Vi stared at him, digesting the words, then slowly held out her hand. "Spence Enterprises? As in Rory Spence?" The coffee she had for breakfast percolated right back up her esophagus.

Marvin shook her hand a tad too long. "Yes. I work for him and his father."

Shards of glass rolled around her stomach. "What's this about?"

The man blinked. "Is there a place we could sit—"

"No. State your business." A growing sense of unease about the man's mission mushroomed inside of her.

"I ... *ah* ... Morgan Spence requests a meeting with you."

Marvin looked at her as if expecting a response, but Vi said nothing.

"Your recent inheritance has come to our attention, and Mr. Spence wants to make you an offer for a tract of land."

"No," Vi said flatly. Her world slid sideways.

"I'm not sure you understand how much money this would mean, Miss Summers. Morgan Spence is willing to offer—"

"Morgan Spence is Rory's father?"

"Yes. He's an entrepreneur here in Val—"

"Does Rory know about this?"

"I'm sure he does. I believe it was Rory's idea. He and his father work together."

Vi stepped back, willing herself not to run away.

"Miss Summers—" Marvin stopped at the look on her face.

Her spine straightened as if hung on a pole. She strove for an even tone. "You can tell Mr. Spence and Rory." Her composure slipped a notch. "My land isn't for sale. Not now. Not ever." Grasping for one last vestige of control, she gritted out. "Please leave."

RORY SAT in a waiting room at the hospital, hands clasped, forearms on his knees, staring mindlessly at the swirly design on the carpet. The interminable waiting had him on pins and needles. *Please save him, God. I'm not ready for Dad to go.*

When the EMT vehicle showed up at the office, the men had assessed Dad and started procedures. From the medical terms bouncing back and forth, Rory figured out they were treating Dad for a heart attack. Everything else blurred as Paige held Rory's hand and Becca sobbed. Then, the EMTs cocooned Dad on a stretcher, hurrying him out the door. Rory gave terse instructions for Paige to cancel his appointments, then he drove to the hospital.

A pair of stylish open-toed heels appeared between his feet. Jolted out of his bleak thoughts, he looked up.

Stella. Why was she here?

He rose, shaking the stiffness out of his legs. "Hey." The absolute last person he wanted to see. Ever.

"What are you doing here, Rory?" One painted eyebrow arched as if he'd trespassed on her turf.

Rory shrugged off her attitude. She'd always had a chip on her shoulder the size of Denali. "Dad's here. Emergency."

Stella's facial features softened the merest bit, and then the dark eyes he'd once thought so enchanting hardened again. "Oh. Sorry to hear."

"And you?" A harmless enough question on the surface, but Rory knew the effect it would have. She never wanted anyone to know her business—especially him.

She flapped a badge. "Pharmaceutical rep."

"Good job." Rory kept a bland expression. Stella would excel at selling drugs—whether people needed them or not.

Heavy footsteps thumped their way. Rory glanced toward the noise, then placed his phone on the chair. His brother Mark hiked toward him, wearing dirty jeans and a nondescript T-shirt. "Your message didn't say much. Why's Dad in the hospital?"

"I heard the EMT guys calling it a heart attack. We were in his office discussing business, and he passed out. Becca called nine-one-one. He's in surgery now."

Mark's face mottled. "Discussing business! What did you say to him?" Fists clenched, he swore under his breath. "This is

Mom all over again." His accusing voice carried to every corner of the room.

The waiting area had fallen completely silent. Adults pretended to look at magazines, but the children stared with open mouths.

Well, why not? Mark resembled an exotic animal with his purple face and long red hair. With matching scent. Stella's avid curiosity irked Rory even more.

Rory sucked a deep breath, addressing Stella. "Excuse us." He turned to Mark. "Let's talk in private?" Without waiting, Rory strode out of the room. No relief came when Mark's heavy tread followed.

Minutes later, Rory returned to the waiting room, desperate to find his phone. He sighed with relief when he spied it on the chair. His brain was a cloudy mishmash of guilt and fear after the morning's events. Mark kept insinuating Rory had brought on Dad's heart attack. Anguish filled Rory at the thought. Dad hadn't been himself, but Rory hadn't helped matters when he realized Marvin's mission. What if Dad didn't recover?

Buck up, Spence. Don't go there.

At least his brother had sort of listened as Rory shared what he knew about Dad's condition. In between growls and accusations, Mark had taken off down the hall without a word. Rory hadn't a clue where he'd gone.

Rory punched a button on his phone. He loved his family, but his aching heart insisted he seek his tribe—the people with whom he shared a connection beyond flesh and blood.

CHAPTER FORTY

Vi wandered around the lake, pausing to watch a pair of woodpeckers hammer on a nearby tree. The day had warmed even more, but her hands and feet remained blocks of ice. Her heart had gone completely numb.

She walked past the birds, her mind lost in Rory's betrayal. He'd played the caring boyfriend so well. When Marvin appeared, she'd naïvely assumed it was a mistake. Then he confirmed Rory's role. Now she knew why Rory had been so helpful about the remodel. So it would be done on her dime. It still didn't make sense if he'd planned to buy it all along.

Her head ached, and unshed tears drowned her insides. It became hard to put one foot in front of the other. A rickety picnic table leaned to one side. She'd sit for a while, then return to Paige's. Sleep sounded wonderful.

Reaching the table, Vi sat carefully to avoid splinters. A white-bellied fish flipped in and out of the water, causing tiny ripples. Harry paddled toward her, honking as if they were long-lost friends, then waddled up the bank. Vi gazed at him. The large stone hadn't inflicted more damage than a crooked gait. Her mouth tilted. The goose couldn't walk in a straight line but zigzagged to her.

Harry rubbed his neck against her legs. Insistent. She held out a hand, keeping her fingers together. Sniffing her hand, he squawked, ruffling his feathers.

Her lips pressed into a flat line. A goose was glad to see her.

She attempted to concentrate on a mental task list so her mind wouldn't fall into the Rory-abyss. Her meeting with Jesse needed to happen. Another practice with Cyrus. She shivered. Preparations were all well and good, but what would she do if real trouble ever presented itself? Wisps of smoke drifted in the air, a reminder she needed to call Tavo about the illegals. Fear poked at her efforts to concentrate. She'd text Silas now.

Maybe the morning's events were all a bad dream. What if Rory cared about her, despite the obvious land grab? The air sucked from her lungs when she considered life without him. Vi scrounged through her pockets for an orange.

Her phone chimed. She pulled it out, glancing at the screen. Rory. She flicked to his text. Surely, he'd explain Marvin's visit had been a giant mistake.

> Vi, sorry to break it to you this way. I've thought a lot about what you said in Houston and have decided it would be better if we didn't see each other anymore. Don't call or text. It was fun while it lasted.

Vi blinked and reread the message. Her phone clattered on the picnic table as she squeezed her eyes shut to blot out the loathsome words. Pain stabbed her heart.

Rory didn't stop with taking her land. He'd waited until he'd gotten everything. Her arms crossed her stomach, and she rocked back and forth on the picnic table, gasping for breath.

Several minutes passed. She wheezed, grabbed her phone, and trod along the path, her vision eclipsed by anguish.

Smoke spiraled into the sky. The scent choked her air passages, but Vi kept going.

BEREFT OF A PLAN, Vi wandered into her room at Paige's with no memory of driving or walking into the house. She needed Cyrus. The large dog stretched and pranced about, thrilled to see her. He jumped on her bed, and she grasped his fur in her fists, burying her face into his neck.

The tears she'd bottled up gushed. She shook with sobs. Cyrus whimpered, anxious to comfort her.

Light footsteps came from the hallway, and Paige appeared at the doorway. Lines puckered her forehead. "*Mija*, what's wrong?"

"Did you know?" Vi asked dully.

"Know what, *Mija*?"

Vi didn't want to talk about it, but the words rushed out of their own accord. "Rory and his dad want to buy my land. And he broke up with me today." She winced at the phrase—such junior-high terminology.

Paige sat on the bed with a bewildered expression. "What? No ... it's not true."

"It is. A man came out to my place today and said so." Vi finger combed Cyrus's fur as if he needed every hair in place.

"Have you talked to Rory?"

"Why would I talk to him?" Vi continued petting the dog. Relating what happened to Paige proved agony enough without piling on more.

Paige perched on the edge of the bed. "Rory's dad had a heart attack this morning. I got updates from Rory for a while, but his phone reception must be bad. I'm leaving for the hospital."

The news jolted Vi out of her misery. "Was Rory with him when it happened?"

Paige nodded vigorously. "Mr. Spence wasn't his normal self when he arrived at work this morning. Everything irritated him, and he grouched at Becca over petty stuff. Later, she told me it's been going on for a while. He and Rory argued. About your property. *Mija*, I heard it. Mr. Spence sent a man out to your place this morning, but when Rory found out the property belonged to you, I've never seen him so distressed." She patted Cyrus on the head.

The nanosecond of hope disappeared when Vi remembered the other blow. She dug in her pocket for her phone and pulled up the text she'd received from Rory.

"Here. Read this." Vi grimaced at their mutual declaration of love in previous texts. "Ignore the other texts. Read the last one." She handed the phone to Paige.

When she read it, Paige looked more puzzled than ever. "Are you sure it's not a mistake? This doesn't sound like Rory at all."

Even though Paige's take confirmed her first thought, Vi sniffed. "It's right there in black and white." She pressed her fingers against her hot cheeks.

Paige handed her the phone. "You need to talk to Rory. Even if he didn't want to see you anymore, he wouldn't do it this way. Something's wrong."

Vi let out a long sigh. "Paige, he says not to text or call him. Sounds pretty final to me." She turned her phone off.

Paige slid off the colorful quilt. "Well, I'm going to track him down. I want to see how Mr. Spence is doing."

"Will his dad be all right?" Despite how she felt about Rory at the moment, she could relate. He had to be devastated.

"Last I heard, Mr. Spence was in surgery. Hoping for the best." Paige left the room, her boots tapping in a steady rhythm.

The woodpeckers she'd seen at the lake earlier had taken up residence inside her head. If she could lay down for a bit, maybe the pounding would stop. Despite restless, negative thoughts, she dozed. Every time she woke up, Rory's text would slam into her consciousness, and the hammering would start up again.

Darkness had fallen by the time any pretense of rest had vanished. Cyrus had snuggled next to her, smelling of lake water. She tried to think about her next move, but the skid marks from her life still burned.

Even the house seemed to hold its breath. No kitchen noise or the sound of laundry or running water in the bathroom. Zip.

Vi stared in the dim light, then rolled over to switch on a lamp. A wrecking ball had swung through her life, leaving havoc in its wake. The one person she'd completely opened up to had stripped her of everything.

She spied Dad's tablet on the end table. One letter remained. She'd cherished the connection the letters provided. As grueling as some of them had been to read, Daddy's perspective had a healing effect. She felt a new strength coursing through her body. Reaching for the device, she thumbed through the file and clicked on his last letter.

Hey, Squirt.

I'm running out of things to say. Already told you most of what I needed to. Only a few more things.

After your ma left, I thought about getting married again. Have to admit, it gets lonesome rattling around here by myself. Glad you're with me now. For a while, I thought about remarrying. With another woman around, it'd make things easier on you. Then I decided it wouldn't be fair, 'cause I ain't never gonna love another woman besides your mama.

All I really wanted was you anyway, so I stayed content at the plant and lived the hobo life. Rat-holed all my money so you could have it.

This land has a special purpose. I never figured it out, but I'm thinking you will. People can get quiet out here and heal. You got firsthand experience with it.

I said all I need to. This cancer's about to get the best of my body. I'm grateful to know death ain't the end of the road. God made a way for the best part of me to go live with Him. Kind of looking forward to it. Pastor assures me I'll enjoy it something fierce.

You go on and have a good life, Red. Don't you fret none over me. I'm going home, and I'll be there waiting for you when it's your turn.

The ache of her father's passing flowed through her tears. "Goodbye, Daddy." The clock on her bedside read 9:17. She'd wept a long time. Now she felt strangely relieved. The piercing grief she'd endured at Thanksgiving had ceased. Daddy's letters, tough as they were to read, had provided closure.

A different grief was swallowing her—the shambles of her life and dreams. The tiny beginning of a life with the man she loved had snuffed out in a day. Rory's zest for life had revived her own. But he'd moved on. Working on the house remodel together had deeply entwined their lives. How could she ever live there now? He had embedded himself into every piece of insulation, sheet of granite, every doorknob and handle.

Despite all the reminders of Rory, Vi had to go out there. Tonight. The lake still maintained its magic. Visions of smoke and trespassers came to mind, but she wouldn't find any measure of peace until she'd seen the lake. She'd take Cyrus and a two-legged walking buddy. She pulled out her phone and turned it on. Several voicemails and texts from Rory. Why the overkill? He'd made himself clear the first time.

She texted Silas.

Meet me at the lake?

A minute later, he answered.

> Be there in 15. Stay in your car until I get
> there.

Vi's gaze caught on the heavy boot next to the wall. She hadn't worn it much since the gala. Her ankle seemed fine. She snatched the jacket hanging on the back of her door. "C'mon, Cyrus."

Rory grew more frantic by the minute as he navigated the traffic. He'd left the hospital because he couldn't reach anybody on his phone. Now he'd gained clear tower range and still no response. Not Paige or Jesse. Or Vi. He'd sent enough texts and voicemails to start a communication center with nary an answer. The lights of restaurants and businesses sparkled and winked at him as if his world hadn't suddenly whipped to a halt. His leg ached, and his thoughts bounced, a virtual pinball machine.

Visiting hours were over. *God, please watch over Dad tonight.* Rory's stomach rumbled. Lunch in the hospital cafe proved a tense affair, with Matt glowering at him in between bites. Rory couldn't remember what he ate.

No twinkling Christmas lights shining at Paige's house increased his anxiety. *Think, Rory.* Nobody home at this hour? Rory jammed the Lexus in reverse and headed to Vi's house. The hospital atmosphere had reduced his brain to mush. The familiar smells and sounds had yanked him back into those awful days of rehab. He'd clawed his way past the pain and despair, only to have it smack him all over again with Dad.

Rory rolled next to Vi's car and stopped. The porch light beamed a pale glow outside her house. Silas's gray pickup was parked on the other side of her yellow bug. Rory's heart plummeted. With blinding clarity, he understood why she hadn't returned his calls.

Climbing out of his car, Rory tried to figure out what to do. If he waited here, surely Vi and Silas would saunter up from the lake. Part of him wanted to get back in his car and drive away. He'd foolishly believed her when she said she loved him.

Hands in his pockets, Rory stepped around to the hood of his car. A popping noise in the underbrush caught his attention. Dry leaves crunching under his shoes, he strode over to the edge of the brush. Smoke engulfed his nostrils, and a sudden blaze of heat seared his skin. He backed away. Rustling sounded behind him. A bright light flashed, and he crumpled.

VI AND SILAS had strolled around the far end of the lake and were halfway to the house. She'd considered spilling the whole sordid story to Silas. Since his uncalled-for hug, however, he'd reverted to his unreadable self. The farther they walked without talking, the easier it became to say nothing at all. Rory may have betrayed her, but Vi had no desire to disclose it to anyone.

Cyrus howled and alerted throughout the entire walk. As they drew closer to their parked cars, the air grew sultry. And smoky. Sizzles and snaps rustled in the brush nearby.

"Vi, you better call nine-one-one. There's a fire."

She hurriedly dug out her phone. "It must have just happened."

A car started. Silas ran the remainder of the path to the driveway. Vi followed at a slower pace, trying to contain Cyrus, who barked and lunged at the end of his leash.

Silas ran back to Vi, taking Cyrus's leash. "Have you got nine-one-one on the phone? We need a fire truck *and* an ambulance."

Vi's fingers shook as she touched her phone screen. "Why?"

Through the haze, Silas's dark eyes pierced hers. "The car that took off belonged to Rory—but he wasn't driving."

Cyrus broke the leash with a yelp, dashing toward the house. In a wobbly voice, Vi answered questions and gave specific directions to the 911 dispatcher. Silas balled his fists and stamped around the property, hollering Rory's name.

Sirens blasted their way within minutes.

***

A WET NOSE nudged the back of Rory's neck. It snuffled around his jaw. With effort, he rolled over. His eyes stung. He coughed, trying to breathe. A relentless tongue licked his face.

Rory squinted. "Cyrus. Good boy." The words came out rough. Thick smoke filled the air. Hot, Rory panted and dry-coughed. The back of his head radiated with pain. His body wouldn't cooperate when he tried to sit up.

He coughed again. Everything went black.

***

FIREFIGHTERS UNWRAPPED HEAVY GRAY HOSES. The underbrush popped and sputtered. Paramedics tramped around, shouting for Rory and to each other. Cyrus barked in the distance.

Silas returned, putting his arm around Vi. "They'll find him."

Despite the heat, a chill enveloped Vi. Rory had to be incapacitated, or they wouldn't have taken his vehicle. She'd called Tavo. Thankfully, Silas knew more about cars than she did. He filled Tavo in, then described the make and model of Rory's car.

Louder shouting ensued, and two men rushed a stretcher into the scrub brush. Minutes passed. Spray from the water hoses hissed. The stench of burning brush filled the air.

The minutes seemed endless until the men returned with the stretcher. Instinct pushed her away from Silas. He caught and held her. "No, Vi. Wait!"

Vi struggled against Silas, kicking at his legs. It had to be Rory on the stretcher, but Silas's arms were bands of iron wrapped around her stomach. "Let me go!"

A blur of black flew at them, snarling. Silas released her and gripped his arm. Red seeped through his fingers.

"Cyrus, down!" Vi shouted. Still growling, the dog backed off and sat.

The ambulance doors slammed shut. She yelled to Silas, "Take Cyrus," and ran to her car. When the vehicle lumbered away, she followed.

Vi needed Rory alive and well, even if he didn't want her anymore.

CHAPTER FORTY-TWO

Last night, Vi had slipped away when the hospital staff wouldn't allow any non-family members access to Rory. When she left, Jesse had ensconced himself in a chair outside Rory's door, pestering anyone who left the room for an update. He and Rory had been through so much together it was only natural. It gave Vi comfort, but she intended to see Rory today, rule or no rule.

Sleep proved elusive, except for a vivid dream about Daddy. He wore a different flannel shirt and a pair of jeans worn to threads at the knees. Between the dream and her own restlessness, Vi had formulated a plan.

An immovable force pulled Vi to Rory despite yesterday's trauma. Her mind fog had cleared, leaving one stark fact glimmering with light.

Vi loved Rory with all her heart.

Her original perception of him as a die-hard flirt had nothing to do with the real person. The man beneath the charming exterior had burrowed into every facet of her life.

During the endless night and Cyrus's snores, she'd read the

texts Rory sent after the first terrible text. He'd sounded upset and frantic. As if he needed her help to deal with his father. Then all communication stopped. Nothing.

The break-up text didn't fit with anything. Vi wanted desperately to believe those mean, flippant words hadn't come from him.

Yesterday, the pain had been so fresh, Vi couldn't bear to know. This morning, new strength fortified her and refused to let go.

Even if Rory trampled her heart into pieces, she would get to the bottom of this.

Vi rubbed her puffy eyes, not wanting to look in a mirror—no doubt she looked atrocious.

Decision made, she flew through her morning routine. Plaiting her hair, she remembered Rory playing with the loose strands. With shaky fingers, she undid the long braid, then pulled it back with a band. She wouldn't go down without a fight.

She donned the outfit from their prequel date and applied makeup. The earrings he'd given her stayed on the dresser. Showing grit was all well and good. Acting like a lovesick idiot? Not so much.

If he meant what he said in the break-up text, maybe she'd hang in Houston awhile to figure out Plan B.

Did that mean Rory was Plan A?

Vi left to find out.

Fingers trembling on the steering wheel as she drove to the hospital, her earlier courage fled as she rode the elevator to his floor. Nurses murmured to each other at the round desk counter. The sharp scent of antiseptic permeated the atmosphere. Machines whirred, and red buttons winked throughout the station.

Her slow footsteps were silent on the linoleum.

Room 361. Rory Spence. The short gulps of air Vi took weren't enough. Oh, well. Breathing was the least of her concerns at the moment.

Standing in the open doorway, a tall man with long red hair carelessly tied in a ponytail glanced at her, then did a double-take.

"Nice hair, Red." He gave her a crooked grin.

Vi's neck grew hot. How weird. She and this stranger possessed the same hair color.

"Who's there?" A deep, achingly familiar voice asked. "Vi?"

Oh, no. Rory was awake. Vi needed him asleep—at first, anyway.

Wistfully, she looked back the way she came. She could still leave.

The man strode to her, gently taking her elbow.

"Somebody wants to see you." His blue eyes remained friendly, but he didn't let go. "He's talked about nothing else, and I'll never hear the end of it if you get away."

Gnawing on her lip, Vi allowed him to lead her in. Whatever made her consider this a good idea?

"Hey, Vi." Rory's hoarse voice sounded tentative. As if he wasn't sure of his reception either.

Vi risked a peek. Rory's eyes drank her in, though dark shadows smudged the skin underneath. The scratches on his forehead and temple looked painful.

"Vi, this is Mark, my brother." Rory cleared his throat and gave his brother a pointed look.

A wry look stole across Mark's face. The expression reminded Vi of Rory. "Subtle, bro—guess I'll check on Dad. Pleasant meeting you, Vi."

A gamey odor tickled her nostrils when Mark passed.

Vi's gaze locked with Rory's, and the silence grew awkward.

"I ... uh ... wanted to make sure you're okay." Vi mustered a brave smile, even as her eyes feasted on every one of his rakish features.

Rory's brows raised.

She bit her tender lip and winced. Massaging a dinosaur would be easier than this.

"I improved the second you walked through the door." Rory patted the covers beside him. "Come sit by me, Red. I've missed you."

Vi looked around for a chair. This conversation was not happening with her on the same bed as Rory, even if they were in a hospital. Settling into the uncomfortable plastic seat, she almost relented at his disappointed look. Instead, her spine ironed itself against the back of the chair. She folded her legs pretzel-style.

"Ankle still doing okay minus the boot?" Rory observed her warily.

Vi tilted her head, recognizing his ploy to help her relax with small talk. "Only hurts when I overdo it."

A thin smile hovered around his drawn mouth. "Sounds about right. Paige filled me in on a couple of things. I hear you're upset about a text I sent."

The nonchalant way Rory said it made Vi's eyes bulge. Every single insecurity she possessed shot to the surface with mob mentality. How dare he put this on her. Scrambling from the chair, she slapped her jeans pocket to find her keys. Coming here had been a mistake.

Sheets rustled. In one fluid motion, Rory moved to the edge of the bed, capturing her hands. "Hon, I have no idea what's going on. Please calm down and talk to me so we can figure out what happened."

Vi stared at his hands, then looked into his eyes. Compassion and determination whispered from the silvery depths. His feathery touch released her when she moved to sit down. She opened her mouth, then shut it. It was on him to explain.

"Tell me about Marvin's visit." Rory swung his legs off the side of the bed, eyeing the prosthetic lying on the window seat as if he might need it.

She took a deep breath, not able to talk about Marvin's visit yet. "Is there an update from Tavo about how you came to be here?"

Rory settled back with a lingering look at the prosthetic. "He says I got hit on the head with a shovel they found nearby. Apparently, a campfire didn't get extinguished. He suspects the illegals knew the fire was out of control and used my car as a getaway vehicle. I just got in the way." Coughing, he twiddled a straw in a water cup on the portable table.

Vi pointed to the IV in his arm. "For hydration?"

Rory lifted a shoulder. "If there were pain meds in it, I'd feel a lot better than I do. At least Jesse brought me a pair of shorts. These gowns don't cover much." He picked at the thin fabric.

Vi itched to check out the back of his head, but she jammed her hands together, interlocking her fingers. No use getting cozy if this wasn't going to end well.

"Tell me about your dad." She forced the words past her clogged throat.

Though his gaze suggested he knew she was stalling, Rory answered readily enough. "Dad came through bypass surgery with a good report. Now he'll tackle rehab like he does everything else. He hasn't been himself since Christmas. We argued when I realized the tract of land he wanted for Peeps belonged to you. That's when he keeled over." What little color in Rory's face vanished, leaving him pale and wan.

His pain pierced her defenses. "I'm so sorry."

Rory sniffed, his eyes watering. "He's got a lengthy

recovery ahead, but—" He spoke with effort, each syllable raspier than the last. "—he's still with us. Give me a minute." He turned his head away from her.

Vi focused elsewhere, allowing Rory a measure of privacy. The washed-out eye color and lines around his mouth suggested fatigue. *You need rest, babe.*

Minutes later, he wiped his eyes on the sheet. "Sorry. The emotions caught up. We lost Mom suddenly, and I'm crying-like-a-baby-thankful it didn't happen with Dad. Tell me about Marvin's visit."

Vi swallowed hard, then sketched the gist of it. She finished in a whisper, then looked down. Rory visibly winced during the telling.

"Vi, look at me." His legs stopped shifting. "I never put two and two together. Dad works the financial end. I didn't know the land we wanted for Peeps was yours."

"How could you not know, Rory? You've been out to the house. Brush covers the far side, but it backs up to Peeps."

"My navigational skills are terrible. Jess says I can't find my way out of a paper bag." The frustration in Rory's voice convinced her. He'd been so dependent on the GPS when they were in San Antonio, it made a weird sort of sense.

"When it first came up, Jess and I planned to check it out. Then Manny's funeral happened, and our look-see fell between the cracks. If I'd known, I would have nixed it from the get-go." Ending on a cough, he drank more water, then pressed the call bell and asked for coffee.

When the nurse appeared, she said, "Mr. Spence, you need to lie flat. And no coffee."

Rory grinned at her engagingly. "I'll lie down once we're done here. And I will have coffee. Please." The last word sounded tacked on. More proof he wasn't quite himself.

The nurse left, her shoes clicking with irritation.

Vi couldn't resist a bit of teasing. "I don't think she's going to bring you coffee, Mr. Bossy."

"Even if she doesn't, Jess knows the drill. He'll bring me coffee." Rory leaned forward, his smug look replaced by earnestness. "As far as your inheritance goes, my *only* concern is getting your house remodeled the way you want it."

His explanation about Marvin's visit made Vi feel marginally better. Aside from enjoying the lake with her, Rory had never shown a smidge of personal interest in her land. The devious agenda didn't fit with the man she knew.

Another nurse entered, checked his IV, and made notations on her clipboard. As she chatted with him, Vi breathed. In. Out. *Hold steady*. In. Out.

"Is there anything else I can do for you, Mr. Spence?" The nurse's tone suggested if Rory asked for a side trip to Pluto, she would find a way.

"Mm. Breakfast—oh, here it is." A blonde in pink scrubs entered, placing a tray on the swing-arm table in front of him. Rory took the cup of coffee, triumphantly waving it at Vi. "Thanks, ladies. You're doing a great job."

Vi brought a knuckle to her lips, hiding a smile as they tittered and bowed their way out the door. *Nice parade, girls.*

Rory's nose wrinkled with discomfort. "They probably think you're my sister."

"Oh, no doubt." Vi's amusement faded. They still hadn't discussed the text he'd sent.

CHAPTER FORTY-THREE

Checkered sunlight shone through the blinds, brightening the room. Rory sipped coffee from the foam cup, seemingly content to watch her. When Vi grew self-conscious under his perusal, he said, "Tell me about this text."

Vi exhaled a shuddery breath but made no move to get her phone.

Rory gave her a patient look, then motioned to the back of his head. "My phone disappeared when this happened. Can you show me the text?"

Oh. Without a word, she took out her phone, pulled it up, and handed the phone to him. Her heart imitated a horse race.

Rory read the text with a sharp intake of breath, then searched her face. "This is why you won't sit by me." His voice wasn't quite steady. "How could I finish your house if I did this?"

Vi tilted her head. "Then how do you explain it?"

His shoulders lifted, and coffee from his cup sloshed onto the sheet. "I can't, but I didn't send it." Folding the blanket over the wet spot, he handed the phone back to her, his brows in a line. "Wait. What's the time stamp?"

She peered at the text. "4:31 p.m."

His lips pressed together. "They'd taken Dad to surgery. I waited in the lobby—" He looked at her. "I saw Stella. Then Mark came in upset, so we left to talk." His mouth flew open. "I left my phone on the chair. When did you receive the text?"

Vi stared at him. "What are you saying?"

He set the coffee cup on the tray. "Stella."

"Stella?"

"She messed with my phone. I started having problems after I saw her. I thought the reception had flaked out ..." A groan worked up his throat. "Stella sent that nasty text to you from my phone, knowing full well it would cause problems. She saw us at the gala, then at my townhouse, and realized you were more than a friend."

"Stella sent me a text?" Vi blinked, still trying to understand.

Rory looked grim. "I'd bet money on it. She sent me similar texts before I blocked—" His mouth dropped open. "Stella blocked my contacts—mainly you, Paige, and Jesse—she's the reason I couldn't get a hold of y'all." His mouth twisted. "In her mind, it would be the perfect revenge. Getting over her made me the bad guy."

Rory shook his head as if to rid himself of a bad memory. His pewter eyes pleaded with her. "Honey, please say you know me better than what that text says."

"I thought I did. But after the I-want-to-buy-your-land deal, I wasn't so sure." Vi couldn't keep the tartness out of her voice.

His lips stretched in a rueful smile. "Vi, I don't want your land. I want you. And no matter how the text looks, I didn't write or send it."

A tingle chased up her spine. Rory's whole being exuded the truth. The text had seemed odd from the beginning. Vi found it hard to believe anyone would deliberately do such a thing, but Rory knew the woman better than she did.

"Red, please get out of the chair." He left the rest unsaid.

Could she do it? If she did, it meant she believed him. Very slowly, Vi climbed onto the bed and sat next to his knees, facing him.

Rory tentatively reached out and fingered the cuff of her sweater. "You wore this on our pre-date. I had already fallen in love with you, but that night I passed the point of no return. You're all I want, Red." His eyes had turned silvery soft.

Stroking her hair, he pulled on the band until the strands cascaded around her shoulders.

Vi shivered. Not because the room was chilly.

His thumb trailed down her cheek. "You're still sitting too far away." He pushed the table away. Bending forward, he hauled her into his arms.

Tucked into his side, she felt his warmth seeping through the hospital gown.

"Better?" His deep voice husked.

Vi snuggled deeper and nodded, still afraid to voice the stream of feelings flowing through her.

He shifted to face her. "Talk to me. Are you okay?"

She touched a red scratch on his forehead. "I'm getting there." A deep breath escaped. Telling him would help. "Do you remember when we first talked about remodeling the house? You said I needed to trust you."

Rory's white teeth flashed between his mustache and beard. "Mm. What I remember is *you* keeping your distance as if I was the Biggest Baddest Wolf ever."

"Your reputation as a flirt preceded you."

His eyes widened with innocence. "All before I met you. Go

back to the part where I told you to *trust* me." He emphasized the word.

A smile tugged at her lips. "Yeah, well, even with the termite issue, your actions showed how serious you were about my best interests. It didn't take long before I trusted you with all the house decisions. You stayed upfront about the cost, even when you knew I'd buck. Every step of the way, you made sure I was satisfied and happy."

She traced a finger along his jawline. "Somewhere between granite and spreadsheets, my heart began to trust you too. With my past. The things I never wanted anyone to know, you handled with grace."

Rory stilled, listening.

"The heart part took longer. When yesterday happened, once I got past the initial shock, I couldn't reconcile the land grab and the text with the Rory I knew. It's why I came this morning—to make sure you were the same man I fell in love with."

Rory tipped her chin up, his eyes moist and red. "Thank you for telling me. My own fear tunneled into the red zone when you didn't answer my calls or texts. I was worried sick you'd decided I no longer fit in your world."

Joy streamed into every nook and cranny of her heart. "Never going to happen."

His mouth hovered inches from hers. "Let me kiss you."

Vi shied away. "The fire. Your lungs ..."

Holding her closer, Rory's breath warmed her face. "Nothing's wrong with my lips."

Her mouth twisted to one side. "If you weren't so downright adorable—"

When his mouth brushed hers, she closed her eyes, and the anguish of yesterday evaporated. His kiss gently erased her doubts and fear, and assured her of his love. The transparency flowed both ways, healing their bruised emotions. Suppressed longing burst forth, and Vi's insides blazed with passion.

Her arms tightened around his waist.

Finally, Rory broke away. Breathing hard, he whispered. "Marry me, Red. I want all of you. All your kisses." He nuzzled her loose hair.

Her arms moved to his neck. Marry her? Her brain threatened to shut down. His beard tickled her cheek, making her pulse race.

"Say it, Red. I need to hear the words." He held her slightly apart from him, his gaze holding hers with aching tenderness.

"Yes, I'll marry you." When Rory's eyes squeezed shut in relief, Vi giggled and kissed his nose. When his lips touched hers again, a loud "ahem" broke into their private world. Befuddled, Vi stared at a man in a white coat and a woman in scrubs. Their eyes twinkled.

The doctor stepped forward, lips stretching from ear to ear. "Sorry to interrupt." He glanced at his chart. "Mr. Spence?"

When Vi made to move away, Rory's arm locked her in place, and he laced his hand through hers. "Yes, I'm Rory Spence." Behind the doctor, Jesse and Brenna stood in the doorway. "And this beautiful woman—" He squeezed her shoulder affectionately. "—Is the future Mrs. Spence."

Jesse, large coffee cup in hand, shouted hoorah loud enough for the entire floor to hear, and Brenna danced in the hallway. The doctor and nurse beamed.

Vi smiled up at her handsome, future husband clad in a hospital gown, of all things. Rory kissed the top of her head and whispered for her ears only, "I'm going to spend the rest of my life lovin' on you, Red."

The last puzzle piece snapping into place, Vi knew what her most recent dream meant. It had been a vision of Daddy, all those years ago, praying for her on a dark, demon-filled night. His letter explained the inadequacy he felt, and his determination to pray anyway.

Vi sighed in pure contentment. Rory's deep voice rumbled beside her as he answered the doctor's questions.

Daddy fought for her that day ... so she could have this day.

It was enough, Daddy. More than enough.

EPILOGUE

Five months later

Rory sat on the bench at the foot of the king-sized bed, unbuttoned his dress shirt, and laid it aside.

Vi came from the bathroom, the color leached from her face. She walked to where he sat and rubbed his bare shoulders. He drew her closer and kissed her. She tasted like minty mouthwash.

He gently tucked a long strand of hair behind her ear. "You're going to get through this, Mrs. Spence." It thrilled him that she shared his name.

Her eyes rolled to the ceiling. "Looking forward to it." Scooping her hair to one side, she presented her back to him. "Button me up?"

"Love all these hard jobs you give me." Rory fingered the lacy buttons and stroked the tat between her shoulders. "The hummingbird needs a maintenance check by yours truly. You need to be still." He affected an innocent tone, delighted his touch made her shiver.

Vi snorted. "As if you didn't do it on purpose."

Her fragrance intoxicated him. He'd finally learned the proper name of the scent. As long as he lived, he'd always associate lavender with Vi.

Fastening the last button into place, he patted her hip. She turned into him again, her eyes soft and dreamy. "What's the menu for tonight's party?"

"Tavo is grilling chicken and beef fajitas as we speak." Rory hid a smile. The tiniest whiff of sausage would send her back to the bathroom for the rest of the evening. "Catered side dishes, dessert, and I made mashed potatoes for you." He grinned at her look of relief.

Dishes clattered downstairs. At her questioning look, he said, "Paige and Brenna are setting up."

She ducked her head. "Sorry. I've been out of it."

Rory's arms wrapped around her waist. "Be patient with yourself, Red. I've loved every minute of taking care of you and getting your nest fixed up."

Shortly after he'd proposed, Vi had told him she wouldn't live in the mess Stella had made of his townhouse. He'd wholeheartedly agreed, but it didn't leave many options. So he'd pulled out every stop, called in every favor, and created several more to hasten the remodel of her childhood home. At first, they'd camped out in the upstairs bedroom and bath. Last week, the downstairs had been finished.

Their friends had insisted on a housewarming.

"I've got news to tell you before we go down." A twinkle hovered behind Vi's pale blue eyes. "Here," she reached for the gray polo shirt lying on the bed. "Put this on so I can concentrate." She playfully smooched his cheek. "All those bench presses make for a great view, Mr. Shoulders-of-the-Year."

Rory thrust his head and arms through the shirt, radiating

with gratefulness. Since their wedding night, his wife had made it very clear she found him physically attractive, an issue he'd struggled with since the amputation.

She smoothed his collar. "You know Mom took me to my doctor's appointment this morning—"

"Yeah, how'd it go? Did it ease the strain between you two for not letting her plan a monstrous wedding? You said it would help."

"Yes," Vi's lips pursed. "I think all is forgiven. Not quite how I expected though." The crease deepened between her brows.

Rory's stomach launched into a whirly-gig routine. "What did the doctor say? Is everything okay with you and the baby?"

The corners around Vi's eyes relaxed a bit. "It's all fine. It's ... I couldn't help it, Rory."

"Help what, Vi?" Rory's voice had risen a notch.

A slight lump traveled up and down her creamy throat. "I wanted you to know before Mother—"

Vi paused, her eyes luminous. She slowly held up two fingers.

A bright light split through Rory's lack of comprehension.

"What? Two ... babies? ... twins!" he sputtered incredulously.

At her slight nod, he stood and picked her up, twirling her around in a dance. "For sure? There's no mistake?"

Breathless, she said, "No mistake. Two heartbeats, clear as day. Mother heard it all, but I still wish it had been you with me."

He sat, tugging her onto his knee. "I get it. Mom being the first to know doesn't hurt a bit." His lips stretched from ear to ear as he hugged her. "I'm so hyped I can't even think straight."

She gripped his shoulders, eyes glistening with tears. "You're going to be a daddy, twice over."

He tucked her into his chest as if she might break. "And you, Vi. You get two babies to love on." His thoughts spinning, he glanced at her pinched brow. "What's wrong?"

She leaned deeper into him. "You have to help me, Rory. My other pregnancy was so ... horrendous ... I get scared." Her troubled eyes tore at him. "Scared I'll get sick again ... afraid the babies won't be healthy ... afraid I won't get to keep them." She buried her face in his shirt.

"Don't listen to any of it." He stroked her hair. "We're keeping these babies. And you'll have a better pregnancy this time because you're happy. None of the stressors you dealt with before factor into your life now. It will make a tremendous difference."

Rory's heart ached for her. Vi still struggled with allowing her first baby to be adopted.

"My turn to give you news." He lifted her, stretched his leg, and settled her back on his knee. "I ... *um* ... spoke to your mom at length at the wedding, then again this morning when she picked you up. She's contacted the adoptive parents of Thomas—"

Vi's jaw dropped at the news. "Is that even legal? How did she manage?"

One side of Rory's mouth twitched with humor. "At our reception, I broached the subject, and she flat-out said it was impossible. Then Rodney, bless his contacts and his clout, told her any sealed record can be unsealed. Once he said that, I knew she would find a way."

Vi's sigh ended in a snort. "No surprise there." She waved a hand. "Go on ..."

"Thomas's parents have given permission for you to write to him—" Rory paused at her look of shock. "And, *when Thomas initiates the idea,* they're cautiously open to him meeting you. You understand?" He searched her face. "It must be Thomas's idea. Acknowledging you as his biological mother is hard for them. If Thomas wants it, however, they're willing, for his sake. He's the key. And it seems he's always been curious about his birth parents."

Tears ran unchecked down Vi's cheeks. Rory cupped her face in his hands. "I can only imagine what this means to you, love, but we can't rush it. All parties must agree. And they don't call him Thomas. They named him Trevor."

Vi wrapped her arms around him. "I don't care what his name is. I only want to meet my son. Thank you. There aren't words …" Her lips found his.

When the kiss deepened, Rory reluctantly pulled away. "If you keep kissing me like that, we're skipping the party."

Her fingers massaged the back of his neck. The aroma of grilled chicken wafted through the ceiling. "Nope. You get to tell everybody we're having twins. The news about Thomas, um, *Trevor,* can wait. I want to enjoy this gift with you and Mom for a while."

Rory's insides uncoiled. Her response promised everything he'd hoped for.

VI SAT AS FAR AWAY from the kitchen as possible with a bowl of mashed potatoes. Cyrus rested at her feet. The dog had accosted each guest at the door and performed a sniff check—apparently, everyone passed inspection. Silas hadn't shown up. He'd not been around much since that night at the lake when Cyrus bit him. Vi frowned. Surely, he knew the dog was protecting her. One good thing that came from the fire had been the exodus of the squatters. Permanently, she hoped. It didn't hurt that Tavo still had security patrols swing by regularly."

Vi took another bite of the buttery treat. It seemed years instead of months ago she'd missed Thanksgiving dinner. Since then, she hadn't been able to get enough of Rory's famous mashed potatoes. Or him.

Close by, Rory held a hand next to his mouth, as if telling Jesse a big secret. "Jess, I highly recommend the state of matrimony. You're going to love it," he stage-whispered.

Jesse wore a look of long-suffering. "Brenna and I are tying the knot next month, Ro. You're the one who got in a big hurry."

Rory smirked in agreement. "You bet I did. Once she said yes, I moved like greased lightning before she changed her mind."

"Said the man who proposed wearing a hospital gown," Jesse teased.

Vi's insides fluttered. She wouldn't trade her small private wedding for anything. Last March she and Rory, surrounded by their closest friends, stood on a freshly painted, beribboned boardwalk and said their vows. A carpet of pink, orange, and blue wildflowers dotted the landscape, and turtles sunned on the lake's shore.

The cool, sunny day was perfect. Until Cyrus decided the goose wasn't allowed and gave chase. For his part, Harry had created enough racket to put the ceremony on hold. Finally, Rory did his alpha-thing, retrieved the dog, and ordered him to stand next to Jesse as canine best man.

Vi's thoughts riveted to the present as Tavo sauntered over, inches taller than Jesse and Rory, who were by no means short. "Gotta go to work, bro. The grill's still warm. Okay if I pick it up tomorrow?"

"You know it's fine, Chief. Excellent job on the meat—your

trademark melt-in-the-mouth style wins every time." Rory saluted with two fingers. Tavo's eyes trailed off toward the kitchen, and he walked away without a word. Jesse and Rory exchanged meaningful looks. Vi angled to see into the kitchen, but Tavo's frame blocked her view. She settled back into her chair, content to listen.

"How's Vi feeling these days?" Jesse asked. He still wanted to move forward with a massage school. Once she got over her all-day morning sickness, she'd be on it.

"*Mm.* 9 p.m. is the new midnight, and as long as she's close to a bathroom, things are peachy." A note of pride rang in Rory's answer. His excitement about her pregnancy helped to allay the fear Vi battled.

"Brenna's already got a case of baby fever, watching you guys, and we're not even married yet."

Rory rubbed his gold wedding band. "Well, Jess, I have confidence you'll figure it out. When you're married, you go home after a long, grueling day, and the house smells delicious. Then you get greeted with a scorching hot kiss and" —He gave an elaborate shrug of his shoulders—"supper can wait."

"I'm right here, Rory." Cheeks aflame, Vi gave him her smelliest stink eye, but he only winked. He loved to wink at her, especially when he was guilty. Jesse avoided eye contact with her but flashed a grin at Rory.

Mom walked up, saving Vi from further embarrassment.

"Hey, Mama." Vi clambered down from the barstool and hugged her. "Rory told me what the two of you have been up to."

"I assumed he would, Violet." Mom's formal words were offset by the smile playing about her lips. Clad in a flowing eggplant-colored skirt with a matching blouse and sandals, she appeared relaxed. "I'm quite pleased with the way the situation has unfolded."

"Thank you for finding a way for me to meet my son." Vi leaned in until their heads touched.

"As if I had a choice." Tru gave a dainty sniff. "Your husband would have taken Houston apart brick by shiny brick to find him. It just happened to be the route he chose. Rory reminds me of your father—the man could charm the rattles right off a snake." Sorrow lurked from the depths of her eyes. "Thomas would have cherished his grandchildren."

A tiny sigh escaped Tru's lips, then she nodded in Rory's direction. "The man adores you, Violet. I'm happy for you, even if the first time I laid eyes on him, he was kissing you in the hospital."

"That's when I became aware of his interest."

"Yes, dear. Rory made his *interest* perfectly clear. And today, he's exceptionally lit up. You've told him about our doctor's visit." Tru's eyes glowed.

Vi couldn't keep the grin off her face. "Of course, I did." She squeezed her hand and their rings clinked together.

"Your dad and I always wanted you to be happy." Mom cleared her throat to cover her shaky voice. "I believe you were going to give me the letters Thomas wrote."

Vi hesitated. "They made me cry, Mom. Are you sure Rodney won't mind?"

"Oh my goodness, no. Violet, I've told you before, Rodney loves me. We're past any secrets between us. I'll let him read them, and we'll both cry. He respected Thomas."

Mom's sapphire eyes brimmed with emotion. Vi hugged her again.

She gazed around her living room, painted a robin's egg blue. Rory talked to his dad and brother. Dad's recovery seemed on point. He always treated her with courtesy and wonder, as if Rory had brought home a long-lost treasure.

Mark looked her way and winked—must be a Spence trait. He'd nicknamed her Gazelle and loved to tell how Vi had been ready to bolt that morning at the hospital. And how he'd saved the day when he escorted her in to see Rory. The story got a little bigger each time Mark told it.

Vi winked back. Barring any embellishment, running had been at the top of her list.

The short few weeks she and Rory dated, or tried to, were an epic rollercoaster. Honestly, it thrilled her the bumpy ride had ended.

Her stomach yowled in discomfort. She weaved her way to the kitchen for a cold drink. In a corner behind the large island, Tavo talked to Paige. The undeniable yearning on his face was painful to watch. Hmm. Nabbing a ginger ale from the fridge, she looked for Rory.

They smiled when their eyes met. Vi thoroughly enjoyed their private world. Rory beckoned her over, then tapped a spoon against a clear glass. The friendly chatter ebbed.

Putting his arm around her, Rory said, "We're so glad you could come and see Vi's Nest." A titter bounced around the room at his pet name for their new home. "Feel free to explore and see all the changes." He looked around the room with an infectious grin. "Recommend me to your friends and sign me on as Valiant's newest home remodeler." Laughter followed his comments.

"As happy as we are to have you here for the housewarming, I have other fantastic news to share." Rory paused, his gray eyes lit with excitement.

Vi took a long draught of the icy beverage and fanned her cheeks. She'd disliked his theatrics at first. Now that she knew the person on the inside, she enjoyed his gift for livening things up. Better yet, once everybody left, Rory stayed. With her. They both loved being married.

"I'll tell you what I heard earlier today. Are you ready?" Shouts of "Quit stallin'," and similar verbiage reverberated throughout. Rory's arm tightened around her. "Okay. My wife had a doctor's appointment this morning." He paused again as hoots filled the room.

"Everybody ready? This is what I know ..." He raised his hand. With dramatic flair, he held up two fingers.

Whoops broke loose as the room erupted in cheers. The noisy response developed into a collective chant. "TWINS. TWINS. TWINS."

Once the backslapping and congratulations quieted down, someone yelled, "Speech, Vi!" Others joined in. Vi's stomach wasn't cooperating in the least. Suddenly, she could hear a cracker crunch. Cold and hot enveloped her. She looked into Rory's concerned eyes. The ginger ale U-turned.

"Make a hole!" Rory's deep voice boomed. Well-wishers hastily cleared a path.

Vi covered her mouth and ran for the bathroom.

***

ALL THEIR GUESTS GONE, Rory and Vi stood on the balcony outside their master bedroom. Another round of mashed potatoes had staved off Vi's nausea. For the moment.

"Feeling better?" Rory's arm rested on her shoulder.

"So far. Too much excitement for these little ones." She patted her small baby bump.

Rory's hand tightened around her upper arm. "You're gonna need more rest, Red."

"Yeah." The idea had no appeal, but her body wasn't taking no for an answer.

They gazed into the night. Even now, birdsong sounded from the scrub trees below. The moon played hide-and-seek among the pale sketchy clouds. Stars blinked and nodded, and a faint barbeque smell drifted to where they looked out over the property.

"Rory." Vi turned to him. "I have an idea for the land."

"What would that be, love?" His voice drifted lazily.

Memories flitted through her mind. The terrifying morning Marvin had come to the property, saying Rory and his dad wanted to make an offer on it. Then, in the hospital, Rory's assurances he didn't want her land.

Vi had taken Rory at his word. His actions had proved he truly had no interest beyond her desires. They'd discussed possibilities more than once, but he'd never pushed an agenda or tried to rush her into a decision. He'd support whatever she wanted to do.

"Daddy always said this land had a healing touch. What if we built your rehab center here? A place where people can come to heal. Get restored."

His sleepy eyes brightened, and then the line between his brows creased. "It's your land, Vi."

"Yes, mine to do whatever. I've thought about it and concluded God gave you the vision ... and He gave me the way to make it happen."

His sleepy eyes were mere slits. "What if we pray about it? Deal?"

"Deal."

They watched the sky and the stars a while longer.

"Rory."

"Yes, love."

"Are you okay living out here in the sticks with me? I mean, we could've lived in the snazzy new subdivision you're developing."

Rory faced her, mouth in a soft smile. "Wherever you are, Red, that's where I want to be. We've already built precious memories in this lovely old Victorian." His hand rested on her tummy. "And it's just the beginning."

Vi snuggled against his warm chest to hear his heartbeat. She shut her eyes with pleasure as he leaned down, claiming her mouth for a long, leisurely kiss.

ACKNOWLEDGMENTS

I'm forever grateful to Linda Fulkerson, publisher of Scrivenings Press, for seeing the potential in my stories. She's responsible for my fabulous book covers and the final editing of my work. Hats off to Regina Rudd Merrick and Heidi Glick of Scrivenings Press for their excellent work on content and line editing. My stories shine because of your expertise. Gwendolyn Gage is my long-suffering critique partner. She never hesitates to tell me when a passage is weak or when character goals aren't cutting it. She also cheers me on like a loyal friend. I love you, girl. And to all the Scrivenings Press authors who regularly encourage me with their writer stories, posts, and memes. Writing is an "onerous task," but all of you make it fun.

My daughter, Nancy Robison, gave me the inspiration for having a massage therapist as a character. Even if your days as a professional MT are long past, your healing hands still provide relief to family and friends. And thanks to Veronica Frank, my ongoing MT at Citizens HealthPlex. I think we're due for another session.

In preparation to write this story, I watched countless videos of vets who returned from war minus a limb. Your stories provided the information I needed to create Rory's character as an amputee. You have my everlasting respect. It was an honor and a privilege to share tidbits about your lives in this work of fiction.

As always, I'm grateful to my husband for letting me spend

ginormous amounts of time with imaginary people. You believed in the dream that God placed in my heart and allowed me the space to make it happen. There's always a bit of you in every male character I create.

And thanks be to God, who planted the dream to write in my heart and patiently led me to a place of fulfillment. Faithful is Your name.

ABOUT THE AUTHOR

Mary Pat Johns' writing career began once she retired from years of teaching speech and writing. She's written devotions for an online publication and had short stories published by Chicken Soup for the Soul. She currently writes a weekly faith column for the local newspaper. *Lovin' On Red* is book 2 of the *Romance in Valiant* series, and she's hard at work on books 3 and 4. God put it in her heart to tell stories of brave veterans and their reintegration into civilian life after suffering the traumas of war. As she kept writing, her focus generalized to include ordinary people who learn how to move forward after devastating events.

Her writing has a strong spiritual thread since she considers a return to faith in God the solution for what ails the civilized world. She lives in South Texas with her husband and their two dapple dachshunds. Her grown children and five grandchildren are useful sorts who keep her grounded with her reading/writing obsession. You can find her at the gym, at her computer, or reading a good book.

Romance in Valiant—Book One

Accountant Brenna McKinley only wants what's best for Peeps, the wildly popular gym in Valiant, Texas. But when money goes missing, and she's the obvious suspect, will she be able to clear her name or face criminal charges? Keeping her dream job matters, but falling in love with her boss isn't part of the plan. Neither is the creepy guy stalking her.

Young veteran Jesse Jacobs manages and co-owns Peeps. He needs help to gain accreditation for the exercise facility, and his new accountant is all in. But is she who she seems? Too bad he's falling

for her like a man with no parachute. When the pressure builds,
PTSD renders him moody and volatile, risking everything he loves.

Get your copy here:

https://scrivenings.link/countinonjesse

Forever Free by Hope Toler Dougherty

Forever Series—Book Four

Phoebe Sinclair combines her love of flowers and teaching to nurture a cut flower business on her grandfather's land. She has her hands full growing the farm, growing her customer base, and dealing with her growing attraction to the aloof man who volunteered to help make her farming dream come true.

Can she focus on her main job, or will a pair of yearning eyes and a hurting heart divert her worthy goals?

Heath Daniels has resigned himself to a life of singleness as he watches his siblings couple up and set wedding dates. Tracking their happiness, however, is more difficult than he expected. A real struggle, in fact.

Feeling old troubles—from the bad time when he dropped out of college to explore less-than-noble pursuits—creep back to tempt him, propelling him to volunteer for manual labor that leaves him exhausted at the end of every day—and out of trouble.

His additional hours of agri-business, however, lead to more struggles with an intriguing farmer. Does he have the strength to resist old temptations as well as a beautiful new one?

Get your copy here:

https://scrivenings.link/foreverfree

***Hope Takes the Reins* by Jenny Carlisle**

Crossroads Series—Book Three

Instead of relaxing during the summer after her first year of college, Kayla Caldwell is attending a memorial service after a plane crash changed her from only child to orphan. Will she ever feel safe, grounded again?

Cody Billings knows what it's like to wake up in a totally foreign world. When his last bull ride left him partially paralyzed, nothing about his teenage life could be the same. Following months of physical therapy and modifications, the loss when he resigned himself to never walking again is still fresh in his mind.

With only the rodeo in common, Kayla and Cody had known each other only as neighbors until now. Grief and loss have matured them more quickly than their friends, but they face the same doubts as they reach the crossroads on the way to their unknown future. Kayla's responsibilities as the young owner of a ranch are multiplying faster than the cattle. Cody is determined to prove to himself and his parents that he can be independent.

Can the two support and encourage each other even as their dreams are being modified daily?

Get your copy here:

https://scrivenings.link/loveneverfails

Rebuilding Joy by Regina Rudd Merrick

RenoVations Inc.—Book Three

Single mom Darcy Emerson Sloan has enough to do raising twins and running a restaurant. She's doing fine on her own and doesn't need the complications of a man in her life. But when her café turns into a crime scene, putting her and her children in danger, she begins to take interest in the handsome young FBI agent that comes on the sene.

Contractor Del Reno is as even-keeled as they come, but even he has his limits. And Darcy Sloan has pushed him too far. Every time he tries to help, it backfires. But now that Darcy and her kids are in trouble, he has no choice but to come to her aid and to protect her. She's just going to have to deal with it. Secret tunnels, organized crime, adorable children, and a wedding.

Just another day in Clementville.

Get your copy here:

https://scrivenings.link/rebuildingjoy

Stay up-to-date on your favorite books and authors with our free e-newsletters.

ScriveningsPress.com

www.ingramcontent.com/pod-product-compliance
Lightning Source LLC
Chambersburg PA
CBHW060623100726
47907CB00006B/1744